WANTED DEB OR ALIVE

OTHER FIVE STAR TITLES BY LAURIE MOORE

A DEBUTANTE DETECTIVE MYSTERY

WANTED DEB OR ALIVE

LAURIE MOORE

FIVE STAR
A part of Gale, Cengage Learning

GALE
CENGAGE Learning

Detroit • New York • San Francisco • New Haven, Conn • Waterville, Maine • London

GALE
CENGAGE Learning™

LIBRARY OF CONGRESS CATALOGING-IN-PUBLICATION DATA

Moore, Laurie.
    Wanted deb or alive : a debutante detective mystery / Laurie Moore. — 1st ed.
        p. cm.
    ISBN-13: 978-1-4328-2540-9 (hardcover)
    ISBN-10: 1-4328-2540-2 (hardcover)
    1. Debutantes—Texas—Fiction. 2. Americans—Mexico—Fiction. 3. Kidnapping—Fiction. I. Title.
    PS3613.O564W36 2011
    813'.6—dc22   2011013268

First Edition. First Printing: July 2011.
Published in 2011 in conjunction with Tekno Books and Ed Gorman.

Printed in the United States of America
1 2 3 4 5 6 7 15 14 13 12 11

To my daughter Laura, stunning
debutante and beautiful bride

ACKNOWLEDGMENTS

Many thanks to editors Tiffany Schofield and Mary Smith at Five Star, Diane Pieron-Gelman, Tracey Matthews at Cengage, and to Roz Greenberg at Tekno Books. And to Randolph Mc-Dorman, El Paso Police (Ret.), and Roger Dominguez, Senior Border Patrol agent for Customs and Border Protection, for law enforcement and technical assistance. But especially to the lovely debutante who inspires me to write.

CHAPTER ONE

"It's insane. You *cannot* go to that lawless, godforsaken place by yourself. Even if you managed to get a trustworthy guide who speaks the language, it's anarchy. The Wild West. Only instead of gunslingers, dance hall girls and cattle rustlers, they have drug cartels, crooked cops, prostitutes and *mordida*—bribes. And there's a serial killer on the loose. Maybe even two of them."

This, coming from Jim Bruckman on why I shouldn't go to Ciudad Juárez, the murder capital of Mexico, located across the border from El Paso, Texas. Not that I didn't expect my boyfriend of three weeks to get upset, him being a detective with the Fort Worth police and all, but I did expect moral support. And since I don't have a ring on my finger, he doesn't actually get a vote in this emergency.

He snagged a pair of clean blue jeans off a hanger and hopped on one foot while he stuffed a toe into one of the legs. My heart skipped and my eyes widened as his muscles rippled wrangling into his denims.

"I take it back," he went on with his rant. "Forget the Wild West. Think Pancho Villa territory—a place that averages fifteen murders on a weekend if you believe the newspapers."

"You act like it's a different hemisphere," I said with false bravado, half-miffed because he didn't understand why I had to leave, half-scared because I didn't want to go. But I had no choice.

A kidnapping is nothing but a euphemism for a murder waiting to happen.

"Not hemisphere—narcosphere. If the criminals don't kill you, the bacteria will. They have turbo-charged mosquitoes the size of Chihuahuas. You could come down with malaria. And never mind the obvious—that you just admitted you're not fluent in any foreign languages."

"That's not what I said." I shot him a wicked glare. Then realization dawned. I'd miscalculated, and in my haste, had started buttoning my blouse on the wrong button.

"Then what, exactly, did you say?" He glanced over at the digital clock on the nightstand as he zipped his pants, then opened a drawer, selected a Texas Ranger jersey and shook it out.

Sigh. The guy could put on a tow sack and he'd still look GQ gorgeous.

The digital clock came to life, chiming to indicate 5:00 in the morning. Which meant we'd been having this same conversation for ten minutes, including the talk time from the frightening phone call I'd just received.

"You asked me if I knew how to speak Spanish and I said I knew enough to get into a good fight—"

"Same thing."

"—then you went all Navy Seal on me and put the kibosh on my trip."

"Like I said, you're not going." He punctuated the comment with a nod.

"You're not the boss of me."

Jim's a Major Crimes detective with the Fort Worth Police Department, so it stands to reason he'd focus on the danger element of what he keeps calling my "harebrained idea." Part of me knew he was right, but I didn't have time to argue. My sister Teensy called, screaming bloody murder. You want to talk about harebrained ideas? This beats all:

On what should've been the happiest night of Teensy's life, she and her best friend, Tiffany, left The Rubanbleu Ball not even five hours ago after making their debutante bows. On a lark, they chartered a midnight flight to El Paso, and crossed the border into Mexico. How random is that? Now, Teensy's lying in a hospital bed, in a third-world country, clinging to life, and Tiffer's been abducted.

When I asked Teensy if she'd called the police, she shrieked that the police were the ones who kidnapped them. That when her ATM card didn't work and the bandits realized they couldn't juice any money out of her, they beat her to smithereens and left her for dead on a dirty, unpaved side road in the middle of Ciudad Juárez.

As for Tiff, well . . . if you live in Texas, those four-inch blurbs occasionally make the newspaper about American tourists being kidnapped and ransomed in Mexico. You never think it'll happen to you. Only this time, it's bleeding over into my family.

Now that I'd properly buttoned my blouse, I'd almost finished dressing after my first marathon night of passion with Bruckman. Last month, after I caught my longtime boyfriend cheating with my boss's wife, Bruckman pulled me over on a traffic stop and tried to throw me in jail. One thing led to another and I eventually figured out I'm in love with this guy. Tonight was supposed to be our first overnighter.

Completely dressed in cobalt blue dupioni silk slacks, a matching silk knit shell and jacket, I took a deep breath and closed my eyes for a few seconds in an effort to de-stress. When I opened them, Bruckman had seated himself in front of his desktop computer. With his face bathed in the blue glow of an oversized monitor, he hunkered over the keyboard and tapped out letters like Morse code. Seconds later, the screen lit up.

He moved the cursor and clicked it several times before reclining against the seat back of his chair. "Read it and weep."

He had one of those *Told you so* looks plastered across his face. Before I could even step over and peer at the information streaming across the monitor, he read portions of the article aloud.

"In the last nine years, over three hundred women about your age have been murdered. And over four hundred girls are still missing. I wasn't kidding about the serial killer. These were girls who blended in. You, on the other hand, will stand out from the rest of the herd like an albino."

"Stop scaring me." I slipped into my blue leather Ferragamos, first one, then the other, and instantly added almost two inches to my height. Which still makes me more than six inches shorter than Bruckman.

"Where've you been?" He eyed me up as if I'd just landed here from an alternate universe. "This isn't a job for the Debutante Detective Agency. This is a job for the cops. Or a recovery specialist. Or the FBI. Maybe a bounty hunter who's not afraid to kidnap a U.S. citizen in a foreign country and bring them back home." He pointed to the grisly picture filling the screen, where one of the victims had a cello stroke to the jugular. In the color photograph, the wound in her neck flapped open, crimson and violent. "Getting someone safely out of a foreign country is a job for Special Forces. Or a hardened criminal." His lips thinned. "Only a hardened criminal isn't trustworthy. You send an ex-con down there to get your sister's friend back, and he's liable to steal her blind, beat, rape and murder her, too. Let the police handle it."

I burst into tears. "But Teensy said the cops are the ones who abducted them." My voice careened upward into a wail.

"Even more reason not to get involved." He eyed me up again. Instead of approval, his expression bordered on contempt. "The way you look makes you vulnerable."

"What's that supposed to mean?"

"You're petite. You're blue-eyed." His jaw flexed. "You're blonde."

"So?"

"Means you don't look Mexican. It's not like you're going to Spain, Dainty, where you might be able to blend in. Spaniards have a lot of northern European influence in their lineage. The people of Mexico descend from Aztecs and Mayans. *Throw the pulsing heart onto the flames.* That kind of mentality."

I blinked. He was trying to scare the hell out of me.

It was working. Except for one thing: The urgent need to rescue my sister and her friend had hijacked my common sense.

"Let me drive you down to the PD, and let's get the El Paso police on the line. See what they can tell us."

"But Teensy and Tiffany aren't in El Paso; they're across the border in Ciudad Juárez."

He expelled a long breath. Wheat-blonde hair stuck out like twigs on a tumbleweed. Piercing, cornflower-blue eyes thinned into slits. His sturdy jaw torqued.

"I know that." Then he spoke with great patience, as if talking to a non-native speaker, or someone with a low IQ, or brain damage. "But if we're going out there, we need a friend on our side who's fluent in Spanish, who isn't likely to slit our throats. I'd trust a brother officer from a Texas police department over a priest across the border."

Wait—did he just say "we"?

He said "we."

Knew he wouldn't let me go by myself . . . thank heavens.

Moi—Dainty Prescott, last year's debutante, society girl, and soon-to-be paid intern at WBFD-TV station—in Mexico? If someone had put this to me ten minutes ago, I'd have said, "Not hardly."

My chest hitched. I know how men are. They end up doing something they don't want to do, and then they blame you. I needed this to be Bruckman's idea.

13

"I didn't ask you to go out there."

"Non-negotiable."

"Like I said, you're not the boss of me."

He'd been staring at the computer, pulling up the website for the El Paso Police Department, when his head slowly turned and his eyes slewed toward me. "You're not going to no-man's-land by yourself. You'll get yourself killed."

"She's my sister."

"You'll get killed, or they'll snatch you and do God knows what until you plead for a quick, merciful death." Then he said what I knew he'd been thinking ever since Teensy's frantic call woke us up. "You need to tell your father."

"No." My death-ray glare should've vaporized that notion.

"Teensy's his daughter."

"My sister made me promise."

"Make an exception. I think you can break this one without any repercussions."

"You don't understand, Bruckman." He'd gone from Jim to Bruckman. And when he lifted one eyebrow, I knew he'd sensed a shift in our fledgling relationship. "Daddy's got a new wife. She's my age—*my age!*" I fisted my chest with passion. To Bruckman, I probably looked like the smallest monkey in the chimp cage. "He doesn't care about Teensy and me anymore. He's so preoccupied with that little gold digger that he doesn't give us the time of day." My chest hitched again. "She talked him into cutting us off financially and now he expects us to stand on our own two feet. So that's what I'm doing. Teensy and I don't need him."

Bruckman sighed. "This is different."

My shoulders shook with sobs. I didn't expect him to understand. Bruckman came from a normal family. If my family became any more fractured and dysfunctional, we'd get invited to be on a talk show.

14

I caught sight of myself in the mirror and disliked what I saw. Bright blue eyes that looked especially disturbing with their lids rimmed red. Pale face with the pink nose of a heavy drinker. Bee-stung lips that'd turned bloodless and hard. Bruckman didn't waste one precious second telling me to calm down. Granted, he didn't know me well enough to feel my grief as sharply as he should've, and his law enforcement background kept him eerily composed in the face of my disaster—like those Brahma cows over in India that don't have to worry about ending up on somebody's plate.

Less than 24 hours ago, my amphibian survival brain had kicked in when my recovering sorority sisters and I barely escaped a grisly end at the hands of a madman. Now it told me to trust Jim Bruckman—he'd been around the block a few times and he'd dealt with bottom-feeders in his job. But I was drunk on fear and needed to keep moving forward . . . needed to get my sister to a safe place, where the people who were hell bent on killing her wouldn't . . . and I needed reassurance, even if it left me with a false sense of security.

As I turned my face to his, he said the only thing worth saying: "I'm in your corner, babe."

"I need a ride to my dad's house, and I could use a lift to the airport," I said through a sniffle.

"So you'll tell him?"

With a little head bob, I averted my gaze, and imagined myself saying, *Yes, Jim, I promise to tell Daddy about Teensy . . . when hell freezes,* so it wouldn't be a totally scandalous fib. After almost marrying a world-class cheater, I wanted this relationship to be open and honest. Lying to Bruckman on what amounted to a continuation of our third official date and my first sleepover wasn't something I relished doing.

"It makes me nervous the way you have these knee-jerk reactions to crises," he said. "I still think we should go there together. Do you have any idea what a mess it'll be to hook up in a few hours?"

I gathered my belongings and stuffed them into my overnight bag. We were wasting precious time, and he still had to contact his sergeant to get permission to burn off a few vacation days. If the detective bureau was shorthanded, then Bruckman wouldn't be able to leave right away. By that time, Teensy and Tiffer could be dead.

"Look at it this way, Jim—" I used my sultry voice "—by the time you arrive in El Paso, I'll already have rented a vehicle and can pick you up at the airport. And if you find an El Paso cop who's willing to escort us into Mexico and act as our translator, I can have him in the car before your plane even lands."

Bruckman stood. He walked over, put his arms around me and pulled me close. I returned the embrace and sensed him sniffing my perfumed shampoo. He pushed me away enough to peer down at me. "I don't want to lose you."

"You won't."

"I have a bad feeling about this, Dainty. Once you get off the plane, you're only a cab ride away from complete anarchy."

Then he took me by the shoulders and forced me into a chair. I didn't expect him to do what he did next. He illustrated his point by scrolling through grisly pictures of dead girls—*maquiladoras*—factory workers who'd been murdered and left, mutilated, in the dirty side streets of Ciudad Juárez.

My stomach clenched. But looking at those photos didn't change my mind. I clicked the cursor and closed the website, pushed back from the desk and walked to my side of the bed to get my Italian handbag.

"If you won't drive me to my dad's and then take me to the airport, I'll use my own car," I said matter-of-factly.

Bruckman shook his head, *Woe is me.* "What're you going to tell your father?"

Was he kidding? The Rubanbleu debutante ball had taken place less than eight hours ago, and my father—who was supposed to present Teensy to the ladies of The Rubanbleu—didn't even bother to show up. A family friend had to step in at the last minute to do the honors.

Daddy didn't even have the common courtesy to let us know he couldn't make the ball. Or to let us know they'd been held up, or missed their flight back from Europe. Or to say he even gave a damn, for that matter. So, no, I didn't intend to tell him anything about Teensy's and Tiffany's predicament. With any luck, I'd find my sister and her friend, and we'd be stateside before anyone was the wiser.

"I don't have to say anything."

"He deserves to know. One of his girls is in the hospital. This time tomorrow, both of his girls could end up dead. You have to tell him."

"Obviously you're not a big hunter." If he had been, he'd know that my father and his gold-digging wife, Nerissa, had probably headed for the deer lease instead of showing up to The Rubanbleu in time for Teensy to make her bow. "Yesterday was the opening day of deer season."

I spent the next twenty minutes in the passenger seat of Jim's truck, deflecting questions, as he drove me from his home in North Richland Hills to the Prescott family estate on the west side of Fort Worth.

True, in a misguided effort to force me to grow up, my daddy cut off my credit cards, locked me out of the house and changed the alarm code without giving me the password . . .

Yes, in order to save herself and Tiffer, my sister gave me the information I needed to get inside the house so I could get the stash of money she'd hidden in her bedroom . . .

No, I didn't need to pick up a change of clothes at my grandmother's house in Dallas, where I've been staying since the sorority house closed this past summer. I could pack a small carry-on at my dad's house, and wear my sister's things.

Bruckman and I traveled Airport Freeway into downtown Fort Worth. When he again suggested we should stop by the police station to place phone calls to the El Paso PD, I pretty much pitched a hissy fit. Every minute was critical. I needed to get into Daddy's house, find Teensy's money, grab whatever else I needed, and call the airport for reservations.

I grimaced.

I have no credit cards. They've pretty much been cut up, right before my eyes, by angry sushi restaurateurs, high-dollar department stores, or rental car agencies.

I looked over at Bruckman. "I hate to ask you . . ."

He slid me a sideways glance.

"I want to make airline reservations before I get to the airport, but I need a credit card. I'll pay you back as soon as I find Teensy's money."

"If you'll wait a couple of hours, I'll buy you the ticket, we can fly out together and you won't owe me a dime. My treat."

Sounded perfect. But I'd take my chances at the airport. "If I can't get a flight, I'll fly stand-by."

His protests lost effect when I scrolled through the telephone numbers stored in my cell phone and tapped the on-button for airline reservations. I still have frequent flyer miles. If there weren't enough, my sister likely had enough cash to cover the last-minute fare.

After giving Bruckman directions to the house I grew up in, we rode the rest of the way in silence. A few minutes later, we pulled off Camp Bowie Boulevard onto Crestline, and finally onto Hillcrest. Midway down the block, I motioned for him to pull over.

The golf course is across the street from the house. Back when we used to be a close-knit family—when my mother was still alive—Teensy and I had our own bedrooms, and the house was fully staffed. Then, after my mother died last year, Daddy started dating Nerissa. When they got engaged, he gave her full rein, whereupon she promptly fired the staff and brought in her own entourage of miscreants, ne'er-do-wells and a few members of her immediate family who weren't Velcroed to stripper poles or doing time in the penitentiary.

Bruckman pulled into the circular drive and shifted the pickup into park. He left the truck idling while I scampered around to the back of the house and inserted my key into a door that opened into the kitchen.

Didn't work.

I blamed Nerissa.

I glanced around for the hide-a-key—a plastic rock with a duplicate house key inside—but it wasn't where we kept it when my mother was alive. I did find a real rock about the same size, which served the same purpose.

As soon as I broke out one of the windowpanes in the door, the "broken-glass" sensor set off the alarm. Suddenly, the neighborhood was treated to the alternating high–low warble of the burglar alarm piercing the dawn.

I needed to move fast. With great care, I stuck my hand through the gaping jaws and un-toggled the deadbolt.

After letting myself inside, I flipped on the light switch, illuminating the room. A quick visual scan of the kitchen hurt my heart. Gone was the hanging rack of copper pots above a butcher-block island. My mother loved to cook. These days, daddy's new wife has systematically tried to stamp out all traces of her.

Reflexively, I threw the deadbolt and headed across the kitchen to the security system keypad. Teensy'd given me the code. I tapped in the corresponding numbers and the alarm shut off. The house fell silent, but the lingering shrill resonated between my ears. Then the telephone rang.

The phone's digital display showed the number for the alarm security center, so I injected a syrupy sweetness into my tone when I answered with a chipper *Hello.*

"Is everything all right?" This, from the company rep.

"Why, yes, it is," I drawled. "We got a new puppy and it has a bark that sounds like glass breaking, because the alarm just went off for no good reason."

"What is your password?" Said sternly.

"Debutante."

"Thank you."

The phone went dead in my hand.

I flipped on a series of wall switches that lit the way to Teensy's room. Sure enough, the wad of cash Teensy'd been hoarding was exactly where she said it'd be—slotted into a bill-sized rectangular hole cut into the pages of her high school yearbook. It was the first time I smiled since my sister's phone call.

I didn't even stop to count it—just crammed it into my handbag and started ransacking her closet for suitable clothes Teensy could change into at the hospital. I also got a change of clothes for myself. Then I rifled through her lingerie drawer. She had a couple of unopened sacks from Victoria's Secret, so I dumped the contents onto the bed. Instead of rummaging through shoeboxes, I picked out a pair of Bally flats in the bottom of her closet that looked broken-in.

I didn't find a single suitcase that wasn't oversized. The last thing I wanted was to waste time checking luggage, or waiting at the baggage claim area to collect it. I needed a carry-on.

At the other end of the house, in the bedroom my daddy shares with Nerissa, I flipped on the light and got a mouth-gaping moment. Instead of the glorious sight of beautiful antique furniture that my mom spent a lifetime collecting, I was treated to a room filled with modern pieces in black lacquer.

Anger blurred my vision. That horrible woman my father married had removed almost every trace of the mother who raised me. I moved to her closet in search of a carry-on, but found nothing. Then I searched Daddy's closet. Nothing there, either.

That meant any unused luggage had been stored in the attic.

I hate attics.

And this one's the stuff children's nightmares are made of: dark and gloomy, with stacks of dusty boxes and holiday stuff like Christmas ornaments and tubs of accordioned fold-out tissue paper turkeys, and other tablescape items; cobwebs and recluse spiders just waiting to sink in their fangs and send venom speeding through your bloodstream . . . rot your flesh . . . maybe kill you. You don't even realize you've been bitten until you roll over in bed one night and see your leg lying next to you. Or the bogeyman, living in your attic, patiently awaiting the day you climb that ladder and . . .

I pulled at the ripcord. The overhead trap door let out a prolonged squeak.

Did I mention I hate attics?

The ladder swung down and I climbed partway up, enough to poke my head above the decking. Sure enough, from my place on a middle step, I saw an unused set of Louis Vuitton luggage stacked up nearby. It probably belonged to Nerissa.

Eyeballing the sizes from my place on the step, I decided on a soft, medium-sized carry-on with roller wheels in the middle of the stack. Once I was certain no vermin were scurrying around, I ascended the steps, removed a hard-shell train case and small duffle bag, and selected the proper suitcase. I put the two smaller cases back in their places, retraced my steps and descended the stairs.

Dragging the soft-sided luggage down the hall was easy. Hoisting it onto Teensy's bed took more effort. When I unzipped it, I found out why.

A book, wrapped in a towel, accounted for the suitcase's extra weight. I set it aside without unwrapping it, packed the clothes we needed inside—including a small makeup kit—and looked around for something to wrap around Teensy's shoes.

The front doorbell rang.

Bruckman. He'd gotten impatient with me.

Instead of ransacking the kitchen for a couple of plastic food storage bags to put Teensy's shoes in, I unfurled the bath towel.

That's when I saw it . . . a journal-type book with the title penned in an elegant hand, calligraphy perhaps . . . almost Victorian script.

The Ladies' Guide to Homicide.

With a subtitle: *Everything You Need to Get Away with Murder.*

CHAPTER TWO

The third time the doorbell rang, I took off down the hall to what used to be my Barbie pink bedroom—now a guest bedroom—repainted in a garish shade of yellow. My personal belongings, including the jewelry box where I kept my passport, had been boxed up and stored in that closet. I pulled out the box marked *Dainty's stuff* in block lettering, ripped open the cardboard flaps and removed my jewelry box.

The expensive gold bangle bracelet my mother gave me for my sixteenth birthday was missing, as well as a pair of diamond and sapphire earrings my ex-boyfriend gave me last Christmas. Still, there wasn't time to do a complete inventory, and I pretty much already had a suspect in this theft. So I pulled out my passport, stuck it in my pocket, and returned the jewelry box to its place.

Now Bruckman was stabbing the bell with the vengence of a serial killer.

I race-walked to the front of the house, dragging the suitcase behind me like a tail. My heart beat a mile a minute. I opened the door to reveal Bruckman's unsmiling face.

"Had to find a carry-on," I said, breathless. "And my passport."

With a curt nod, he took the overstuffed suitcase by the handle and rolled it to the pickup, leaving me to turn off lights, reset the alarm and lock up my childhood home. As for the broken glass, I'd explain later.

I met him by the truck, collapsing the soft-shell luggage's telescoping handle. Then he hoisted it into the back of the pickup. It landed with a *thunk*.

"What's in here? Bricks?"

"Clothes, shoes, makeup. Enough for both of us."

He expelled a long sigh. Then he came around to the passenger side and wrapped me in his arms.

"I won't be able to do this once we get to the airport," he said warily. "I wish you'd reconsider."

"She's my sister."

Even in the shadows, misery shone in his eyes.

"It's not that I don't think you know what you're doing. Believe me, I respect you for it more than you know. To tell the truth, I'd probably do the same thing. But it'd be better if you waited a few hours. Then I could go with you."

"We're wasting time."

"Alert your father. You said yourself he has all kinds of connections. Try using a few of them now."

I shook my head. Trying to pull away only made him grip me tighter.

For no good reason, he kissed me like our lives depended on it. I've never been kissed that way before—a desperate, hungry kind of kiss that transcended mere passion and lasered me straight to the core. My chest clenched with a love so strong it whipped my breath away.

Then he pushed away, leaving me gasping for air.

"Jeez, Jim, you act like you're never going to see me again." My heart tried to beat through my rib cage.

He said nothing. Just helped me up into my seat and shut the door with an authoritative clunk.

We traveled to the airport in relative silence; Bruckman with his eyes on the road, me with my head resting against the window, watching the scenery unfurl. A vision of Teensy with her straw-colored hair reflected in the glow of flickering gas sconces popped into mind.

Six hours ago, Bruckman and I were saying good-bye to everyone at the country club where Teensy'd made her debut into Fort Worth society at The Rubanbleu's annual debutante ball. She still had on her gorgeous white designer gown made of heavy silk. And the gloves that rose above her elbows gave her such elegance that it was hard to remember Teensy as a tomboy climbing trees, and running with a pack of neighbor boys on our street. She looked so beautiful in her white ball gown—all of the debutantes did. Each wore white dresses with long white kid gloves that extended from their fingertips to the middle of their upper arms. But Teensy's gown was fabulous, with a beaded bodice like the breastplate of a gladiator. When the spotlight hit it, thousands of crystal beads cast off tiny rainbow prisms.

Each debutante carried a bouquet of fresh flowers and performed an extravagant curtsy with a dramatic flair known as the "Texas dip" before the members. When the orchestra struck up the first strains of "How Lucky Can You Get," Teensy came on stage and made this low-court bow with Swan Lake maneuvers in front of The Rubanbleu doyennes. It was all very posh, and her perfect complexion radiated with happiness. Of all the debutantes put together, Teensy exuded glamour.

But not as glamorous as *moi* when I made my bow year before last.

I twisted in my seat so Bruckman wouldn't see me, misty-eyed, and stared out the window, watching the smear of street lamps along the freeway shut off in sections as dawn broke. Pink clouds striped the purple horizon.

"Is your cell phone charged?" Bruckman glanced in my direction.

"Not so much."

Through the silence, my thoughts free-associated. Bruckman, on the other hand, clearly wrangled with his conscience. When we arrived at the departure area, airport security urged drivers to keep the stream of traffic moving. Bruckman could go no further.

"Here, Dainty. Give me your cell phone and take mine. I'll get a charger for it when I get back into town, and we can exchange phones again in El Paso."

But as I dug into my purse, I couldn't focus on trading cell phones. Until now, I didn't think anything could divert my attention from Teensy's trouble, and how to find Tiffany and get them back home.

Now all I could think about was that book.

It certainly didn't belong to my mother, a saint of a woman. So why would Nerissa have what appeared, at first glance, to be a "how-to" manual for murder?

Chills swarmed over my body, electrifying my skin and causing the downy hairs on my arms to stick straight up like tiny needles.

Then the security guard slapped his hand on the hood of Bruckman's truck, wanting us to hurry. Next thing I knew, Bruckman shoved his credit card into my hand.

"I know the restaurant cut yours in half."

And not just one restaurant, either. Thanks to Daddy, merchants had systematically shredded all of my credit cards.

Then I was standing on the sidewalk, outside the entrance to my gate, with suitcase in hand, watching my new boyfriend watch me recede in his rearview mirror. The disturbing feeling that I might never see him again turned the air around me so thick and oppressive that I fought the desire to claw right through it.

CHAPTER THREE

¡Hola amigos!

I held a handy-dandy English-to-Spanish dictionary purchased at a book store in the terminal, a boarding pass for the red-eye to hell that I got with the frequent flyer miles I'd been stockpiling for an impromptu trip to Europe, and, according to my eighteen-carat gold Piaget wristwatch, it was a few minutes before seven o'clock.

With the sunrise a bloody thumbprint on the horizon, I found a quiet corner in hell's waiting room where I could sit, unaccosted, and plan the rendezvous with my sister. At least if things went badly and I ended up on the front page of the local newspaper—or on television, CNN maybe?—the image of me looking like I stepped off the cover of *Vogue* would be branded in the public's memory. In a bucket chair near the jetway, I contemplated the horror that'd propelled me into action. Inside my head, Teensy's voice came from an impossibly long distance.

When the early morning phone call came in, my mind must've played a trick on me in self-defense. It telegraphed a message to my ears to garble her plea. Now that the tension in my neck muscles had subsided, the distortion in my sister's cry evaporated and I made out the words I should've understood hours ago.

Wracked with sobs, in a voice barely audible, she appealed to me in a plaintive wail. *"Dainty, help me."*

A shiver zipped up my spine, bringing with it a chilling

premonition that made me edgy enough to jump through a plate glass window. I should've listened to Bruckman. Would a short delay getting to El Paso have made a difference? He should've tried harder to stop me. Who'd he think he was dealing with, anyway? A Ph.D. from the Sorbonne?

The devil may wear Prada, but he speaks *Español,* so I spent the time buffing up on Spanish phrases as I waited for the announcement to board. I had no idea in what condition I'd find my sister, and I really didn't want to think about it. Eight hours ago, Teensy looked so beautiful. But images of raccoon eyes and a head wrapped in gauze kept springing to my mind, and I had to battle them back to keep from screaming. The alert part of me wanted to turn around and run out of the terminal, to a place outside where my cell phone could get a clear signal so I could start tracking down my father. The part of me that had gone numb after Teensy's phone call sat as inert as a gas. I'd deceived myself into thinking I could handle this on my own, knowing I was headed to a country that everyone in my social circle thought of as "enchanting Mexico."

Everyone but me, that is.

Did I mention I hate Mexico?

The term "apprehensive" didn't begin to cover how I felt about crossing the border. I was frightened for Teensy and her best friend. But I was just as frightened for me.

The intercom crackled to life, shearing my reverie.

A disembodied female voice came over the loudspeaker, effectively torpedoing my thoughts. *"Buenos días pasajeros . . ."*

My mind went blank. As she rattled off more Spanish, I pinpointed a woman behind the airline counter speaking into a hand-held microphone. I sat, slack-jawed, with my dictionary opened to the *Hola* page and realized my unblinking eyes had gone dry. I'm so out of step with this language barrier problem. Snippets of the announcement seemed familiar. Seizing on a specific word, I thumbed through my dictionary. About the time I looked up the translation for "board," fifty Mexicans rose from their seats and formed a line.

Then the lady repeated her greeting in English. "Good morning, ladies and gentlemen, we're now boarding Flight One Twenty-Three to El Paso International Airport."

I snatched my carry-on by the handle and rolled it across the room, merged with the line and pulled out my boarding pass.

I didn't get the exit row seat I'd requested, and ended up in the rear of the plane in a seat with less legroom. By way of their girth, two people on either side of the middle seat were already competing for my space, so I pleaded with the flight attendant to place me in a different row. By the time I settled in and waited for the plane to taxi down the runway, I'd memorized most of the Spanish curse words.

Then I started a crash course to re-learn the basics: Where's the police station? A good restaurant? Taxi? The bathroom? How come there's no toilet paper? Where's the ATM? Telephone? I have the right to have a lawyer present during any questioning by police. How much will it take to buy my way out of this . . .

Cobweb clouds peeled back, floating from a gray ceiling. The plane gave an untimely jolt. My eyes shifted to the little window to see if we were moving, and I caught the man seated next to the window staring at me.

Hand to chest, I sucked air. Dressed all in black, he had the density of an anvil and looked like an escaped felon. *Hello, Clarice.*

"Brushing up on your Spanish, are you?"

"Je ne parle pas Anglais." I don't know much French, either, but it's a strategy I use to discourage strange men from bothering me. I was flabbergasted when he engaged.

"Ah—" his eyes lit up *"—vous êtes Français?"*

"Nein," I used my best fake German accent.

A middle-aged female flight attendant had moved to the front of the plane, accompanied by a lean, bronze-skinned male assistant holding a demonstration seat belt and an air mask.

All bright-eyed, crisp and perky, she keyed the mike and welcomed us aboard. "This is a no-whining, no-complaining flight. Guillermo—" hand gesture introducing slender, tawny man "—will be coming through the cabin to ensure that your seat belts are buckled, and that your shoes match your outfit."

I barked out a laugh. Being the best-dressed person on the plane—well, let's face it, I'm usually the best-dressed person anywhere—I couldn't help it.

Guillermo demonstrated how the seat belt worked. He tended to be clumsy, and made it look like rocket science.

The gregarious flight attendant gave him a heavy eye roll. "For those of you who are unmarried and looking for a husband—"

Why's she honing in on me? Do I look desperate?

"—Guillermo's so gay he may burst into flames any second. If you'd like to purchase an adult beverage, the price is ten dollars. If you don't have the exact amount and overpay, consider it a donation because you will not receive change. Guillermo needs it for his sex-change operation."

Great. I'm flying Hyena Air.

I'd like to think my life's in the hands of calm, capable pilots when it comes to flying—like that Captain Sully, who had to ditch his aircraft in the Hudson. Now, there's a hero. But then, he's a Texan. This comedy team looked like they came from Illegal Aliens 'R Us.

"In case you hadn't noticed, this isn't a charter flight and you're not the only one on the plane, so no hanky panky beneath the blanket. I don't care if you want to be in the mile-high club, keep your clothes on. If you hear us paging for a doctor or see us stampeding down the aisle with the defibrillator, that's not the time to ask for an extra pillow. In case of a bumpy ride, pipe down and nurse your drinks. We'll return for your trash before the flight careens into El Paso."

Guillermo did a bored little head bob for effect, and switched out the seat belt for the yellow mask.

"Should the cabin pressure change in flight, these oxygen masks will drop down. Stop screaming and slip yours on over your face. Do yours first, then do your kid's. We don't like kids. If you're traveling with children and you keep hearing bells, it's not your hearing. Keep your kids' fingers off the call button."

My shoulders tensed.

"If the plane goes down, bend over and grab your ankles. And don't pretend you've never done that before. If there's a crash, and the plane doesn't explode on impact, an inflatable slide will pop out. Use it. The exits are here, here, and here—" more hand gestures "—or just use the nearest hole once the flames die out."

I'm known around my sorority as the designated driver for the world, but I could've used a drink right about then.

"If for any reason we ditch in the water, your seat cushion turns into a life preserver. If you're not unconscious or dead, use it." She laughed without humor. "I know what you're thinking. That we're flying to El Paso. But the Rio Grande is on the border, and let me tell you, if we ditch in the Rio Grande, you'll need more than a life preserver. Try tetanus shots. Have you smelled the water on the Mexico side? Just saying."

The long-suffering Guillermo waited for her to finish. He had no more gadgets to demonstrate and kept checking his watch as if he had another engagement. Or maybe the ticking time bomb in the belly of the plane was about to go off. When he glanced toward the window, I saw earphones sticking out of his ears and realized he hadn't heard a word she said.

31

"Just so you know, Cagney and Lacy are flying the plane, so if you get out of order you'll be summarily shot. Instead of a burial at sea, you'll receive an air burial through one of the six exits that are located here, here, and here." Again with the hand motions.

"If you skipped your anti-psychotic medication and don't understand what I've said, just refer to the handy-dandy little card sticking out of the seat pouch in front of you. Except for you people sitting in the bulkhead. You're screwed."

Ohmygod, I'd boarded a plane with crazy people. The pre-flight presentation seemed to bear that out.

The plane's engines spooled and then we were airborne.

This isn't so bad, I tried to reassure myself. *It's like being a sardine in a very long, very crowded tin. A tin that could drop to the ground and kill us all . . .*

The man next to me kept trying to engage me in a conversation I wanted no part of. The cadence of his respiration when he looked at me made the hair at the nape of my neck stand on end. I sat as far away from him as I could without crawling into the next seat over. Finally, I closed the dictionary, leaned into the aisle and flagged down the closest flight attendant.

"Can I move?" I sent her a trembly smile of hope.

She shifted her eyes from me to the escaped felon and back. "There's a spot in the bulkhead."

I tugged my carry-on from under the seat, stepped out into the narrow aisle and traipsed clumsily up the passageway as the flight attendant addressed my former section mate.

"Something to drink, Father Michael? A soda? Bottled water?" She grinned. "Spirits?"

My inability to judge people's character perfectly illustrated why I should *not* be going to Mexico. Once I got to the bulkhead, it didn't take long to realize why the space was available. I'd traded a seat next to a priest for one next to a woman of indeterminate ancestry with a screaming toddler who had a cry so piercing that I expected it to trigger an aneurysm. To make matters worse, the girl seated directly behind me used the tray table attached to my seat as a trampoline to bounce her infant on.

Babies shouldn't be allowed to fly. Neither should their parents.

With my nose buried in my English-to-Spanish dictionary, I suffered in silence, adding more curse words to my repertoire.

Trading phones with Bruckman had seemed like a good idea at the time. Thirty-five thousand feet above ground, it suddenly dawned on me that Bruckman had access to all my telephone contacts, including numbers for Daddy. Knowing Bruckman the way I do, it wouldn't surprise me a bit if he placed a call to my estranged father.

As we flew over Abilene, I ordered a handful of those little whiskeys and tried to pass them out to the children around me. The mothers were bitches and refused to go along with this. I'm pretty sure once drinks were served the entire crew parachuted off the plane, because we didn't see them again for the duration of the flight. Either that or they hid in the back.

By the time we were over Midland, I longed for the special moments I'd spent with Father Michael and his paraphilias, and considered asking for an ice pick to drive through my left eye to make myself feel better.

Short of a plane crash, this was the worst travel day I'd ever experienced. My nerves were shot as the plane touched down in El Paso, but I could string together a handful of sentences that would virtually ensure that I'd either navigate my way around Ciudad Juárez, or end up in jail.

As people behind me raised their seats to the upright position in anticipation of our landing, I relived my last hours at Bruckman's house. After the ball was over and we returned to his place, he swept me into the full depths of his lovemaking. Afterward, I fell back onto my pillow, sated. Until I drifted into slumber, I had to be the happiest girl in the world.

Then the cell phone rang for the Debutante Detective Agency, and life as I knew it went to hell in a hand basket.

I closed my eyes and relived the five-minute phone call that caused my world to tank.

"Wait. What? I can barely hear you."

With the phone pressed tightly against my ear, and the other ear plugged with a fingertip to mute the rush of acclimatized air whispering over my body, I'd struggled to make out the caller's words.

"Who's calling? No, who are you?"

The light on Bruckman's nightstand switched on.

"International operator?"

I nodded along, hanging on every word. The lady had a thick accent, and I hadn't come fully awake.

"She's phoning from where? Mexico? Sure, I'll accept the charges. Put her through."

But I was thinking, *Wait . . . what? Is this a joke?*

As I listened, chills swarmed over my skin. I knew in an instant this call would change my life, and not in a good way.

I covered the mouthpiece. *"Jim—I have to leave. Emergency."*

I sat up rigid and listened while my peace and serenity came unraveled.

A thin, high-pitched voice pealed down my ear canal, tinny and distant. *"They want money."*

It sounded like Teensy on the other side of the planet.

"Who wants money?"

"The kidnappers who took her."

"Took who?"

"Tiffer."

My blood curdled.

"*Somebody took Tiffer? I don't understand.*" I checked Bruckman's bedside clock and noted the time of her call—about four forty-five in the morning. "*That's impossible. I just saw y'all . . .*"

. . . five hours ago.

"*We hailed a cab and they just took her.*"

Words piped into my ear canal were slow to dissolve, as if my brain had shifted into protective mode in an effort to void the entire conversation.

"*I don't understand. Somebody took her from the cab? Where'd you get a cab?*"

"*Ciudad Juárez. I'm in a hospital. At least I think it's a hospital. They drove us to the ATM and forced us to get the money out. They took it and they took her. They beat the hell out of me. Dumped me on the side of the road like garbage. Left me for dead.*" The small voice broke with sobs. "*I didn't have credit or debit cards. They got so mad.*"

"*Call the police.*"

"*That's what I've been trying to tell you, Dainty. The police are the ones who took her.*"

That's when the telephone connection went dead.

CHAPTER FOUR

Five hours after I'd received Teensy's phone call, the plane touched down in the untamed west known as El Paso, Texas. Even though I was running on "E", pure adrenaline worked on my body like rocket fuel. At ten o'clock that morning, I had one goal—getting my sister out of that hellhole. My mind shifted into overdrive. From the airport, I took the shuttle to the nearest car rental agency and tried to rent a car to take across the border.

We'd pretty much formalized the paperwork when the car rental girl dangled the keys within reach and said, "You can't take the vehicle into Mexico."

My mouth gaped. "That's the whole reason for renting the car."

She threw back her head and cackled. "Auto theft's a huge problem in Mexico. They average about thirty car thefts a day in Ciudad Juárez. There's no way we're letting one of our vehicles go across that border."

"Then tell me where to buy Mexican insurance."

"Even with Mexican insurance, there's no way you're driving our car across that border."

"But my sister's in a hospital. Her best friend's missing. I have to find them."

"Wow. That's too bad," she said, but her expression said, *Not in our car.*

"What am I supposed to do?"

"Well, first, if you're hell bent on going to Ciudad Juárez, I suggest you take out health insurance."

Health insurance?

I did a little face scrunch. "But I'm not sick. And I won't be there that long. In and out. That's the plan."

"That's what they all say." She smiled as if she were a scientist trying to communicate with a lab chimp, and no matter how many times her mouth formed the words, she still couldn't penetrate the language barrier. "Bottom line—once you cross the International Bridge, if you need medical attention, you're probably not going to get it."

I blinked.

"And I suggest you eat in El Paso before you go. You can pick up parasites that only a doctor specializing in tropical medicine can cure. And for heaven's sake, don't drink the water."

I blinked again. I'd heard this in Bruckman's crash course on the way to the airport. But I wasn't feeling the least bit hungry, and I could always drink something out of a can if I got thirsty.

"Don't even let the waiters give you ice for your soda," she went on. "It still comes from the same polluted water source—only in frozen form. If you're going to do that, you might as well drink out of the toilet. Speaking of . . ." Her eyes took on a speculative gleam. ". . . once you cross that bridge, hygiene as you know it is a thing of the past."

With the car rental scuttled, I reclaimed Bruckman's credit card and hailed a taxi. On the way to the El Paso police station at One Civic Plaza, I thumbed on Bruckman's phone. It immediately chimed with a message alert. He'd probably called while the plane was airborne to give me the name of my contact at the El Paso PD.

I pressed the message button and listened to the first of five messages.

"Hi Jim, it's me—Stacey."

Okay—not for me. I should've skipped it and gone to the next message, but the devil on my shoulder forced me to listen.

"I dreamed about you again last night . . . about how you . . ."

I sensed my eyes crossing. The traffic in front of the PD turned into white noise as I listened to Stacey describing bedroom gymnastics with my new boyfriend. I looked around for a paper bag to wheeze into, and saw a cast-off wine bottle in a sack that'd been tossed beneath a shrub. I pushed the skip button. There'd be plenty of time later to discuss Stacey in person—B.D. or A.D.—Before Dainty or After Dainty.

Voicemail cycled to the next message. Work related. I thumbed the skip button.

The third message was worse than the first. A woman identifying herself as Sugar had either gotten stuck in quicksand or she was making slurping sound effects to entice my boyfriend.

Delete.

Oops. Sorry 'bout that.

Again, I reminded myself: B.D. or A.D.?

The fourth message came from Bruckman.

"I just got off the phone with El Paso PD. Our contact is Lieutenant Armando Vásquez. He won't be in until ten this morning, so maybe you can grab something to eat and find us a hotel while I finish up here at the office. My flight lands at noon, so if you can pick me up at the terminal, well, hey— that'd be great. Love you, babe."

The fifth message was Bruckman again, also for me.

"Hey, Dainty. I love you. I just wanted you to know that. You're the greatest thing to ever happen to me." Long pause, while my eyes went all misty and my heart said, *Before Dainty.* "And it's because I love you that . . . I called your dad."

You did what?

My soaring heart hit the ground like an eagle dropped with birdshot. I sucked air.

"Your dad says he'll handle it. Well . . . that's not exactly how he put it. I'm omitting the profanity." Deep sigh. "All right, I see why you didn't want to tell him. He said not to let you touch anything. Called you a major fuck-up." Another sigh. "Okay, so don't do anything until I get there, and we can discuss it with this Sergeant Valdez guy. Wait . . . did I say sergeant? I meant Lieutenant Velásquez. Whatever. Just wait for me. And Dainty . . . I love you."

Love you long time, GI number ten.

My mind seethed with indignity. How dare he?

And wait—didn't he say my contact was Lt. Vásquez?

Infuriated, I thumbed off the phone.

Bruckman had been teasing me about the Debutante Detective Agency ever since my boss at the TV station hired me to chronicle his wife's activities. "Spy on" is such an ugly term. Then Tandy, one of my recovering sorority sisters, hired me to dig up the dirt on her mother's fiancé, Alex Garrett, an imposter who'd actually re-invented himself as Alex Garrett, since the real Alex Garret turned out to be dead.

Didn't those jobs turn out okay? Damned straight, they did.

I got on television for capturing one of the FBI's Ten Most Wanted—that would be Alex Garrett, AKA Robert John Taylor, AKA Jerry Don Grayson; and I made the front page of *The Dallas Morning News, moi,* Dainty Prescott, posing beside my silver Porsche, wearing a hot pink Escada suit since pink's my signature color now, and matching Gucci pumps.

I peeled off two tens from Teensy's wad of cash and handed it to the cab driver as he pulled up to the curb in front of the Central Regional Command building of the El Paso PD.

Across the street was the El Paso County Detention Facility, a dull gray concrete structure that consumed an entire city block and soared twenty stories or so into the air. Females of all sizes, in all states of sobriety and all manner of dress were standing about, waving and attempting to communicate with incomprehensible hand signals to their worthless boyfriends and husbands who may or may not have been able to see them through the small slits in the concrete walls. Sadly, a few of them dragged along little kids, also waving. I waited for a raggedy-dressed lady with seven or eight raggedy-dressed stair-step children to pass, each holding onto a rope that had been knotted at intervals. As the woman—who, incidentally, was built like a switch engine—dragged this train of offspring along the sidewalk, she wove a tall tale about how they were "going to visit Daddy at work." Once the caboose-child of this rope train finally cleared my path, I trotted up the steps and into the PD.

Inside, I halted in my tracks, scanning the lobby for where to go.

For a Sunday, the place turned out to be a hotbed of activity, full of people, noise, and odors. Just inside the two entry doors, a small museum area with three glass display cases had been arranged in a square against the wall. These cases contained police artifacts, including old photographs, badges, pistols, vintage leather gear and documents pertaining to the history of the PD. A large room that contained restroom facilities, tables and vending machines lay to the right. Various certificates, memorials and other items hung on white-over-blue walls in what appeared to be a clean, comfortable space. To the left, a large counter with a couple of civilian clerks behind it ran the length of the wall. From what I could see, they were manning a sign-in log, administering passes, and otherwise assisting those members of the public who had arranged interviews by summoning police personnel to escort them to different parts of the building. As best I could tell, this administration had made homeland security a fetish. It didn't appear that anyone got past the lobby without a building pass and an authorized escort.

I clinked an invisible toast in my head. *Hear, hear.*

Some of the people at the counter were being funneled off to the right, to the Public Records window, where copies of accident reports and criminal reports were available for a fee. Across from the Public Records window and to the left were approximately ten or fifteen chairs where people were waiting patiently—or impatiently—for their number to be called. Just past the Public Records area, I saw a main security door that appeared to be accessible only to authorized police personnel, since in order to gain access one needed a security badge to swipe against a keyless reader.

I took a number from the dispenser and wandered over to an unoccupied seat, glancing around for the memorial to fallen officers that Jim—who's a huge police history buff—had told me about. Apparently it was on display within one of the secured areas of the building, because I didn't see anything remotely connected to the twenty-three fallen officers in the public area of the lobby. For awhile I alternated between fidgeting in my chair in anticipation of having my number called, and watching all kinds of weird people entering and exiting the building. Finally, I heard my number called out and practically bolted to the head of the line.

A harried white woman wearing civvies—civilian clothing as opposed to a uniform—gave me a pointed look and beckoned me over to her station. As I sidled up, a man I couldn't see called out from some distant place behind the counter, "Line two, Dottie. It's your son again."

Dottie gave me the universal *Just a second* finger measurement to indicate the call wouldn't take long. She picked up the telephone receiver and I was treated to a one-sided conversation that clued me in as to how her day was going.

"What now?" she demanded, followed by a short pause. "A nail went through your foot? How'd you do that? Stepped on it? Well go get the pliers and pull it out." Her jaw torqued. "Quit bellyaching. Jesus had one in his foot and you didn't read about him whining, did you?

Ordinarily, one might think that'd put a period to the conversation. But no. Apparently the kid's response completely fouled her mood.

"Just pay the damned ticket," Dottie said. "Don't act so outraged. You weren't a suffragist in the right-to-vote movement, you ran a red light." Hazel eyes searched the ceiling as if reading her next few lines off the invisible teleprompter mounted overhead. Then her head bobbed and she said, "Uh-huh. Uh-huh. Uh-huh," in a way that suggested her son might be losing ground. "Stop being so damned dramatic. You act like it's a five-car pileup with fatalities. It's a flat tire, not a Shakespearean tragedy. Call a tow truck . . . you don't keep a number handy? Well then, I guess that makes you an idiot." Another pause and the conversation at my end turned lively. "Hey, hey, hey! Stop low-rating the cops . . . Fine. Next time you're in trouble, call a coke whore." Down went the phone, and her attention turned to me.

No small wonder I looked at her mouth angling up in a snarl and thought, *If this is how she talks to her son, just think how nice she'll be to me.*

"This is Sunday," I announced after a chipper *Hello.* Shouldn't it be more laid back? What's with all the people moving in and out?

"You may have noticed the jail directly across the street—although it's more PC to call it a detention facility."

Sarcasm resonated in her tone and, fully appreciating the chaos, I said, "Is this a Sunday morning circus, or an everyday event?"

"Daily event. You'll find females loitering in the area—although we don't call it loitering, because that's no longer a violation, and also not PC. So we refer to it as the Tammy

Wynette syndrome."

Being familiar with Tammy's hit song, "Stand By Your Man," I barked out a laugh. This woman reminded me of Rochelle LeDuc, WBFD-TV's assistant to my boss and station manager, J. Gordon Pfeiffer. While Rochelle and I had something of a tenuous relationship, there existed a modicum of respect between us, and I knew how to get around her when the need presented itself.

"That's funny." I wanted to build rapport.

She blew out a long-suffering sigh. "Yeah? Well, Sundays are visiting days. Surely you saw all those mothers showing up to visit their innocent sons, and the baby mamas here to visit their wayward love interests. Most people who work here go out of their way to avoid coming down here. I myself wouldn't even be here on a Sunday morning if I had a better attitude—or so my supervisor tells me." This, she said with a glint in her eye and a plastered-on smile.

I asked for Lt. Vásquez.

This lady informed me that they didn't have a Lt. Vásquez working there.

I instantly panicked. "There must be some sort of mistake. I flew in from Fort Worth, and I'm supposed to meet a Lieutenant Vásquez. Or Velásquez."

The clerk, who'd by now had her fill of me, motioned to a nearby uniformed officer who was seated behind her and off to the side. Until the interruption, he'd been having a passionate affair with his cup of coffee. This information officer, a light-skinned Hispanic with dark close-cropped hair and intense brown almond-shaped eyes that angled up in a slight Asian tilt, appeared to be in his early forties. He pushed back from the desk and hobbled up to the counter with a spit-shined leather shoe on one foot and a Velcro cast on the other. *Light duty.*

The Rochelle-lookalike handed me off with a smooth, "She'd

like a second opinion, doctor."

The officer bellying up to the counter resembled a little general in his midnight blue uniform shirt accented with French blue epaulets on the shoulders and French blue pocket flaps. The shield-shaped shirt patch near the shoulder of each sleeve was edged in bright yellow thread; it had an orange sun complete with flaring rays rising up from the bottom and embroidered into the sky blue background of the patch. The word *POLICE* was stitched in bright blue thread across the sun's rays, and *EL PASO TEXAS* was stitched into the sun. The uniform trousers were also French blue. A silver nametag above the right pocket flap identified this officer as RODRIGUEZ.

Then the big blue enameled Texas centered on the badge pinned above the left pocket caught my eye—Jim's FWPD badge has a panther at the top—as did the three gold longevity stripes sewn between the elbow and cuff of the man's left sleeve. This was no rookie.

Officer Rodriguez corkscrewed an eyebrow. Let's just say I'm not accustomed to people scowling at me.

I repeated my request to speak to Lt. Vásquez. Or Velásquez, or maybe it was Valdez. A "V" name, I explained.

"We don't have a Lieutenant Vásquez."

"Sergeant Vásquez." Inclining my head closer to the counter, I did a quick scan for an employee directory.

"Don't have one of those, either."

"Lieutenant Velez."

"Nope."

Midway through my game of twenty questions, I learned they had a Captain Velásquez—but unless I had an appointment, he was handling a press conference about a shooting and couldn't see me.

"Hold my place in line," I said, "while I listen to this phone message from my boyfriend again. I'll get right back."

He did a little head bob, and I stepped out of the way as the next number was called. A chair scraped back and an old lady with an ice pack pressed against one side of her head waddled up to the counter, explaining that she had an appointment to talk to a detective.

Good luck with that, I thought.

With one finger drilled into my ear canal, I listened to the message a second time, but each time I thought I had the exact name of the policeman I was supposed to meet, rowdy conversations from people milling about drowned out Bruckman's voice. Before another person muscled me out of my place in line, I approached the information desk a second time.

"Look, I'm pretty sure my boyfriend spoke to a Lieutenant Armando Vásquez."

"Like I told you, ma'am, we don't have a lieutenant named Vásquez."

"Valdez. Try Valdez."

The Rochelle lookalike thoughtfully touched a fingertip to her temple. "We had a Valdez," she chimed in, "but he retired to Colombia. I think he sells coffee beans."

No question why she'd been assigned this plum role as information goddess.

Officer Rodriguez took over again. "I repeat, we have a captain named Velásquez, and he can't see you this morning."

"But he's supposed to find me a bodyguard to take me across the border. If there's no Lieutenant Vásquez working here, and Captain Velásquez isn't the one who's arranging this for me, then who's in charge of stuff like this?"

"Our job is to protect the public, not get them killed. The last thing we'd do is hook somebody up with a bodyguard to go into Cuidad Juárez." While I stared, slack-jawed, he became more animated. "Just this past weekend, they had eighteen murders—mostly drug lords cutting each other down with machine guns. In case you've been living in a cave, they have a serial killer loose over there, too."

"I want to talk to the captain. Let me speak to the captain, and I'll get out of your hair."

Resigned sigh. "What's your name?"

"Dainty Prescott."

Dull-eyed, he moved to the desk, lifted the telephone receiver, and stabbed in a number on the keypad. "Rodriguez here. There's a Dainty Prescott here to see you—no, that's actually her name." He appraised me with a head to toe glance. "Yeah, I guess so . . . I don't know, it's hard to tell . . . she looks pissed. I don't know. I'll ask—" he turned the mouthpiece of the phone into his shoulder "—where'd you say you were from?"

"Fort Worth."

"Right." He un-muted the receiver and parroted my information. "Right." Eyes that had previously seemed approachable thinned into onyx beads. "Right."

He hung up the phone and braced his arms across his chest. For no good reason, I looked around and saw that a long line had formed behind me—people with scowls wanting to take care of business, becoming impatient over an out-of-towner without an appointment.

"Capt'n says he doesn't have an appointment with a Dainty Prescott from Fort Worth. That he didn't procure a bodyguard to squire you around Mexico. That if I had any more trouble with you I should call the mental health officers and have them transport you to the county hospital for a psyche evaluation."

He lifted his gaze past my shoulder and, with a couple of finger-crooks, beckoned the next person up to the counter. "Yes, sir, how can we help you?"

I gave him a dedicated eye blink before stepping aside to let the guy behind me advance. With my mind hurtling in confusion, I returned to a chair and tapped on Bruckman's wireless.

My call cycled to voicemail. Judging from the time on my wristwatch, he was probably already in the air. Then I realized I'd changed time zones and reset my watch back one hour. I tapped on the phone again to listen to his messages.

That's when a fight broke out at the front desk, and the people who'd been standing in line behind me jumped aside to reveal the old woman I'd been sitting next to earlier, beating a man over the head with her purse.

It's also the precise moment my life intersected with that of Amanda Vásquez.

CHAPTER FIVE

"Dainty Prescott?"

I looked up expectantly. "Yes?"

A small, dark-skinned woman of indeterminate age and origin, with a complexion so black it seemed to have a purple tint, stared at me through reptilian eyes. With the hide stretched taut across her chiseled face, she couldn't have weighed more than ninety pounds nor stood much taller than four feet high. I'm only five feet four inches and 110 pounds—all right, 115 pounds but the last five pounds are mostly muscle—and when I rose from the chair, I towered over her like the jolly blue giant. Clearly, she didn't take cover quick enough when the glitter factory blew up, because the pair of super-high silver platform shoe-boots she'd slung over one arm had enough sparkle beneath the fluorescent lights to temporarily blind me. Since the long platinum hair didn't go with her complexion, I assumed the tangled mess of curls cascading past her shoulders was a wig. Never mind the sheer black blouse that didn't conceal the red lace bra underneath, or the short, red latex skirt that screamed *streetwalker* so loud that it assaulted three of my five senses.

"You're Dainty Prescott from Fort Worth?" She had a gap-toothed grin with a space between her teeth so big you could insert a filet mignon in it. And she talked with a kind of *je ne sais quoi*, exaggerated, over-modulated cadence of a drag queen, with flamboyant hand gestures. Her broad, flat nose flared as she spoke. When she talked, she spoke in exclamation marks. She must've thought she was communicating with Helen Keller, because she prompted me with, "You're looking for a bodyguard to take you across the border?" As she twisted a spiral of crimson lipstick and applied it to her mouth, *sans* mirror, limpid black eyes searched my face.

"Yes?" My skin tingled. Chills prickled the hairs on my neck, and I clutched my purse a little tighter to my chest.

"You're here to see me?"

My mouth formed the word *What?* while my mind screamed, *I don't effing think so.*

She swept the room with a furtive glance and returned the lipstick to a small clutch purse. Then she gripped my elbow. "Let's not talk in here. We'll go outside, okay?"

I have no idea what off-balance dimension of my personality allowed her to steer me beyond the glass entry and beneath the portico overhanging the front doors, but when we got outside, she plopped down on the top step and jammed a toe into her right thigh-high boot. I inwardly winced at the ripping sound it made when she zipped it up past her knee.

"I'm Lieutenant Amanda Vásquez." Her speech patterns had an interesting kind of rhythm to them, with an upward intonation at the end of each sentence that made her statements seem like questions. She slipped into the other boot and zipped it with another head-splitting rip. Then she stood and steered me away from the foot traffic in and out of the PD, toward a couple of wire news racks that held the *El Paso Times* and the *Border Observer.* Now we were almost the same height.

The morning sun beat down on the street, heating up the pavement as locals hurried to work. The woman held out her hand.

Against my better judgment, I clasped it. Instinct prompted me to demand whether she owned a full-length mirror; etiquette restrained me. Instead, I reminded myself what I'd come here for. "Wait—what? This is weird. You don't look much like a lieutenant."

"Lower your voice. I understood you needed a bodyguard. To take you into Mexico." Ebony eyes coolly narrowed.

I'd angered her. "I'm confused. I thought I was meeting a policeman—" emphasis on *man* "—named Armando Vásquez."

With a flick of the wrist, she fanned away the notion. "Happens all the time."

A couple of uniformed officers exited the front doors. One glanced our way and did a double take. Then he tapped the other's arm and gave an authoritative head jerk in our direction. As they strolled over, the lieutenant visibly tensed.

"Well, well, well, if it isn't Canary Tanzanite, darkening our door again. I thought I told you we'd better not catch you hooking around here again," said the steroid-munching bodybuilder of the two, "Or we'd lock your ass up—"

The partner finished his thought. "—and throw away the key."

"Aw, come on, baby," Lt. Vásquez said with a wink. "You don't mean it."

"You bet your ass we mean it. You'd better not be panhandling, either." To me, the big guy said, "Is this old raggedy-ass thing bothering you, ma'am?" leaving me speechless as the lieutenant prolonged the adversarial conversation.

"*We* are having a private conversation that does not include *you*. Now why don't you two hyenas get back to work. I'm sure you have places to go, people to see . . . lives to ruin."

They walked away with their heads close together, snuffling with laughter as if they were sharing an inside joke, or conspiring. The lieutenant flipped them a stiff middle finger.

My jaw went slack. "What was that all about?" I watched them climb into a patrol car that had been curbed beside a No

Parking zone.

"All part of the show."

"Canary Tanzanite?"

"My street name. Everybody needs a street name. Even you." She gave me the visual onceover. "You look like a . . ." The gears turning inside her head must've had sand thrown in them. ". . . well, don't worry, it'll come to me."

"Are you in Vice or something?"

"Not in it. In *charge* of it. Look, there's a coffee shop down the street. Tastes better than the mud they serve inside." She did an over-the-shoulder thumb gesture at the melee taking place inside the building.

"Sure." Still confused, I trailed her by a half step as she led the way. For no good reason, I channeled the voice of my dead mother: *Leaving with a stranger, Dainty? Have you lost your ever-lovin' mind?* My inner voice nagged, *Are you nuts?* My outer voice translated. "Wait—could I see your badge and ID?"

With a walk that was more of a strut, she'd advanced a few steps ahead of me. Stopping abruptly, she pivoted on one heel, whipped around, and planted a fist on her hip. After giving me the eye, she virtually stomped back to where I'd rooted myself on the concrete sidewalk, making the hoof-clopping noises of a Clydesdale.

"You can call me Amanda. Or Mandy. I don't care which. And no," she dropped her voice to a whisper, "you may not see my creds. I'm undercover, and I don't carry identification when I'm on assignment."

"Pardon me for saying so, but you don't exactly look like a decoy." The words were hot-wired to my tongue. On some level—a primal, amphibious level—I worried that she'd cold-cock me with that fist.

"What's wrong with the way I look?" She reared back her head.

51

"Well . . . for one thing, you could use some fashion advice."

"Is that so?"

"Like those boots, for instance," I said, looking at her garish shoes for effect. "You might rather invest in a pair of high-quality boots. I have a pair of Christian Louboutins, myself—in alligator. They're really showy."

"What else?"

"Well . . . you could use some makeup tips. Iridescent blue eye shadow isn't really your color. A nice mushroom over dark brown would be better. And the ladies of The Rubanbleu always wear muted colors such as cream or camel . . ."

"I like the way I look," she said defensively. "And what I don't have to spend—what the police department doesn't have to spend—in the way of money for clothes, I make up for in other ways. I know how to work it, girlfriend. Johns love me."

"I'm sure they do," I said, cutting off my statement and leaving off the *Not* part.

"Come on. I need coffee, and I'm hungry. And if we hurry, I can still order breakfast."

And that's where we cemented our deal, with me on one bench of a vinyl-covered booth, and Lt. Amanda Vásquez sitting opposite me. The woman appeared to be close to fifty, judging from the tiny strands of gray that poked out from under the wig near the temples.

I said, "Did you talk to Jim Bruckman about taking me across the border?"

She nodded and flagged down a waitress, a sturdy brunette woman wearing a colorful pink smock stitched with the name *Helen.* "Black coffee for me." Lt. Vásquez turned my way. "Order whatever you want."

"Could I get a mocha cappuccino with cream—lots of cream—and maybe some of those little chocolate shavings over the top of the foam? Not sprinkles—shavings. And can you make sure they're thin shavings? Because if they're too thick, they don't melt, and when you chew them, they taste like wax."

"Sure," the waitress said dully. She scrunched her brow. "We'll call in our best cappuccino consultants right away."

"*Dos cafés,*" Lt. Vásquez said, "*y un trozo de pastel para mí.*" As I stared, dumbfounded, she turned my way. "Dainty, would you like a piece of pie?"

I took the advice of the rental car lady about eating before crossing the border. "Yes, please."

"What kind?"

"Whatever you're having."

Lt. Vásquez rattled off more Spanish. The waitress shoved her pen behind one ear and bustled off, disappearing behind a swinging door with a glass portal in it.

"What, exactly, do you need from me?" asked the lieutenant.

"Well . . ." Unsure as to how much Bruckman had told her, I drew in a deep breath and slowly exhaled. "Last night, my sister Teensy chartered a plane to El Paso with her friend Tiffany. Apparently, they caught a cab across the border. Now my sister's in a hospital and her friend's missing. My sister said the Mexican cops did it."

Lt. Vásquez nodded pensively. "What do you plan to do about it?"

Air seeped out of my lungs. I didn't even realize I'd been holding my breath, waiting for her to back out.

"Look, I have to get my sister and her friend back. My boyfriend says I shouldn't cross the border without a guide." I checked myself. "Actually, he says I shouldn't cross the border, period. But I figure if I have someone who speaks the language and knows how to deal with the police, it'll work out fine. So I was thinking if you could match me up with a huge, football player–sized translator who knows how to handle the Mexican police . . ."

Coffee and pie arrived. When the waitress left, the conversation resumed.

I unfurled my napkin and spread it over my lap. Lt. Vásquez shook hers out with a whiplike snap before tucking it into the front of her see-through shirt.

Lacking an appetite, I ate anyway.

The lieutenant picked up her fork and let it hover over the slice of pumpkin pie. "I'm your translator."

"You?" My eyes bulged. I barked out a laugh. "What—*you?*" I howled like a coyote. "You're no bodyguard. You're like— *what?*—four feet tall?"

"Four-eight." Dark eyes thinned into slits.

"Wait. You're like—okay, I'm sorry, but I don't know any other way to say this—you're like a midget, and you're going to protect me?"

"Pygmy."

"What?" I must've misheard.

"I'm not a midget. I'm a pygmy."

Now that was funny. I had a rollicking good time. Tears of mirth filled my eyes. I wiped them away with my napkin.

"I'm sorry." I gulped back a chuckle. "I'm not laughing at you. I just realized my boyfriend played a practical joke on me." Which wasn't such a bad thing considering my muscles had been in knots ever since that phone call from Teensy. I caught my breath. Fanned my face with my napkin. Did a little eye roll to show her I was fine with the prank. "So who's really going to take me across the border? Because I want a big, swarthy kick-ass Mexican with a Fu Manchu mustache who'll scare the crap out of the bastards who tried to kill my sister and stole her friend Tiffer."

The pygmy held me in her steady gaze. She lowered her fork, carved off a piece of pie, lifted it to her mouth and chewed. It went on so long I lost count . . . five, six . . . ten. Swallow. Cup of steaming coffee to mouth. Swallow. Cup to saucer. Second verse, same as the first. She never broke eye contact.

I blinked. "Wait—are you kidding me?"

Carve. Eat. Count. Swallow. Sip.

"Ohmygod. Are you serious? I can't go with you."

"Why not?"

"Because . . . you're . . . well . . ." There was no nice way to put it. "Too small."

There. I said it.

"The cops won't sanction your little catch-and-release program. The only reason I'm willing to stick my neck out for you is because your boyfriend asked nicely, and I need the money. He said you'd be fine with the thousand dollars."

"A thousand dollars," I shrieked. People at nearby tables paused in mid-bite. Eyes moved in a collective shift. I forced the rest of my words out in a whisper. "I'm not paying you a thousand dollars to walk me across the border."

People were looking at me like I should be using my inside voice.

"That's extortion," I hissed. "Why would I pay a thousand dollars for someone to accompany me across the border and rattle off a couple of Spanish phrases?"

It was a stupid question and a completely inane response, but apparently I couldn't process what she was telling me any other way. In the end, I knew I'd enter into an agreement with her. I had to get my sister back. And since Lt. Amanda Vásquez happened to be the only taker for this suck-dog assignment, we were about to be shotgun-married to each other.

She locked gazes with me and wiped her mouth with her napkin.

"That's highway robbery." I tried not to blink, despite the fact that my eyes had dried out five minutes ago.

"You're absolutely right." Lt. Vásquez spoke in a low voice.

"Hire anybody you want, and pay them as little as you want. And when they get you across the border and turn you over to their cousins, or their drug dealer and what-not, or cut your throat and let the dirt soak up your blood like the *maquiladoras*—the poor factory workers—well . . ." She shrugged. "Think of the money you saved."

She was spot-on, of course.

"How do I know I can trust you?" Again, the words were hotwired to my tongue.

"You found me at the police station, right?"

I started to answer, but the waitress returned with a huge steaming meal: steak, mashed potatoes, fried okra, a huge glass of iced tea and Texas toast—thick slices of bread buttered to a fare-thee-well and browned to a golden crisp. I blinked. Amanda opened a new napkin and fanned it out across her lap.

"You just ate pie," I reminded her.

She squeezed a lemon wedge into her tea glass, then turned the sugar dispenser over. I watched as the bottom of her glass filled up with an inch of granulated sugar. When she'd doubled that amount, she upturned the container and pushed it aside. As she stirred, the teaspoon clinked noisily against the glass.

She said, "Know anything about pygmies?"

Big headshake.

"Short life spans." She picked up the steak knife, stuck her fork into the meat and sawed off a hunk. "I eat dessert first." She popped the steak into her mouth and chewed, making little grunts of approval as she devoured her meal. "Did you know the oldest documented pygmy was thirty-seven when he died?"

"How old are you?"

"Thirty-five." She carved off another piece of meat and stuffed it into her mouth. "Don't be sorry, that's just how it is. I told my kids to marry Americans."

"Aren't you in the wrong country? Shouldn't you be in Africa?"

"Shouldn't you be in Sweden or Norway or Holland or one of those countries where brown-haired, brown-eyed people are in the minority?"

Touché.

She explained how, years ago, her father moved the family to Mexico and became a bodyguard for the Mexican president. Since pygmies were small and lithe, they could walk along and see other people's hands at eye-level—people who might want to assassinate *El Presidente.* I could tell she was self-conscious about the gap between her teeth from the way she tried to keep from smiling. Sure, it was big, but it's not like you could see it from the rooftop of the El Paso jail.

I said, "Doesn't the PD have a height requirement?"

She wolfed down a few more bites and then dabbed her mouth at the corners with her napkin. "Here's the thing . . . I have skills. I speak four languages. I'm a catch." She grinned big enough for me to notice a missing molar, and went back to her food.

She had me over a barrel.

Bruckman would be here in another hour or so, and I needed to get across that border. I didn't like the idea of spending a thousand dollars of Teensy's money, but Amanda Vásquez had me backed into a corner. And she had kids. And—I tried not to think about this next part—she didn't expect to live long.

"Fine. We have a deal. You get a thousand bucks, and I get my sister back. Then you help me find her friend."

She shook her head. "The thousand is for getting your sister out. I want two thousand to get your sister's friend back."

"What?"

People raised their heads. Eyes riveted on us in a collective shift.

57

The lieutenant did a one-shoulder shrug. "Suit yourself."

The cell phone chirped. It was Bruckman, waiting standby for the next flight to El Paso.

"I don't understand." My voice corkscrewed upward. "They run flights to El Paso every hour. What's the problem?"

"Mechanical malfunction. I tried to get on the last flight, but nobody wanted to give up their seat. Imagine that. El Paso's become a hotspot for tourism and business."

We both knew that was a laugh.

"Can't you pull some strings?" I didn't want him stuck at the airport. "Why didn't you just flash your badge and demand a spot on the flight?"

"Well . . ." he drawled out the word to prolong the agony, "I imagine if I was working with your daddy on this, he might've chartered a plane for me."

Oops. Sorry. Long pause.

"I hooked up with Lieutenant Vásquez. If you're not on the next flight out, we're going across without you." This gambit allowed me to flex my inner-courage muscles. In no way did I actually plan to go through with such a veiled threat.

"Dainty, listen to me . . . your father knows a recovery specialist—"

"Don't worry, I have everything under control." *Houston, we have a problem.* "So if you'll just get on the next plane, everything will be fine." Which anyone within earshot knew meant not so fine.

Tiring of the conversation, I pulled the cell phone from my ear and held it at arm's length. "What? You're breaking up. I can't hear you. Uh-oh—tunnel." I switched off the talk button and let out a deep exhale.

Right or wrong, I'd made my decision. And I'm nothing if not decisive.

Our waitress buzzed by and slapped the guest check on the

table. Instead of picking up the tab, Amanda Vásquez shoved it across the Formica.

"Are you kidding me? You're sticking me with the tab? I had a slice of pie, and you ate like a horse. I'm not paying this. You invited me, remember?"

"Yeah? Well, if you were smart, which I'm really starting to have my doubts, you'd have ordered a big, fat hamburger and gorged yourself on it. The restaurants across the border are viral and bacterial palaces. Since I don't particularly feel like being holed up in a motel room with a sick person, waiting for Montezuma's revenge to run its course, you should've taken my advice and stuffed yourself." She snapped her fingers. "Diva Delight. That's your street name."

"Do not call me that. Ever."

"Can I trust you?" Her voice dropped to a whisper. She glanced around and did a quick, conspiratorial lean-in. "As an undercover officer, I intentionally walk around without money. I don't want to get rolled. We're working a big case—organized crime—can't really talk about it. Very hush-hush. I can't afford to have my cover blown. So pay the damned check and let's get out of here."

Chapter Six

Since I didn't get a rental car, Lt. Vásquez hailed a taxi. We piled into the back seat and listened to the door locks snap shut.

"To the Bat Cave, Alfred," I said feeling suddenly upbeat after making a plan and cementing the deal with the cop.

Obsidian eyes slewed to the rearview mirror. A chill rippled up my neck. The tiny hairs at the base of my skull stood on end. I was pretty sure I'd seen the driver's mug shot on the bulletin board back at the police department. Or he was one of the Ayatollah Sistani's men, fled to the states for political asylum. And why not? Border towns are crime cesspools.

The lieutenant inclined her head toward the taxi driver and rattled off a few phrases in Spanish. He gave a perfunctory nod and whipped the cab into traffic. My head immediately snapped back. We'd apparently lucked into getting the only cab driver who was gearing up for the NASCAR tryouts. All we lacked was the smell of burning rubber and racing fuel. We were pulling about four-Gs, me with my back flat against the seat and Lt. Vásquez gripping the headrest on the front passenger seat for stability. I felt the blood being suctioned from my brain.

Good news, though—that much force can either be fatal, or make you slip into unconsciousness. Either way, I derived a smidgen of comfort knowing I'd probably be unconscious or dead when he plowed through the red light at the upcoming intersection.

Posted signs clearly indicated curves in the road and warned motorists not to pass, but our driver seemed hell bent on overtaking every vehicle in our path. On the rare occasions he couldn't pass them, he'd try to intimidate them by riding their bumpers and honking.

"What'd you say to him?" I asked.

"I told him there's an extra hundred in it for him if he can get us to the border in the next half hour."

I blinked. Twisting in my seat, I tried to look out the back windshield, but centrifugal force held me in place. My head must've weighed twenty pounds. For a moment, I actually felt the skin on my face sagging.

"Wait. Isn't the International Bridge behind us?" I thumbed over my shoulder, and the vector force almost pulled my arm out of its socket. This car had no shock absorbers.

The lieutenant rattled off more Spanish. The cabbie cornered on two wheels. For no good reason, he slammed on the brake, and the car fishtailed. He drove over the median, completed a mid-block U-turn and we careened into a residential area.

Vásquez said, "Slow down—*stop*. I'll get out here." The locks popped open, and she grabbed the door handle.

I clutched her wrist and tightened my fingers until she winced. "Where are you going? You're not leaving me here. What's going on?"

"I'll be right back."

"I know, but where—" By the time I delivered the rest of my sentence, she'd wrangled free from my grasp and was gone, swishing up the sidewalk at a brisk, exaggerated pace.

She returned five minutes later, looking eight months pregnant. It was like watching time-lapse photography, only without the video. As soon as she climbed into the back seat, she delivered a matted, undernourished bichon puppy.

At her command, the driver whipped the cab into the

intersection and roared off down the road.

I stared, horrified, at the dirty, quaking canine. "What's going on?"

"Just rectifying a situation."

"What kind of situation?"

She dove to the floorboard, taking the dog with her. For a second I thought she might be having a seizure. Then I observed a cop car roaring past on the opposite side of the divided roadway.

The farther we drove, the more property values declined, and the more rat-trappish the houses looked. We ended up in the barrio, a desolate spot with ramshackle houses that weren't much bigger than a roach motel. Midway down the block, she directed the cabbie to pull over.

"Wait here," she said, as if she actually thought I'd leave the sanctuary of this taxi without a gun pointed at my head. She took the dog with her.

Meantime, the meter on the cab ticked off another five bucks. Somehow, I knew I'd get stuck with the tab.

Twenty minutes passed before the El Paso cop returned. She emerged from the house looking like a baboon wearing heavy mascara and purple-blue eye shadow, and had changed into a cheap denim skirt from China, the kind that'd leave an inky black trail like an octopus if she got caught in the rain. She also wore a dark blouse, faded from too many spins in the washer, with a loose-weave sweater that swallowed her. With her closely cropped hair and orthopedic shoes laced tight, she could've passed for a factory worker. This was the last thing I expected of my guide, to be dressed as a homeless woman, carrying a small tote filled to capacity and slung over one shoulder.

I didn't ask what she had in her bag of tricks. I didn't really care since the outfit she'd chosen was the lesser of the evils. Those glitter shoe-boots and that platinum blonde wig made her look like a circus clown. If she'd added a jaunty little beret and climbed out of a tiny car, we could've sold tickets.

She fired off a couple of Spanish commands to our driver, and then twisted in the seat to face me. "You need to change clothes."

"What's wrong with the way I'm dressed?" It was pretty, it was silk, it accentuated my curves and brought out the vitality in my complexion. It was the kind of gem-tone, dress-for-success clothing I wore to my internship position at WBFD-TV Channel 18.

"It screams rich *turista*. You don't want to attract unwanted attention."

"So you'd rather I looked frumpy?" Of course she envied me. I get that a lot. What other explanation could there be?

"I want you to blend in. People across the border don't dress like this. You need different clothes. Old stuff."

The executive decision I made was predicated on the fact that I was tired and cranky, and we still hadn't left the United States. "We're wasting time. I'm wearing this. We don't have time for me to change clothes."

"Let's get a few things straight," said the lieutenant. "First of all, you need to get rid of that cell phone."

My mouth gaped. I wasn't about to sever my umbilical cord to the free world. Apparently she picked up on my hesitation, because she said, "Fine, keep it. Just don't blame me when you become the profit center for all the telecommunications towers that have to route your calls. You can leave your little suitcase here."

As if. "This is Louis Vuitton. Where I go, Louis goes." No need to mention *The Ladies' Guide to Homicide* inside. Besides, we'd gotten off to a rocky start, and I might need to read it.

She ignored me. Then she tapped the back of the driver's seat, and he pulled away from the curb and out into traffic. We rode to the International Bridge in relative silence.

On occasion, Amanda made small talk. "So you live in Fort Worth? What's that like?"

"It's only the greatest place in the whole world. You should visit sometime," I said politely, while thinking, *Like that'll ever happen,* as the scenery rolled by.

"Is that an invitation?"

I gave her a sidelong glance. "Sure." *Not.*

On occasion, Amanda described our surroundings.

"Here's the 'tortilla curtain'." She thumbed at the wire mesh barriers of tightly woven rebar springing up along our route.

Before Homeland Security managed the border situation, cyclone or chain link fences separated the two countries. New twenty-foot-tall rebar fences with their two-inch by two-inch holes made it almost impossible to cut or otherwise circumvent. According to Amanda, drug smugglers who formerly used bolt cutters to open the chain link fences had to modify their tools by filing down the metal snippers until they looked more like needle-nose pliers in order to slip the cutters through the two-inch holes.

While I was looking out the window, a Border Patrol officer overtook us along the same route.

Amanda said, "There's *La Migra.*" She meant Immigration, now under the auspices of Homeland Security.

"What do they do, drive up and down the road looking for illegals?"

"They have bike patrols, too. We might even see them riding horseback in this area."

Between Amanda and our cab driver, I learned that tracking illegal aliens and drug smugglers had become a complex, high-tech operation. The Border Patrol had even installed seismic sensors to discern movement in areas where "wets," "beaners," or "tonks"—pejoratives used to describe undocumented workers—might cross into the United States. These sensors were so sophisticated that they could make the distinction as to whether the movement that triggered it walked on four feet or two.

"So the fence stretches all through El Paso?" I asked. My imagination conjured up a scenario where Teensy and I couldn't get back into the U.S.A. via conventional methods. It might pay off to learn as much as possible about these barricades.

"Little-known fact," Amanda said, "there's an area called Cement River Park that doesn't have this barricade. It'd cost too much to put the metal fence up, and the old stuff would have to be torn out. Nobody wants to go to the expense. But the barriers exist in major parts of El Paso. That's the main thing." She fell silent, leaving me to contemplate these attempts to fortify our border.

"How long do you think this will take?" I asked, referring to my sister's rescue operation. "A few hours?" No response. "All day?" Nothing. "Hello? Are you listening?"

Apparently, I'd developed a superpower—invisibility—because I sensed her ignoring me. My blue-haired grandmother does that—either completely ignores me, or talks over me when I'm speaking to her. It happens with such frequency that I've started carrying on conversations with imaginary people while she does this. Like day-before-yesterday when Gran went off on me while I was trying to have a discussion with her about The Rubanbleu ball, I said, "Okay, doesn't look like she's going to let me finish what I was saying. Par for the course. Guess I'll just sit here and talk to myself." That woman is so self-absorbed she doesn't even hear me acting like I've got a split personality. Seriously, it's a wonder I didn't develop an imaginary playmate when I was young.

Whatever. Let Amanda tune me out. Silence is golden; duct tape is silver.

Ever since the unwelcome commentary on my designer clothing, I'd grown tired of the pygmy's horsey attitude. At least this way I didn't have to slap tape across her mouth to stop the rude opinions about my ensemble. No one will ever catch *moi*, Dainty Prescott, wearing used clothing from a thrift shop. *Ha!* Dress down indeed.

Now that I'd become the invisible woman, I started thinking of ways to use my new gift.

Finally, our cabbie stopped on the U.S. side of the bridge to let us out.

Amanda emerged from her coma. "Pay him."

"I'm not paying him. We're not across the border yet."

After a staccato conversation between Amanda and our taxi driver, I got a rude awakening.

"He says there's no way in hell he's crossing into Mexico."

I immediately suspected he might be an undocumented alien, afraid that he couldn't get back across the U.S. border.

"This is crap," I said out on the curb, watching the taxi speed away in a swirl of brown exhaust.

"Mexico is crap," said Amanda.

There's a distinct difference in the air quality in the U.S. when you're standing by the bridge that leads to a border town. At this particular moment, the breeze changed course and I whiffed a vile mixture of raw sewage combined with the cloying smell of sugar.

My nose slammed shut in self-defense. "That's disgusting. It smells like an outhouse."

"Oh." She nodded knowingly. "I thought you were going to remark on the sickeningly sweet odor coming from the crematorium."

I blinked.

"When the wind shifts, it floats over here."

"That's revolting."

Her eyes thinned into slits. "Are you sure you want to do this?"

"You'd better not be chickening out on me," I said.

"You can't have a play in hell and expect to have angels as actors. I'm not scared. You just make sure you're not." Amanda started walking toward the bridge. I trotted to catch up, and as we fell into step, she gave me a crash course in what to expect. "Listen up. Never, ever, hail a cab from the street. That's where your sister and her friend made their first mistake. Only use the authorized cabs."

"How do you know what's an authorized cab?"

"I'll show you when we get across. Street cabs—what're known as gypsy cabs—are usually green VW Beetles. They're known as the Kidnapping Express. They'll hold you hostage and make you withdraw money from the nearest ATM."

A deeper understanding of what happened to Teensy and her friend soaked in. It left a creepy residue in my memory, as if I'd touched something viscous and vile, and didn't want to sniff it to identify it.

A cold wind coming off the Chihuahuan desert whipped my face. The lieutenant was a good ten steps ahead of me.

"Try to keep up," she called over one shoulder.

"What? *Me* keep up with *you?* Are you kidding? You can't even keep up your pantyhose." I chuckled without humor.

Instead of looking down at the little folds around her ankles, she plodded on without comment.

A ragged sigh escaped my lips. My joke went right over her head.

Well, what'd I expect? She's a pygmy.

I barked out a laugh. Sometimes I just crack me up.

Amanda whirled around to see if I was a lunatic. She paused long enough for me to catch up. "This'll require us to work together. I'm talking so close you'll think we're Velcroed at the hip."

Ha! Your hip to my knee.

"I know what you're thinking . . ."

Apparently Amanda had developed a mind-reading super-power of her own.

I snorted. "Don't tell me you're claiming to be telepathic."

"By the time we're through here, I'll be able to read your mind before you can say what you're thinking."

Flake. "Well, I'm sorry you had to hear that," I challenged her, my tone surly. I get cranky when I haven't had enough to eat. Sarcasm oozed. "I'm sure you have the kind of mind that can bend spoons."

I wasn't at all certain this shotgun marriage to a pygmy would work out. But when there's precious little to choose from, well, you get the picture.

The river lay as smooth as glass. The dead air felt thick and compressed beneath the gunmetal gray sky. Almost halfway across the bridge, Amanda said, "We can always turn back. It's not too late."

"You said you weren't scared."

"I lied. You'd have to be stupid not to be scared."

"Then I'm probably the smartest natural blonde you ever met, because I'm scared to death."

"Try not to act like you speak English. Every border town in Mexico is crap. The remedy, if you must go, is don't speak to anyone and maybe they'll think you're a deaf mute and leave you alone. Do not act like you're from America." She gave my ensemble the onceover. Then she dropped her gaze to the Louis Vuitton on roller wheels. "Oh, wait, what am I saying? They're going to take one look and peg you for a rich girl. We should've bought you a black wig, girlfriend. And brown contact lenses."

"My vision's perfect."

"And that's another thing, we should've gotten you a pair of clear glasses without a prescription to ugly you up."

"There wasn't enough time."

"Well then, girlfriend, all I can say is when we get across the border, you'd better attach yourself to me like a two-year-old special needs child."

A black-and-white rendition of communist hero Che Guevara had been painted on the Mexico side of the river. Seeing this mural mocking the U.S. infuriated me.

"I thought our governments were supposed to be working together for better commerce. You'd think they'd send someone out to paint over that."

This triggered a heavy eye roll on Amanda's part, and a sarcastic thought on mine. *Thanks, Bill Clinton, for giving us NAFTA.*

I didn't think anything could pique my irritation radar beyond the Che Guevara mural until I saw the huge and overpowering Mexican flag fluttering at the top of the bridge next to the U.S. flag. According to Amanda, who'd suddenly morphed into a tour docent, this 162-foot-by-93-foot mega-*bandera* flew atop a 110-ton, 339-foot-tall flagpole.

Then we came to a line on the bridge. Amanda called it the point of no return—if we crossed that line, we were in Mexico.

She dug into her tote and fished out a pack of cigarettes. Then she shook one out and lit it. As we stood on the bridge—Amanda with smoke snaking out of her nostrils, me with my nose prickling from the vile smell of raw sewage wafting up from the river—she told a story.

"Not too long ago, a Border Patrol officer chased a smuggler across this bridge," she said, straining her conversation through her cigarette. "When they got to the top, the Border Patrol agent caught up to the smuggler. They got into a struggle, and the agent called for backup. But guess what? The smuggler had backup, too. The Mexican police were on the Mexico side waiting to see how it'd all play out."

In Amanda's scenario, the agent crossed the dividing line and ended up on the Mexico side. Mexican police arrested him and seized his weapon. Negotiating his release began at the top of both nations' capitals, and ended up in a trickle-down effect where diplomats of both countries worked to secure the agent's freedom.

"Somebody got paid off?" I asked.

Amanda lifted one shoulder. "I'm not sure how these things work. All I know is that you don't want to end up in a Mexican jail. If that means paying people off, so be it." She continued with an abbreviated survival course. Her cigarette had burned halfway down, and I could see she wanted to finish it. When she finally took her last puff, dropped the filter and toed it out, she said, "You know how it is when you get too much of a good thing?"

Thoughts of South Padre Island and a case of raging sunburn came to me in a flashback. I nodded.

"When you think of Mexico," she said, "moderation is the key."

But I'd already taken it one step further, as in, *Less is more, and none is perfect.*

CHAPTER SEVEN

We came to the end of the bridge, to the mouth of a tunnel, with Amanda, athletic and physically fit despite the cigarette habit, and me huffing and puffing. Amanda stopped and turned my way.

"Are you sure you don't want to go back?" When I didn't answer, she said, "If you decide to rent us a car and anybody tries to pull you over—"

"Who'd try to pull us over?"

"Fake policemen." Without warning, she grabbed me by the shoulders and gave me a gentle shake. "Stop talking, diva, and listen. This is critical. Everything I'm telling you now is critical. If anybody tries to pull you over, you keep going. Do not pull over."

The sick, sinking feeling I'd felt on the U.S. side of the bridge stuck in my gut.

As I entered the graffiti-tagged tunnel with the Louis Vuitton bouncing down the steps behind me, I took one last longing look over my shoulder at the Cordova International Bridge, at the cars stacked up behind filling station awnings, waiting for the green signal to proceed into the country. While descending the steps, I thought about what Amanda had just said, and tried to imagine what a fake policeman looked like, and how to tell a counterfeit cop from a real one.

It took all of 90 seconds before we ended up on Mexican turf.

71

Bienvenidos a Mexico. Welcome to Mexico. Land of coups and uprisings and crises.

I did a heavy eye roll. Border towns are crime cesspools.

At the border crossing, Mexican customs officials sat in chairs, nodding at pedestrians as they stepped onto Mexican soil. The guard asked if we had any fruit or vegetables to declare.

Uh, no.

Then he waved us through. No interrogation, no questions, nothing. Nobody wanted to have a look inside my suitcase. I guess nobody in his or her right mind would be coming into the country; therefore, nothing I might be smuggling in would have any value.

Almost the instant the tunnel disgorged us, we were accosted by beggars, children hawking chewing gum while screaming, *"Chicle, chicle,"* and people with some of the most grotesque deformities I'd ever seen. I wanted to help them all, but I didn't have money to spread around, and I didn't know how long what I did have might last.

"There." Amanda pointed.

I tracked her finger to where a dozen or so taxicabs—clearly individually owned according to colors and logos—had lined up in the rotation waiting for fares.

"Take a good long look. Those are authorized cabs."

"Let's get a cab and find out where the hospital is." I angled over to the first vehicle in the queue.

Amanda grabbed my sleeve and held me back. "Not that one."

I shot her a wicked look and shook off her grip. Nobody manhandles Dainty Prescott. "Fine. Which one do you want?"

"It doesn't work like that. They take people in order. I want that one." She pointed to a white cab with a picture of a bluebird on it, where a fat-faced, dark-skinned man with a spidery mustache sat behind the wheel. "We'll just stand here and act like we're talking while other people take the cabs in front of that chubby guy."

I stepped aside, waving away exhaust fumes that spiraled into my face. Far be it from me to challenge another's superstitions. Besides, it didn't take long before the one she wanted pulled in beside us. We stepped up to the taxi, and the driver got out and opened the trunk. As I thrust the Louis Vuitton at him, Amanda slapped away my hand.

"What are you doing?" That made the third time she'd put her hands on me. At this rate, we'd end up in a cage fight. "This might be a good time to warn you . . . my pet peeve is people who put their hands on me without permission."

"Yeah?" Dark eyes shrewdly narrowed. "Since we're sharing, my pet peeve is people who whine in car trunks."

She rattled off a bit of Spanish. With one of those *Don't say I didn't try* looks spreading across his mournful face, the driver shrugged, palms up. Then he opened the back door for us.

Amanda grabbed my suitcase, shoved me inside, slung the luggage in after me, and hopped on in.

"What was that about?"

"Hey—we don't know these people. He could've thrown it in the trunk and sped off. Now *cállate la boca*. That means shut your mouth."

Dark eyes cut to the rearview mirror.

"I'm talking to her," Amanda said, her gaze locked with his as she continued to mother-hen me. "Where's the nearest hospital?"

The driver shrugged his shoulders. *"No ingles. Solamente español."*

Even *moi*, with my limited Spanish vocabulary, knew he denied speaking English. "Ask him to take us to the hospital."

It was a simple question. The answer took longer than it should have.

Amanda said, "He wants to know if you mean hospital or clinic."

"Hospital."

"He says there are five hospitals in Ciudad Juárez. And dozens of clinics. Also private clinics. But he says the private clinics won't treat gunshot victims because the cartel hit men often show up to finish off victims of their attacks."

"My sister was beaten."

She translated. Even before our driver finished answering, Amanda was shaking her head. "He says it doesn't matter. If the cartel did this, she's as good as—" she abbreviated the grisly thought "—he says we should check the morgue."

Tears blistered behind my eyeballs. "No."

"He's got a point. If you rule out the possibility that the girls are there . . ."

What my mind heard her saying was, "She's dead," and those horrible words were just too huge to cram into my ears. Starting our search at the morgue would've been the logical thing to do, of course, but my mind closed off that option in self-defense.

"No," I said with an edge. "Tell him to take us to the nearest hospital. And tell him to wait for us."

The driver floored the accelerator. My neck instantly snapped back. Once again Amanda had chosen the one cab driver in the queue who was practicing to be a Formula One racecar driver. I curled my perfectly manicured fingernails into the door padding and tried to right myself. I'm pretty sure we were pulling a couple of Gs—not that it mattered. I wouldn't be able to tell anybody, since we were going to die.

Palm trees popped up on either side of the road, but pine trees lined the medians. A smear of old buildings appeared in my peripheral vision, as well as old cars belching brown smoke. Mexican gasoline is different than what we have across the border—cheaper, too—and you can sure tell from the choking smell of exhaust. One thing for certain, these vehicles could never pass inspection in the United States. I'm not kidding.

Murals of the Virgin Mary appeared on buildings as we careened through the city. Altars with candles and photos of loved ones appeared on sidewalks and near street corners, commemorating the deaths of victims of street crimes.

Then traffic bottlenecked and we slowed to a crawl. Inside the cab, the air thickened. The gridlock was starting to seem worse than having a root canal in Tijuana.

While Amanda carried on with our driver, we passed Chamizal Park—a public park. She paused in the middle of their conversation long enough to explain that the locals dubbed it "Central Park" even though there already was a Central Park elsewhere in the city. It was beautiful, with tiered water fountains and plenty of palm trees and benches. Shadows from the palm fronds made lacy patterns on the sidewalks, as well as on the faces of people strolling through it. But I knew from reading the newspaper that this lovely park had become a dumping ground for dead bodies—victims murdered by warring cartels. According to one article, a missing finger on the latest body had been severed and stuffed in the victim's mouth—a killer's nonverbal message accusing the dead man of being a ratfink.

While we were stopped at the traffic light, a disconcerting sight appeared in front of us. A Humvee filled with military men dressed in camouflage fatigues drove through the intersection, holding what looked like AK-47s. Not that I'd actually seen an AK-47 up close. But the weapons looked Russian, and they looked evil and threatening.

The light turned green. The driver behind us tapped the horn and the cab lurched forward. Up ahead, traffic slowed for the octagonal red sign marked ALTO. I quickly learned that nobody stops for these, except for the truck in front of us that bore Texas license plates. It had a camper shell covered in dust.

Someone had written a message across the grit on the back windshield that read, *I wish my wife was this dirty* . . . whereupon someone else added, *She is* . . . *when you're at work.*

So sue me, I laughed. At this point, the grimy pickup had been the best part of my day.

As I sat contemplating this journey, a fireworks display of grand proportions went off all around us. Another explosion every bit as sharp as the first one followed.

"They let you set off firecrackers inside the city limit?" I asked.

But Amanda wasn't listening. Our driver had said something. She grabbed me by the neck, pulled me toward her, and shoved me onto the floorboard. Then she threw herself on top of me. Tires screamed against the pavement, and we were moving again; me with my face getting rug burn against the floor mats, and Amanda riding me like a rented mule.

Ugh. I can't feel my legs.

"Get . . . off . . . me." Dazzled by an inner vision of colorful pyrotechnics, my eyes flicked around in search of anything I could use to create a fulcrum to pry her off me.

The taxi banked to the right. My stomach lurched.

Then Amanda climbed back up into the seat. "Are you all right?"

"Am I all right?" My voice spiraled up in volume and pitch. "Am I all right? Are you crazy?" No reaction from the pygmy. "Three things. Three. Things. First thing: Don't be grabbing me. Second thing: Don't climb on top of me. Third thing: Don't slap or hit me. Got it? I'm paying you to translate and to act as my bodyguard, not to get physical with me."

"I was looking out for you. Deal with it."

The cabbie spoke. Wide, dark eyes connected with ours in the rearview mirror.

Amanda nodded understanding as she translated. "The gangs

have taken over the borders, the highways and the cops. They have shootouts anytime and anywhere. Count your blessings. We were just in one."

"What?" I said dully.

"You saw that truck back there? The one with Texas plates?" I nodded, and she said, "Shot full of bullet holes."

This was how I imagined the Middle East would be, only without the turbans.

She helped me up from the floorboard and dusted me off. My cheek burned from being rubbed raw against the nasty carpet, but I was here and I was alive, and for now, that's all that mattered. I know in my state of despair, I only imagined the next part of this, but I swear I heard my dead mother's voice.

"God protects children, dogs and stupid people."

CHAPTER EIGHT

Thanks to the gunfight at the OK Corral, we'd strayed off the beaten path. A cyclone fence of considerable length appeared ahead of us and to the right. Coat hangers hung from the wire mesh, displaying clothing in festive shades. We'd entered upon the world's biggest yard sale.

Amanda said, "We should stop and buy clothes for you."

"I'm not wearing that stuff. It's used."

"You stick out like a sore thumb, diva."

"I'm in a taxi. Unless these people have X-ray vision, nobody can see me."

"Suit yourself." She laughed without humor. "Get it? Suit yourself?"

I just stared at her. *Hello Night, this is Day.*

Once we were back on a paved road, smells of Mexican food leaked into the cab. Our driver lifted a sausage finger and pointed as we passed a restaurant.

"He says that's a good place to eat."

Probably friends with the owner. "I want American food."

The driver made eye contact with me through the rearview mirror, but he spoke to Amanda. *"Señor Pepe,"* he said, and rambled on for several minutes before she said, *"Sí,"* and turned to me.

"He says the college kids from the United States like Señor Pepe's. I've heard of it. They serve American food."

"Thought he said he didn't understand English. He knew

what I was saying." I darted a look at our driver. Accusations flew from me in French. I know it sounded stupid, but hey—it's a Romance language, so I figured his mind could make the leap. "*J'accuse!* You knew what I was saying. You understand."

"Stop it, Dainty. You're not even supposed to be talking."

"I don't like being lied to."

"He saved our lives."

The cab pulled to a stop. I looked out the window and saw the word *Hospital* on the side of the building. It didn't look much like a hospital. Except for the carved marble statue of the Virgin Mary standing near the wrought iron fence, it looked more like a dilapidated warehouse.

We'd arrived at Catholic hospital hell, located in the Enema section of Ciudad Juárez.

Amanda jolted me back to reality. "Pay the man."

I hadn't converted my U.S. dollars to those worthless Mexican pesos, so I expected him to make change. He gave me a handful of Monopoly money, and I grabbed my Louis Vuitton by the handle and stepped out of the cab. Then Amanda had a lively conversation with our driver, complete with hand gestures. She got out of the car, shaking her head.

"Wait for us," I said, certain he understood more English than he let on. It wasn't until I got halfway up the sidewalk that I realized he'd ripped me off with my change. His tires smoked pulling away. I looked over at Amanda. "What did you say to him?"

"I asked where to get a gun."

"Have you lost your mind?"

She shook her head. "You can't bring them into the country or you'll get arrested. But we need one—just in case—and they're supposed to be easy to buy down here."

"Maybe not that easy."

"I'm not going to discuss this with you anymore," Amanda

said, and clammed up.

We stood in front of a set of iron gates that hung on an eight-foot high fence, staring through the bars like prison inmates. Except we were actually trying to get inside, not escape. It was as if hospital personnel had taken precautions to fortify the place, and I found this disconcerting. The lock mechanism wasn't that complicated, just foreign to me. But Amanda figured it out and in mere seconds, we were inside the courtyard and walking into the building.

Imagine . . . 1948 to 1952. Gnawbone, Oklahoma. With linoleum floors in colored tiles, checker-boarded into an unidentifiable pattern; metal beds from vintage WWII; walls painted a shade of pale green that had dulled with the patina of neglect; a single bare light bulb hanging from the ceiling . . . then you have an idea what a Mexican hospital is like.

As I looked toward the front counter for a receptionist, a shadow fell over me. For a second, I thought it was an eclipse. When I turned, a hulking man who appeared to be descended from Aztec ancestry stood in front of the window, silhouetted within the frame. He held a push broom in one thickly cal-loused hand. In the other hand—well, there was no other hand. Thin, dark eyes narrowed into slits.

Chief Bromden. *One Flew Over the Cuckoo's Nest.*

So it was true. Old actors never died. They just lost their parts.

Amanda pushed past me. She engaged a woman behind the counter in quiet conversation. The woman, who had eyes the color of melted chocolate, listened attentively. When Amanda said, "Teensy Prescott" and "Americana" and a couple of other words that I recognized, the woman's eyes grew wide. The longer Amanda talked, the more those helpful eyes hardened into black walnuts. Fearing she'd turn us away, I opened my purse and dug for my wallet, rummaging through it until I found a photo of my sister. I thrust it at her.

"*Mi hermana.* Teensy." I wanted her to see what my sister looked like, in case she'd been admitted without being able to tell them her name.

I knew in my heart things were going badly once the head-shaking began, and their Spanish exchanges came in staccato bursts. I touched Amanda's sleeve—I needed to know—was Teensy dead? The lieutenant shook off my grip.

"She's dead, isn't she?" My voice warbled. The air thinned. I needed oxygen. Fresh air. I needed to get back outside.

I ran for the door, gasping for breath, pulling the little suitcase behind me.

I have no earthly idea why I did what I did next—flung open the doors and stepped out into the front courtyard screaming my sister's name at the top of my lungs.

"Teensy. Teensy Prescott. I want my sister. Give me my sister, you sons-of—"

Someone clapped a hand over my mouth, lifted me on tiptoes and dragged me back inside the building.

Chief Bromden.

As soon as the doors closed me in, he let go and I fell to the floor. Silence engulfed me. Seconds later, the quiet was broken by footsteps. A doctor stood next to Amanda—at least he looked like a doctor . . . he had the white coat with the squiggly doctor symbol on it. The caduceus. Or the rod of Asclepius. Whatever. Snakes on a staff. That symbol.

It was embroidered on his white doctor-jacket. And I have a theory about doctors: The one you pay to treat you today may turn out to be the one who pulls your plug tomorrow.

Amanda said something to him, and then came over to help me up. "We're going with him. He wants to talk to us."

"In English. Make him talk to me in English. He's a doctor. He'll know. American doctors probably educated him. Make

81

him speak English."

We took the elevator to an upper floor. As soon as the door screeched closed, I knew we should've taken the stairs. The rickety lift hummed, air whooshed, cables grated, and the bell dinged. When the door slid back, the elevator stopped six inches above our level.

Minutes later, we were sitting in uncomfortable chairs in a small office.

"I don't know about you," I mumbled, "but I'm taking the stairs when we leave."

Amanda nodded. Then she told the doctor to speak to me in English.

"You are not the first to come looking for this girl . . . this Teensy Prescott." He held my sister's photo between his thumb and forefinger. "The cartel. They come to take her. They want to kill this girl. To . . . how you say? Finish her off? But we don't have her."

Deceit swam in his eyes.

"You have her."

"We do not have this girl." Big headshake.

"Yes," I nodded, "you do. Give her to me."

"Miss . . . Prescott? You must listen to me carefully. We do not have your sister."

"Then where is she? What did you do with her?"

Amanda touched my sleeve. "That's enough, Dainty."

My eyes never left his. "Where's my sister?"

"We could not keep her."

His voice went tinny and distant between my ears.

His mouth was moving, but the only sound I could hear was a thin, high-pitched buzz, like the whirring of a dentist's drill. Tears spilled over onto my cheeks. Heat flushed my face. Amanda was right. We needed a gun. If we had a gun, this man would tell me where my sister was.

Amanda grabbed me by the shoulders and shook me hard. "We need to leave. Now. We're endangering these people's lives. They can't help your sister if they're dead."

"But they know where she is. You know where she is," I yelled as Amanda pulled me up from my chair and dragged me toward the door.

He nodded. "Even if we had her, she is not well. You cannot take her yet. She would never make it to the border." Although I heard what the doctor said, I didn't grasp the darker implications, nor why his apprehension hardened into icy despair until he added, "They would find you before you made it to the crossing. They would execute her. They would execute you."

"You have her," I whispered, all punctured and deflated and eerily calm. "She's alive."

"For now, Miss Prescott." To Amanda, he said, "You must go out the back way. People will come." He looked me dead in the eye. "Because of you, Miss Prescott. They are everywhere. They are here. They are not going away. And they want to intimidate us. So you must leave."

"When can I have my sister?"

"Three days, *más o menos.*" He flip-flopped his hand, *More or less.*

"I'm sorry. I'm sorry I yelled. I didn't know. Please forgive—"

"Out the back, Miss Prescott. Quickly. Before they come."

CHAPTER NINE

We left the hospital, but not before the doctor returned my sister's photo. I knew that small gesture had nothing to do with kindness, or with not wanting to deprive me of my memento of her. He did it because he didn't want any evidence lying around that would incriminate him or his hospital.

I couldn't imagine being in this hellhole for three days, but since that seemed to be the general consensus, I pulled out my cell phone to call WBFD-TV, to let them know I wouldn't be in.

Rochelle answered the phone in a voice full of fake cheer. I knew it was fake because I've had my fill of these phone conversations. Her *modus operandi* is to either put you on hold until you give up and redial, or toy with you until you finally crack. I was in no mood for either.

"Gordon Pfeiffer, please?" I disguised my voice.

"Is this Dainty Prescott?"

Got me. "Listen carefully, Rochelle, I'm not in the mood. I'm in serious trouble and I won't be in for a few days."

"Are you in jail?" I could almost hear her saying, *Look at Aspen Wicklow and all that trouble she got herself into.* Aspen was the newest anchor at WBFD.

"I'm not in jail. I'm in Mexico. Which is worse than jail."

"You're telling me."

"Yes. Well." Deep breath. "I need to talk to Mr. Pfeiffer."

Amanda gave me the universal, twirling-finger, *Wrap it up* signal.

"I have to go, Rochelle. Tell Gordon I won't be in. You can tell him why, but if my father calls the station looking for me, or my grandmother—" Jeez, I'd forgotten all about Gran "—please don't tell them I called, or that I'm in trouble."

"What kind of trouble?"

I gave her the abbreviated version of Teensy's disappearance, and asked her to pass it along to the boss. Instead of agreeing, she said, "We'll send a film crew out to cover the story. We're coming up on sweeps month again, you know? It'd make a great piece."

Part of me wanted to sever the connection.

Cover the story?

My stomach lurched.

Teensy and I? Debutantes? With our faces splattered all over the metroplex? I don't think so. Especially since I very well might end up in a Mexican jail before this was over. And the words "Mexican jail" and "Dainty Prescott" should never be used in the same sentence. Ladies of The Rubanbleu do not make the news unless there's an award involved.

Award. Not reward.

The part of me that didn't want to sever the connection burst into tears. "Please, Rochelle. I've never been more serious in my life. Don't talk to my father. I'll be back as quick as I can. Just please tell Gordon. I don't want him giving my paid internship to one of the SMU girls."

I got a visual of her drawing her finger through the air while saying, "Breaking news tonight—WBFD-TV's college intern, Dainty Prescott, Fort Worth debutante and hoity-toity, high-society member of The Rubanbleu, landed herself in Mexican prison squalor—" complete with subtext, "What an idiot—and now we've had to fire her."

A burst of gunfire stitched a nearby wall. I heard the *zing* of bullets ricocheting off metal. I looked at Amanda, who grabbed my phone and my hand, and pulled me down a dirty side street behind the hospital.

She told me to run, but she needn't have said anything. This happened to be one of those times when my amphibian survival brain kicked in. On instinct, I took off in the same direction, bound only to her clasped palm. If I'd had a magic genie, I'd have wished for our speed demon cab driver back.

I don't know how many blocks we ran, or where we ended up, except that when we rounded the next corner, we were standing across from the police department.

"Let's go in."

Amanda held me back, squeezing my wrist until I felt the blood back up into my upper arm like a clogged drainpipe.

"No," she snapped. "It's not the same as the United States. You can't trust them."

"They can't all be on the take," I challenged her.

"Wait, Dainty." She took another run at my ebbing common sense. "I got the names of some bars the college kids like to go to when they come across the border. Let's check out those. Then we can go get something to eat and find a hotel."

But I wasn't listening. Pumped into fearlessness after realizing we'd stumbled onto the police station, I shook off her grip and angled across the street. Grubby children who should've been in school were carrying squeegees and buckets of water, hollering, "Watch you car, señor, watch you car, señor," to anyone who'd allow them to run a wet rag over their vehicle.

Amanda caught up to me. She growled, "What're you doing, Dainty? What're you doing?"

"Going inside." I shaded my eyes against the glare of the sun.

"The drug cartel killed a policeman every two days until the chief of police resigned. So these people don't go to the police anymore. Going to the police is like wearing a bull's-eye on your chest. You wanted me to come with you for a reason. We do this my way."

"We should just explain what we're here for," I panted, trying to shake her off me.

"That would be the answer to *'What is the stupidest thing I could do?'* "

"Fine. Then I'll go in and ask what they know about this kidnapping. They can't all be corrupt. And if they don't know anything, I'll file a report."

"That's a great idea." Amanda chuckled without humor. "And after that, why don't you taunt them until they shoot us?"

"Your problem is that you don't have any faith in me. I can be a very persuasive speaker when I want to be."

I'm not exactly sure how she responded, because I'd already walked away, and she didn't speak to me in English. But I think she might've started a prayer. Or called out to me in her castigating Spanish.

Before we called any more attention to ourselves out in public, I trundled up the steps to the police station with Amanda breathing down my neck. Missing-person posters littered the walls. I knew many people believed that most of the *maquiladora* murder–torture cases were related to gang initiation rituals, but the cartels were killing off police officers at an unprecedented rate, too.

I'm not exactly sure what I expected would come of my brazen act, but I think I thought this would be like making a report at the El Paso or Fort Worth PD. Not much help, no solved-in-48-hours deal, but at least I'd have an opportunity to get all the facts down on paper and maybe exchange information, right?

I expected to see uniformed cops, but was surprised that the

Ciudad Juárez police uniforms resembled the El Paso PD's. Only instead of that pretty French blue that didn't look gay at all, the shirts here were light blue, above dark slacks with a pale blue stripe on each hip that ran the length of the trousers. At first glance, they reminded me of those wooden nutcracker dolls my mother used to line up across the fireplace mantle each Christmas. Except for the dark brown skin, swarthy mustaches, and low-slung gun holsters known as widowmakers.

We sauntered deeper into the building. Mexican police were lined up like blue jays on a clothesline. We'd hit the trifecta of trouble—local cops, *federales,* and military police—standing with their arms braced and blood in their eyes. The ante had just gone up on this poker game.

The desk between us and them served as the perfect metaphor for why we weren't going to get anywhere in this hunt for Teensy and Tiffany. That, and the black mesh bag in the center of the blotter like the webbed sacks used to aerate produce. This plastic fishnetting contained a man's severed head, and everyone had stopped to look at it. For a city nicknamed "The City of the Dead," it'd so far lived up to its name.

My heart banged against my ribcage trying to get out. I could hardly hear over the drumming in my head. Eyes that had been boring holes in the decapitated head were now leveled at me like a firing squad.

Amanda, who'd been eavesdropping on a nearby conversation, spoke in a stage whisper, "Nice going. They think we're vigilantes." Her words were accompanied by unmistakable sarcasm. Completely unnecessary, I might add. "Next thing you know they'll be trumping up charges to get payola from us."

I couldn't help it. The need to get my sister and her friend back had short-circuited the trip switch to my common sense. In my fascinating journey to clarity, I'd made a huge tactical error. The problem is, I have no street creds. I prayed for a quick and successful end to my asinine mistake, and instead, got a generous dollop of jeopardy flambé.

"The vigilantes are focused on taking matters into their own hands." The voice came from behind and to my right.

The last thing I wanted to do was turn around. It was cold outside, and I wasn't properly dressed for the weather, but I could feel sweat stair-stepping down my ribcage, and my shirt tacking itself to my back.

My voice trembled with the effort of speech. "I'm looking for my sister."

The man behind me came front and center, brushing against my shoulder, obliging me to move beyond the lunge area.

"You girls need to go back home," he said in the face of government ineffectiveness.

"I want to make a report."

"*Por supuesto.* Of course." He had an intimidating stare, and a finger-crippling handshake. "One moment."

When he left the room, sighs shuddered up to the ceiling. He returned a minute later with a pen and a report form, handed over both and offered me the use of the desk with the head on it.

By this time, I was more than ready to end this ongoing flirtation with law enforcement. I told him I'd return after we had lunch—it was late afternoon—and bring back the report form completed. I gave back his pen. The last thing I needed was to rot away in a Mexican jail with a pending theft charge. That, or pay out the rest of Teensy's money on a bribe.

"How very nice. I look forward to seeing you again soon." Radiating contempt, he practically loomed over us while I talked myself out of keeling over in a dead faint. His face creased into a smile. Actually, it was less a smile and more a baring of teeth.

I smiled back, because neither of us meant a word we said,

and we both knew it.

As we left the building, a swarm of children rushed us, shouting, "Chine, chine," wanting us to let them shine our "choos."

I didn't have Choos. I had Ferragamos. What can I say? Italian shoes are my Kryptonite.

And they didn't need shining, although I paused on the sidewalk long enough to give the grubbiest child an American dollar, even though Amanda warned me not to.

You'd have thought that would've made him happy. Instead, one of his little friends ran down the steps of the police department and snowplowed me.

That's the fine how-do-you-do I got for my trouble.

CHAPTER TEN

"Nice job, death wish." Amanda was smoking hot as we left the *policía.*

Once she heard me tell the policeman we were getting lunch, she actually thought I meant it. Now, she couldn't pull me away from there fast enough.

My mind hearkened back to the severed head. "How can you even think about eating?"

I was all but convinced Amanda had a tapeworm. After all, I'd watched her gorge herself like a field hand. If she had her way, we'd spend the majority of our time eating in these restaurant Petri dishes.

We were near *el mercado,* the market, and I wanted to see if I could find a scarf so that my blonde hair wouldn't be so noticeable.

"That's not the reason for me wanting to go to the restaurant," she said. Which was like saying pregnancy wasn't the reason for fast-forwarding the bride's wedding date a few months early.

She looked at me sternly. "We should eat, yes. But I also need a restroom. And we'd better find a hotel before the sun goes down. Once it gets dark, we're not getting out again. Understand? There's still a lot left to do today."

I'm not sure why, but a chill went up my spine.

Since Amanda assured me *el mercado* was within walking distance, we headed that way. While walking the dilapidated streets, we passed a scary tattoo parlor. The greaser running the place apparently mistook Amanda for a man, because he asked if she'd like him to show her where to find the dog and pony show. As we walked, I contemplated a theory: the more broken the sidewalks, the more plentiful the prostitutes.

"Is this where people go for prostitution?"

"People from Texas?" Amanda shook her head no. "It's called Boy's Town. *La Zona Rosa.* The red light district. And if you go, you can get your throat slit."

Naive *moi.*

The public bus system consisted of old school buses repainted blue or green. In addition to cabs and mopeds, there were horse-drawn carriages for the romantic to get around in. And there were pickpockets. Amanda warned me to guard my purse. She told me pickpockets liked working crowds and would often jostle or bump you while one of their cohorts distracted you.

For once, I was actually glad I didn't rent a car. Driving in Mexico is absolutely insane. People drive like maniacs. But the worst thing is, after you've been here awhile, you want to jump in a car and drive violently as well. I know I did. It's like road rage is legal here.

And the *cantinas—ay-ay-ay. Dios mío.*

Juárez is home to the seediest bars I'd ever seen. What could those girls have been thinking? I couldn't imagine going into one unless I had a gun to my head, which figuratively speaking, I kind of did.

The odors around us suddenly changed. We'd reached our destination.

The Juárez city market was a kaleidoscope of colors, sounds and smells. The air trapped inside it was also noxious with human waste, body odor and auto exhaust. Flies buzzed around sides of beef that hung from meat hooks, much of it still seeping. Thick drops of blood pooled on the concrete like spilled paint. Some droplets had turned a dull shade of brown; some still glistened crimson. Street vendors sold cigarettes out of modified suitcases, by the carton, pack, or individually. People were lined up in front of storefronts selling lottery tickets; after all, the National Lottery was up to nine million pesos.

Storefronts replete with the special accoutrements of the *Día de los Muertos*—Halloween, back in the U.S.A.—still displayed all manner of skeletons and other macabre toys, including intricate tissue paper cutouts called *papel picado*, candles and votive lights, and edible goodies in the shapes of skulls and coffins that were made from sugar. Having lost my mother less than a year ago, this creeped me out.

The sugar part I liked. When Egyptian slaves constructed the first food pyramid, they left off the most perfect food in the world. Cotton candy. It's pink—my signature color—and it's tasty. Also deceiving to the eye. Because when you think you've eaten a whole paper cone of cotton candy and are full, you've really only eaten maybe a teaspoon. Cotton candy makers can spin a smidgen of granulated sugar into an airy concoction that's a thousand times its original size. As for those liars who say it'll rot your teeth, I call them dentists.

I gave the little skeleton heads a second look.

Seeing me shudder, Amanda said, "If this gives you the heebie-jeebies, imagine what the altars inside the homes look like."

"It's ghoulish. And I'm not imagining it, because I'm not going into anybody's house."

"Yeah? Well, don't be so sure."

We saw cheaply manufactured clothing in storefronts. For the record, there's a huge difference between a cheap garment and an inexpensive one. Some people believe you can get really great deals on clothes down here. These are obvious lies spread by the manufacturers, the Mexican tourist bureau and the Taliban.

I caught Amanda's eye. "This stuff is junk."

My eyes slewed to a jewelry display. For no good reason, my thoughts turned to the severed head on the blotter back at the police station. I figured we should take a moment to appreciate the irony of buying gold-plated trinkets when all the gold chains in the world didn't mean a thing if you didn't have a neck to wear them around.

Amanda's eyes flickered past my shoulder and went suddenly wide. She gave me a palsied headshake that meant *Shut up.* I looked behind me and saw a Mexican man around my age dressed in blue jeans, an unbuttoned long-sleeved plaid shirt worn loosely over a wifebeater T-shirt and a belt. He was holding a walkie-talkie to his lips, and flinging daggers at me with his eyes.

He lowered the two-way radio enough for me to see his lips and said, "What are you talking about?" in English.

I darted a look at Amanda, who rattled something off in Spanish. She flashed a couple of hand signs at me, and I realized she expected me to play deaf. So I did. After a few minutes, he got bored with us, and ambled off in the opposite direction.

"What the hell just happened?"

"*Sicarios,*" she said on a long exhale of relief. "Like the cab driver told me about. They work for the drug lords. They're all pretty much dressed like he was, so you should be able to spot them from now on."

"What do they do?"

"They wander around talking to each other on those little radios. But what they're really doing is intimidation. Like the doctor said, they're creating a show of force that says, 'We're here, we're not going away and there's nothing you can do about it.' "

We were walking through the aisles when something shiny caught my eye. I halted in my tracks and veered off to a little stand with a jewelry display box filled with rings.

Amanda pulled me back. "You don't need that."

"You don't know that."

"Even if you find a piece of nice jewelry you can afford, you shouldn't wear it. You'll only call attention to yourself."

"You're no fun."

"And you're supposed to be deaf. Act like it. Oh, wait," she said, as if she'd just had an epiphany, "I guess you *are* deaf, because you keep ignoring me when I tell you to stop talking."

She pointed to a booth with scarves and shawls hanging from an overhead rack, similar to the one that held copper pots and pans and hung from the ceiling in my grandmother's kitchen.

We were met at the display table by a matronly lady whose face looked as worn as the simple housedress she had on. With graying hair strained back from her face and pinned into a bun at the nape of her neck, she seemed world-weary and sad as she got up from a little stool where she'd been fraying the edge of a scarf she'd made, trimming the fringe to even its length.

I pointed to a particularly boring scarf on the rack.

"No, no, no," the woman said with a vehement headshake, and took down a more festive one in a lovely shade of blue that happened to perfectly match my eyes.

Amanda intervened before she could drape it over my head. She selected a brown and black shawl in a tropical-weight wool, and the lady removed it from a stack of others with similar weights and textures.

Amanda made hand signs as she spoke to me, alternating between Spanish and English. "I just told her you were deaf. Put this on. She thinks you read lips."

I nodded.

"I'm telling her this is for your *abuelita,* your grandmother. She thinks you want to try it on, so do it."

The lady pointed to a mirror and I lifted the scarf up enough to be able to whisk it overhead. She carried on a conversation with Amanda while I tried it on. I riveted my head when the woman called me *"la Americana"* and commented on my *"ojos azules"*—my blue eyes.

I caught Amanda's reflection over my shoulder. She lifted a simple wraparound dress from the next booth to her neck, and the contrast of her dark skin was made more luscious by the pale blue outfit.

The elderly woman manning the next booth nodded in approval. Age had hunched her shoulders; pleated skin hung in folds on her face and neck. But her hooded eyes twinkled seeing Amanda get carried away by this simple frock.

Then Amanda inclined her head in my direction. "She likes your jacket."

Our gazes connected in the mirror.

The lady at the scarf stand seconded the thought. "I like you jacket. It fit me." She reached over and touched the material, rubbing it between her thumb and forefinger. She smiled, exposing the remnants of lunch mortared between her teeth.

"Muchas gracias," I said reflexively. Amanda withered me with a look.

The scarf lady pointed a finger at me before turning it on herself. "You give to me?" Brown eyes glittered with anticipation, like a game show contestant watching the wheel spin around until it wound down and landed on Bankrupt.

I shot Amanda a hard look though bugged eyes, hoping to telepathically message her to thank the woman for the compliment, but let her know I wasn't parting with my clothes. No damned way. Had I strained any more, my eyes would've popped out of their sockets like champagne corks.

Amanda said, "Give it to her. She just gave me some useful information."

"No," I said, not caring whether anyone heard me. "I intend to pay for the scarf. That's plenty."

"We're busted. She already knows you're looking for someone. The word's out."

"You give jacket to me?"

I was slipping into shock as I shrugged out of my jacket.

Then a *très, très* bad thing happened.

The frail, elderly woman manning the stall where Amanda picked out the blue dress let out an audible gasp.

"*¡El Mortero!*" she cried in a raspy voice, and clapped a parchment hand over her mouth.

Tracking her gaze, I saw a man who appeared to be in his mid-to-late fifties, and stood at least a head taller than everyone else. The hair on the back of my neck stood on end, followed closely by the pale downy ones on my arms. For no good reason, he stopped in mid-stride. I felt a thrill of terror as his internal radar honed in on something, or someone, with pinpoint accuracy. He slowly turned in my direction.

My stomach gave a nasty flip.

I lifted the gauzy scarf in front of my face, effectively obscuring my features from view. Silhouetted behind the fabric, I watched him as he faced me head-on. Behind the loosely woven, tropical-weight wool, I saw the outline of a cowboy hat. As he turned and gave us his profile, I lowered the scarf enough to peer over the top. From the neck down, he wore a black longcoat over a black shirt; and as he slowly continued his journey, looking, listening, scouring, scanning with the precision of a Geiger counter, I realized I'd been holding my breath. My eyes closed. I inhaled deeply. If there'd been a chair nearby, I would've dropped into it like a sandbag.

Amanda noticed him, too. She drew in a sharp breath. *"El Mortero,"* she whispered.

Then the woman with the scarves turned to see what we were looking at. She sucked air. *"Dios mío, El Ladrón de Cadáveres."*

"What's that?"

Amanda didn't answer. Just visually tracked him as he walked away doing his human Geiger counter thing. The old lady made the sign of the cross. I realized she'd been holding her breath too.

Needing clarification, I nudged Amanda with my elbow. "What's a *Mortero?*"

"Undertaker."

"He's an undertaker?"

"No. That's what they call him. I've heard of him. She called him the bodysnatcher." Amanda grabbed my scarf and threw it on the table. "We need to leave. Now."

Her words carried a bit of hang time.

She said something to the lady, and the lady handed the scarf back to me.

"Even exchange," Amanda said, "her scarf for your jacket. Come on."

Next thing I knew, we were out of the market, running, searching for a place to hide.

Chapter Eleven

Out on the street, we quickly weighed our options.

I say "we" despite the fact that Amanda had clearly taken charge. When she said, "This way," I followed in her wake, falling a few steps behind her.

For no good reason, I remembered studying the components of a slasher movie while working on my Radio-Television-Film degree at Texas Christian University. The formula hinged on the "safety in numbers" theory. Once a member was culled from the group, unspeakable things happened. I knew how these horror flicks ended, and didn't want that to happen to me, so I picked up the pace until I was practically race-walking to catch up with her.

For a short person, Amanda demonstrated gazelle-like speed. Even so, we were both winded by the time we reached the corner, me with my Louis Vuitton and her with the pale blue dress. She probably stole it. Not that it mattered at this point. We might as well have worn blinking neon signs around our necks to call attention to ourselves. If I ever have to do anything like this again, I'm getting a trainer. I used to have one, but I had to get rid of him. I hired him to whip me into shape, not to induce a heart attack.

We lingered at the corner while Amanda poked her head around the building and took in our route.

"We need a cab," she said, pushing me back when I tried to look.

"You said we should only get one in the queue."

"No. I said we should only get an authorized cab."

Hello, I already know that. It's the reason I'm here now.

Once again, Amanda won out. She'd been right from the get-go. I should've stuffed myself until I was as bloated as the Macy's Thanksgiving Day turkey before we crossed the border, because now that my adrenaline rush had worn off, I was hungry, cranky and tired.

"So how do we tell if it's an authorized taxi?"

"People will be riding around in cabs from the bridges. The market's a hot spot for tourists, so when they get dropped off, we'll jump in. Those should be the same taxis from the queue. Now cover your hair with your shawl, halo-head."

I whirled the scarf over my hair, flipping the fringed edges back over my shoulders.

"We have to go back tomorrow to see that lady. She had something important to tell us. She was just starting to talk when *El Mortero* showed up." Amanda pointed to a cab rolling up in the next block. "Run for it. When those people get out, we'll hop in." She grabbed my suitcase and took off in the direction of the cab.

Inside the taxi, she gave instructions to our driver. Bossed him around, more like.

Apparently, the traffic devices in Mexico were more advisory than cautionary, even though posted signs clearly indicated obstacles ahead in the road. They warned of men working, and cautioned motorists not to pass, but this cabbie wanted to overtake every vehicle he came across. Either that, or intimidate them by riding their bumpers and honking. I should've known Amanda would find this exciting.

Our driver pulled up to a stop sign. Traffic had stacked up ahead of us, so we weren't able to clear the intersection. He twisted his head and asked Amanda a question, which started a long, drawn-out exchange. This time, I didn't understand any of the Spanish words. Not that I cared—that's why I brought her with me.

She still had my cell phone and I asked for it back. Even though it only seemed like forty-five minutes since I'd spoken to Bruckman, a more accurate count would be five hours. I needed to know if he'd made it to El Paso. But instead of returning my wireless, Amanda held it to her chest in a protective crush. She skewered me with a look. "Who're you going to call?"

"Ghostbusters."

"You can call your boyfriend when we get to our hotel."

"No. It's my phone. Give it."

"What is wrong with you? We have more important things to do, and I can't have you distracted. We need to exchange those Andy Jacksons and Ben Franklins—"

She must've figured our driver knew English because she'd started talking in code, putting air quotes around the code words when pig Latin might've worked better.

"—and we need to do that before the you-know-what closes. We also need to eat. I'm starving."

"You have a tapeworm," I said with cutting reserve.

"Which reminds me, it wouldn't hurt to stop at the pharmacy for, well . . . you know."

Lost me there.

"Also . . . wouldn't hurt to stop off at the M-O-R-G-U-E and have a look around. But we need to do that before they close. So which do you prefer? To go before or after we eat?"

Was she kidding? I didn't want to go there at all.

Traffic began its slow crawl forward. As our driver pulled ahead, twin white vans marked SEMEFO on the back and *Unidad Espezializado de la Escena en Crimen* on the side pulled in front of us. It didn't take an interpreter to know these were crime scene vans, but Amanda translated anyway.

Our driver commented.

Amanda translated. "They had a shooting here about an hour ago."

"And the cops are just now getting here?"

"Don't act so surprised, Toto. You're not in Kans—"

"Don't say it."

Then I saw the reason for the rubbernecking. A man gunned down in front of an icehouse, or convenience store, formed a crumpled human display against bullet-riddled glass. My breath caught in my throat. I looked away and closed my eyes, but the image popped back up behind my eyelids. The dead man lay on the floor with his back propped up against the store front.

When I opened my eyes, Amanda was staring at me. She'd been talking to our cabbie again, and from that conversation I learned that the men climbing out of the vans were part body collector, part crime-scene investigator. And that these Mexican gun battles were the equivalent of military small-unit combat. The cartels weren't much different from military operations with their grenade launchers, night vision goggles, .50-caliber sniper rifles, body armor, and Eastern European machine guns like the AK-47. More important, they had the capacity to intercept cell phone and radio traffic, and armed their soldiers to the teeth using state of the art equipment.

Apparently Amanda bought into whatever our driver was telling her, because she said, "These paramilitary groups know our playbook because we trained them." She meant the Americans.

"Get me out of here." Seeing this dead man left me badly shaken and suffering from sensory overload.

"Fine. I'll tell him to take us to the morgue."

"No." If I couldn't handle seeing the body of a man I'd never met, how could I handle identifying Tiffany or my sister? "Make him turn."

I needed to think. What'd I gotten us into?

He veered off down a dusty, unmarked street, on the fringe of what turned out to be a horrible part of town known as Riviera del Bravo. Rows of cinderblock houses, built close to the curbs and covered in graffiti, lined the streets. As our taxi driver related details about the area to Amanda, I subsequently learned that the police had abandoned this neighborhood when the cartels took over, and only responded to murder, kidnapping and extortion calls.

We passed by a memorial to a murder victim that'd been placed in front of an elementary school. The school had bars on the windows and doors. It appeared the children who lived here were growing up in an environment of lawlessness, violence and drugs.

Now newspapers were reporting severed heads found in the area. My stomach roiled as my thoughts careened back to the mesh bag with the man's detached head. He probably had a family who missed him at this very moment. I squeezed my lids shut and tried to replace this dreadful image with good visions—happy recollections—like birthday gifts and Christmas presents. But that only triggered memories of how Teensy and I used to set the alarm clock so we could sneak downstairs in the middle of the night and peel back the gift wrap on our packages enough for a quick peek. Then my mind conjured up visions of my sister wrapped in bandages . . . which caused the tears I'd tried so hard not to shed for two dead people I didn't know to leak out anyway.

Our driver slowed for dozens of women who were crossing the street. Their facial expressions ranged from numb to angry. He and Amanda had a lively discussion, and from that exchange, I learned that due to apathy on the part of the police, these women had gotten together for a town hall meeting to discuss ways to avoid the Juárez serial killer. According to our driver, they'd do this several times a month. The last time they gathered, while they were out searching for missing bodies, they found the remains of two members from their own group.

"I really think we should go to the morgue. Get it out of the way. If your sister's friend isn't there—"

"Stop," I said. "Stop the car." I recalled the word from the red octagonal street sign. *"Alto. Alto. Alto."*

Dust churning, the taxi skidded to a halt.

"I want to talk to those women." Forcing a wad of cash into Amanda's hand, I said, "You tell this man to wait for us. Pay him the fare, and then tell him there's more money if he'll wait."

I piled out of the cab and headed toward the women. Common sense told me I was making a spectacle of myself—*come on, Dainty, you don't even speak decent Spanish!*—but common sense and I had parted ways hours ago. "Please," I heard myself say as I approached the nearest member of the group. Tall and striking, she'd turned to watch me with what I read as curiosity. *"Por favor . . ."*

"¿Sí?" She sounded brisk, efficient, ready to dismiss me in a heartbeat. Helping out some crazy Anglo stranger wasn't on her agenda for today.

I plunged ahead anyway. This woman and her companions knew about the local serial killer; maybe they knew about other local crimes, like Teensy and Tiffany's disappearance. Anything was worth a shot.

"My sister . . . *mi hermana.* I'm looking for my sister." My heart thudded. Where was Amanda, damn it? She should be here, playing translator. What was taking her so long?

I trailed off and just looked at the Mexican woman, seeking some clue of facial expression or body language that I'd made myself understood. I viewed her in stages—carefully lined eyes; lids shadowed with the palest hint of green that set off limpid hazel irises; impressively thick lashes that needed no mascara to lengthen them; a lightweight shawl that looked like cashmere but probably wasn't; a cream-colored blouse and camel-colored skirt that were fitted, yet tasteful; and simple brown leather shoes that had probably been made in one of the local factories.

"I am Maribel," she said abruptly, in heavily accented English. *Thank you, God.* "Maribel Espinoza. Your sister—what happened to her?"

I swallowed. "She was kidnapped. By the police."

Compassion flooded her face. "If *La Policia* took her . . . then there is no hope." She started to turn away, to follow the rest of her group down the street.

"But—" I caught her sleeve, desperate. "You must know something. You, or them." I waved a hand toward the other women, most of whom had stopped to watch by now. "You're out here protesting against crime in your city. You might've seen something, or . . ."

She was shaking her head, but I thought I saw guarded hope in her eyes. "Not me. But others . . . maybe."

And that's how we found out about *Los Commandos.* "Vigilantes," Maribel said, as Amanda came over to join us. "They have sworn to kill a criminal a day until the government gets the cartels under control. If anyone knows anything, they do. The cartels are in the police, you know. So if *La Policia* took your sister and her friend . . ." A shudder went through her. "They give the bodies to *El Cocinero.* He leaves no trace of them."

" 'The Cook'," Amanda translated. "That's what the newspapers call him. I've heard of him . . . he disposes of kidnap and murder victims in vats of acid." She looked, if anything, grimmer than Maribel. "If he got ahold of your girls, there won't be anything to find at the morgue."

I swallowed hard to tamp down the contents of my stomach, meager though they were, and focused on the one thing

Maribel'd said that promised a glimmer of hope. *Los Commandos,* who helped innocent people that got cross-wise with the cartels, or the human traffickers, the drug smugglers, or the police. . . . My mind whirred with possibilities. Maybe Teensy was with them? "So how do I find *Los Commandos?*"

Without warning, she grabbed my arm and yanked hard. "Black widow spider."

I glanced down at the crack in the dirt road, to the two-inch black spider with a red hourglass on its back tracking its way across the dust. This stranger'd saved me from a violent, venomous bite. As I gaped, she stepped forward and toed it with her shoe until it became a writhing, unidentifiable mass.

This inhospitable land took my breath away. Dry-throated, I croaked out my appreciation, *"Muchas gracias." Once this ordeal's over, I'm not coming back here. Ever. I'm not kidding.*

Maribel eyed us both for several seconds, as if she could see inside our heads. Whatever she saw there must have looked trustworthy; her next words were, "There's a safehouse here in the city. I can tell you where. But you must not say to anyone where it is." Hazel eyes darkened. "These people could die helping you."

"I swear I won't tell. Please help me get my sister and her friend back." I held up my hand and molded my fingers in what I hoped was the Girl Scout symbol. I've never been a Girl Scout. Not even a Brownie. To me, brownies are food. The closest I ever came to being part of an organized group outside of private school was when my parents enrolled me in etiquette class for budding debutantes. I have the certificate to prove it.

I pulled out a pen and paper while Amanda translated—the complicated directions apparently being beyond Maribel's English skills. Since so many of the streets weren't marked, I ended up drawing a map. As Maribel lingered to help Amanda and me, the rest of the women fanned out just beyond the neighborhood, walking slowly toward the desert where descan-sos—small crosses left to memorialize the dead, many of them pink—jutted up from the baked, tan earth.

A few yards away, our taxi idled, boiling blue smoke rings out of the tailpipe. While Amanda took down the name of our safe-house contact, I glanced over at our driver. I needed to reassure myself of two things: one, that the money I'd promised was enough to keep him from abandoning us on this lonely, desolate back street; and, two, that no spectators were keeping tabs on us.

In the distance, the faint scream of a siren heralded another disaster. I looked over and saw flashing lights. An ambulance rolled down the road, pursued by several vehicles.

"Maribel likes your suitcase," Amanda said.

With my eyes riveted on the emergency vehicle being overtaken, I pretty much ignored her, other than to mutter a cursory, "Yeah? That's nice."

"I said—" she gave me a pointed look, speaking more emphatically the second time around "—Maribel likes your suitcase." Emphasis on "likes."

My eyes flickered to Amanda. She fixed me with a harsh look.

"No."

"I think you should give it to her." Said sternly.

"For clarification, you might want to rewind and listen to the 'no' answer I just gave you. Besides, I don't have anything else to carry all my stuff in."

After a short conversation with Maribel, our new pal removed her shawl.

Amanda turned to me. "She says you can wrap your stuff in this."

Maribel looked at me Bambi-eyed.

Hello, what else could I do? I love my sister.

"Fine." A sigh huffed out. "Take it."

What happened next had all the characteristics of a pack of jackals devouring an impala. In seconds, Maribel and Amanda had my belongings out of the suitcase and tied into a fat pouch, including *The Ladies' Guide to Homicide*. I blinked in disbelief while these two women turned me into a hobo.

When I looked back toward the ambulance, all vehicles had rolled to a stop. This reminded me of recent police chase footage I'd viewed at the TV station where the Texas highway patrol boxed in a fleeing felon. Only in this case, a half-dozen armed men dressed like jack-booted ninjas bailed out of SUVs and swarmed the emergency vehicle. One of them dragged out the driver and held him at gunpoint while the rest of the men opened the ambulance's rear doors.

I'd never seen anything like this before, and couldn't tear my eyes away. Blood whooshed between my ears.

My heart drummed as they extracted a person lying atop a gurney. Automatic gunfire filled the air. The ambulance driver and paramedics lay as dead as the man who'd been singled out for this firing squad, their blood coursing into cracks in the baked, scarred desert.

A strangled-cat cry reached my ears. It wasn't until Amanda grabbed my arm and yanked me toward the safety of the taxi that I realized the origin of this ghastly sound.

It came from me.

For no good reason, the gunmen opened fire on the town hall women. Bullets stitched the ground. Pulverized clods of dirt and sand shimmered upward. Some of the ladies ran back toward us; others dropped to the desert floor like deer carcasses. Others too slow to react merely stood, rooted in place and resigned to their fate.

I'd blanked out from sheer terror. For an instant, I wondered if a person could die from fright. Legs that had supported me when running from *El Mortero* now weighted me to the Earth like bridge abutments.

Amanda snatched the hobo sack from me and slung it across the seat of the taxi.

My next memory was of our cab driver pulling a mid-block U-turn and retracing our route, flooring the accelerator to speed us away from the crime scene. Centrifugal force pinned me to the seat. I looked out the back windshield in a state of shock.

El Mortero had just rounded the corner of the street we were fleeing.

CHAPTER TWELVE

The tires of our taxi churned up dust. I wanted to cry for those innocent people but couldn't even squeeze out a single tear. I'd heard of post-traumatic stress, and figured I'd just gotten a dose that would last me a lifetime.

Amanda gave the driver instructions. I picked up on the Spanish word for morgue, and tuned up in protest.

"I've seen enough killing in one day. I want to go home." Then I cracked, sobbing under the weight of the images that kept replaying in my head.

"You want to leave without your sister?"

"Not without my sister. I just . . ." In my lightheaded rush, I watched as Amanda placed her palms to her head, massaging what had become an obvious headache. ". . . want to go eat."

Actually, eating was the last thing I wanted to do. What I really wanted was to erase the last ten hours and take Bruckman's advice, call Daddy, have him hire the best recovery specialist on the planet and put him on this case. Someone familiar with kidnappings and guerrilla tactics who understood this strange culture of *mordida* and death, and knew what needed to be done to pull off a no-casualties rescue.

Meanwhile, if we took sanctuary in a restaurant, it'd give me time to mentally regroup, not to mention maybe avoid the morgue altogether. After all, if I picked at my food long enough, we'd find the morgue closed for the day, right?

I am so out of my element.

At the mention of food, Amanda instantly perked up. Her tapeworm probably sensed it was mealtime, and was wondering what to order off the menu. Guided by this internal parasite, she spat out new instructions in Spanish and the driver wheeled us onto a paved road. I heard "hotel" and "cantina" and knew she was already plotting our next move. Now I knew why so many of these Mexican people walked around lifeless and numb. Danger and killing had become a way of life.

I relaxed against the seat, closed my eyes, and let my control-freak of a guide call the shots.

That's why I got the surprise of my life when I felt the car slow, and opened my lids. Not a hotel, not a cantina, but the morgue.

Amanda told me how much to pay the driver. I threw in a little extra, and we got out of the cab. As she tugged out the hobo sack, I mentioned I'd given him a bonus.

She gave a derisive grunt. "*Idiota.*" No translation necessary. "I already factored in a tip. Plus the extra you promised if he'd wait. Now he thinks you're rich."

"Who cares? We'll probably never see him again."

"I care. You'd better hope he doesn't start dogging us."

"Seems like a good thing, always having a taxi at the ready."

"Are you crazy? We should be taking different cabs every time we're on the move. Makes us harder to track."

"Oh," I said dully. So much to learn, so little unused memory left in the internal hard drive.

"I'm guessing your sister's the smart one and you're the pretty one."

Amanda must've been relying on the law of logical argument—meaning anything's possible if you don't know what you're talking about.

"Are you calling me stupid?" I asked, building on my irritation. "Because I'm the one paying you."

"I didn't say you were stupid. I just meant it's a good thing you're pretty because otherwise, people would just think you're a dumb blonde."

Had we been on the other side of the border, calling me a dumb blonde would've been enough to start trench warfare. I knew this wasn't the time or place to set the record straight, but I couldn't help myself. "I'm not a dumb blonde."

"*Ha,*" Amanda huffed. "Two more minutes in the incubator and you'd have been completely retarded. You may be bankrolling this little jaunt but I'm calling the shots. So you can do one of two things: You can either do it my way, or you can do it my way mad. I don't need your input. You're twenty-two years old with zero street smarts—"

"Twenty-three."

"—Fine. Twenty-three. I'm still not looking to you for advice. When I want your opinion I'll ask for it."

What began as a spirited discussion had evolved into street theater that focused unwanted attention on us. Amanda was about to fuel the fire when she unexpectedly turned and saw vacant stares coming from people who'd lined up outside of the storefronts. That's when it dawned on me what they were gawking at.

Much to my—and everyone else's—surprise, we had a challenger to the hideously deformed bell ringer in the Quasimodo look-alike contest, and I found this frightening. I looked at the sudden growth protruding out from the back of Amanda's shirt and had to assume, for my own sanity, that she'd stuffed the powder blue dress down her back. I had to. The alternative notion that someday that'd be me, hunchbacked from calcium deficiency, was just too scary to process.

In an attempt to deflect this sudden interest in us, I spoke in a hypnotic tone. "Well, at least we're going to eat, right?"

"Wrong." She pointed to the building behind me. When I

turned to look, she said, "Better to get it out of the way now."

We lingered in front of the morgue.

The air around me thinned. Carnal panic set in. "Please don't make me go inside that awful place. I can't—"

"Don't tell me you can't." She snipped off her words like fingernail clippings. "Do *not* tell me you can't. You can, and you will. Because if your sister's friend is inside, then we don't have to continue to search for her. We can concentrate on getting your sister out of here. Maybe even go back tonight, and return for her in a few days. Now come on." She left me standing on the sidewalk, fighting off a panic attack.

She was right, of course. I trailed her like a puppy, hauling my chew-toy beside me.

I was totally unprepared for life at the morgue. Since Amanda was doing all of the talking, we ended up in a work area where the coroners were tending to autopsies. We learned the coroners had fallen behind, and that two hundred bodies were crammed into two refrigerators made to hold eighty cadavers. Rows of zipped white bags, holding bodies, were stacked up like firewood. While doctors performed autopsies to Mexican love songs playing in the background, the whir of Stryker saws cut through bone. Across the room, a coroner was carefully laying out clothing on a plastic sheet.

The room smelled like what I imagined Cambodia smelled like after the release of tracers and Agent Orange. This prompted me to run for the toilet. The bathroom smelled like Calcutta in August.

When I returned, pale and clammy, fresh bodies were being wheeled into the pungent, formaldehyde-infused morgue. The sheet didn't quite cover the tennis shoes and blue-jeaned leg of one of the victims, but I figured it belonged to the man who'd met his untimely death at the convenience store.

As we waited to speak to the senior coroner, a cell phone

went off. Nobody bothered to answer it. A moment later, a different ring-tone came from inside one of many cardboard boxes stacked to the ceiling in the crime lab. These boxes had people's names written on the sides in black marker, and as best I could tell from the items poking out, held bloodstained cowboy boots, cell phones, bulletproof vests, and whatnot—the possessions of the deceased.

"Isn't somebody going to answer that?" I asked, more as an observation than expecting an answer.

One of the older coroners, dressed in a shower cap and wearing a blue medical robe, looked up from his work. "It's somebody's mother looking for her son or daughter, or somebody's husband or wife looking for their spouse. There is nothing we can do for them."

I blinked in astonishment. This man spoke fluent English.

I swallowed hard. "Don't they deserve to know?"

"Maybe this way, it will give them another night's sleep, *mi'ja*," he said tenderly.

How many cell phones went off during a typical workday? How many survivors paced the floors each night, waiting for loved ones who'd never come home again?

"But you could at least tell them . . ."

"They may not be here for long." Mournful eyes drooped at the corner. "Drug traffickers know investigators can track killers. They have raided morgues and carted off bodies at gunpoint. Let people take comfort that their families are still alive. They won't find the bodies."

I got an ugly visual of the monster they called The Cook, and found it hard to digest this line of thinking. "Can't you guard the place?"

He explained how they occasionally brought in soldiers to guard the morgue if they thought they had a well-known cartel member among the dead. As he zipped the remains of the cadaver he'd been working on into a body bag, the doors opened. Workers wheeled in another dead man. The coroner pulled off his gloves and placed them in a discolored porcelain sink.

"Come with me," he said, and escorted us over to a walk-in refrigerator. Steel shelves held stacked bodies like bunk beds.

I shuddered. The last thing I wanted to see was Tiffany with her face frozen in an unbreakable death mask.

"I hope we don't find her dead body." I realized that statement came from me, and that I'd been talking to myself as we walked toward the refrigerator.

"It is not very likely," he said.

I looked over expectantly. From the moment we'd arrived in this south o' the border hellhole, I'd operated under the assumption that my sister and Tiffer were alive. But this was the first ray of hope I'd felt since we'd arrived here.

"So you don't think she's dead?" A drop of sweat descended down my back and into my underwear.

"No, I *do* think she's dead. I just think they'll dispose of her body in a vat of acid like the other three hundred people they've killed."

Hand to mouth, I suppressed a loud intake of air. The severed head, the dead man at the convenience store, and the women I'd watched get cut down in a hail of bullets paled in comparison to this latest abomination. The last time I experienced a feeling this visceral, I'd rushed into my parents' bedroom to announce that I'd made the Dean's List and discovered my mother lying dead on the floor.

"Why couldn't these girls have gone to a resort in Cancun?" I announced to the room at large.

"It's no safer there." He gave a dismissive flick of the wrist. "A Mexican general who was sent in to clean up the drug cartels was tortured and killed. His wrists and ankles were broken. The only difference between Cancun and here is that Cancun is prettier to look at." He wasn't being facetious. He was being brutally honest.

The click-clack of low-heeled pumps coming down the corridor caught his attention. A female assistant handed him a thin file and said, "This one came in last night." Then she pointed to the white bag at the top of a stack.

I swallowed hard. Tiffany could've fit inside that zippered body bag. It was about the right size. Chills crawled up my spine and settled at the nape of my neck. The hairs there stood on end. More than anything else, I didn't want this to be Teensy's friend.

The body bag made a ripping sound as the coroner unzipped it. Then he peeled back the flap. Life is filled with harsh truths and I was about to experience one: No matter how much you love someone, you always move back when their blood inches toward you.

I gasped. A painful whimper slipped out. Lightheaded, I looked at the face—at eyes that were frozen in an unbreakable death gaze.

It wasn't Tiffer.

Thank God, it wasn't Tiffer.

CHAPTER THIRTEEN

I hate Mexico. I love Mexican food. Huge difference.

We agreed we'd eat at the first restaurant that looked clean from our place beyond the morgue's threshold. We settled for an intimate café with typical Mexican décor near Chamizal Park. This one had terra cotta floors, high ceilings and frescoed walls painted in beige over rust, with arched entryways trimmed in festive, hand-painted tiles. They'd even incorporated old pieces of decorative iron fencing to partition off dining areas, and had a scene of a town square with fountains and botanicals painted on one wall.

While a mariachi quintet strummed guitars and shook maracas in the background, Amanda told the maitre'd my requirements—table in the corner where I could keep an eye on the door (I learned that from Jim), clean utensils, clean glasses and a cold Mexican Coca-Cola. Mexican soda pops are made with real sugar cane, and taste different from the ones back home. And I needed it to be chilled because I knew better than to write off the "don't drink the water" warning as an urban legend, kind of like the pet boa constrictors and pet pythons released into the wild by irresponsible owners in Florida, now full grown and slithering around in the Everglades.

Note to self: If ever in Florida, stay out of the Everglades.

"Reckless—party of two—your table's ready," Amanda muttered under her breath as we were shown to the corner.

Sarcasm is so unbecoming.

Well, so what if she was irritable? It didn't escape my notice that she wanted to have control over the decision-making process.

Well, hey—I'm bankrolling this operation, so you just need to zip it. And quit bugging me about going to the pharmacy. Or farmacía.

I didn't say these things, of course. I was trying to keep the peace.

But what could she possibly want at the pharmacy? I mean, whatever we bought, we'd have to haul around in this hobo pouch, which I'd started to think wasn't such a hot idea. Admittedly, I should've brought nothing into this hellhole of a country except my purse and its contents, and you see where that got me. But seriously, where was I going to leave that book?

Which reminded me.

I studied the shape of the book through the fabric. Why would Nerissa even own a book like that? Was it fiction? Non-fiction? A how-to manual?

That "how-to" stuff got me to thinking uncharitable thoughts. Daddy's beyond rich. And that awful woman insinuated herself into our lives right around the time my mother became ill. I wondered if there was a connection.

Amanda was talking to me and I'd missed what she'd said.

"What?"

"I asked what you felt like eating."

"We just visited the morgue. What should I feel like eating?" I said nastily.

All right, she didn't deserve that. I was getting neurotic.

But, *hello,* I'm in a foreign country where people are dropping like flies, a scary-looking dude called the Undertaker keeps surfacing at inopportune times and I'm supposed to play deaf but I'm not sure Amanda's asking the right questions of people. Who wouldn't be neurotic? Besides, I couldn't stop brooding about the words those women at the market used to describe this Mexican bogeyman: *El Mortero.* Thief of cadavers. The bodysnatcher.

The waiter came and I ordered soup. I didn't have to worry about looking like a cheap tipper since my crazy pygmy guide pretty much guaranteed him a whopping gratuity by ordering practically everything on the menu. While we waited for our meal to arrive, I excused myself to use the restroom.

"Watch my stuff," I said as I pushed back from the table. "Do not let anything happen to that." I thumbed at the hobo pouch, which I'd placed on one of the extra chairs at our table.

Amanda was chewing on a piece of bread and had her mouth full, so I didn't get any back-talk from her as I left my things in her custody. As I moved further out of range, I shot her a backward glance. She was washing down bread with a beer, even though I wasn't at all sure we should be introducing alcohol into any situation down here. She caught me staring and frantically waved me back.

Whatever.

I had to get to the *cuarto de baño*—the bathroom—before it became urgent, so whatever inane thing she needed to discuss could wait. I chose the door marked *Damas* because of the little wooden cutout on the door of a stick person wearing a dress. As soon as I stepped inside, I glimpsed myself in a mirror mounted in a large punched-metal frame.

When I saw my reflection, I wondered why the café people had even bothered to seat us, much less serve us. I certainly didn't look like a debutante. You'd think with my privileged upbringing, I'd awaken to the chirps of cartoon birds swirling around my head, tying satin ribbons in my hair. But no, I'm in a swill pit of a place called Mexico, covered in grime and carting around other people's stuff, hiding out in a third-rate restaurant, in a third-world country with a pygmy, wondering what third-rate hotel I'd be checking into within the next couple of hours.

Oy vey.

The wasp nest in the corner of the bathroom added a new dimension to my misery since wasps started dive-bombing me like crop dusters. The commode was nothing more than a composting toilet fabricated from cement. I'd read about these contraptions . . . how the solids are separated from the liquids by design, and the liquid drains into the Earth through a rock filtration system, whereas solids sit for 6 to 12 months in a waterproof bin and come out as pure dirt. I wanted no part of this. What I *did* want here in the ninth circle of hell was to take a picture with Bruckman's cell phone camera to turn in for the judging of the office's weekly *How bad do you need to go?* contest held by the photographers at WBFD-TV.

Once inside the restroom, I quickly realized that I'd made a huge tactical error. Why would any percentile of Americans want to come to Mexico on vacation? Oh, I know—*Let's use public toilets and bring our own toilet paper because they don't have any.*

For the love of God, what'd these people do in such situations? Use their hand? Their shirttails? Hems of their skirts? Now, I've always disliked being around negative people, so I tried to look at this latest fiasco in the best possible light and think happy thoughts. Such as, I couldn't begin to tell you how happy I was that nobody in my social circle knew I was down here in this God-awful place. And one more thing—I was happy, happy, happy that I'd brought my purse in with me, since a couple of old dollar bills would do the job . . .

Almost pulled a butt muscle running out of there.

In my absence, the mariachis had migrated over to play a song for Amanda. I hung back a moment and watched the musicians in their tight black pants and bolero vests trimmed in silver thread—picking and plucking acoustic guitars, running a bow across a bass fiddle, fingering keys on an accordion—until they turned and strummed their way to a table at the far end of the room. Horrified by my latest experience, I returned to our table fuming over the lack of toilet paper. The steam coming off the soup I'd ordered couldn't compete with the coil of smoke coming off the top of my head.

Amanda addressed me innocently across the table. "What's wrong?"

Glowering, I shook out my napkin. "You could've at least warned me."

"About what?" She couldn't pull off "doe-eyed," but she did present a good poker face.

"The toilet paper issue."

"There's a toilet paper issue?" A diabolical little smile formed at the corners of her mouth.

"Don't play innocent. You know what I'm talking about. There's no toilet paper. You should've warned me before I got myself in a jam."

"You ask me, you're lucky they even had a bathroom. Most restaurants and bars don't have indoor plumbing. You're expected to relieve yourself behind the building in the dark."

The soup wasn't enough to slake my thirst or quell my hunger, but it was piquant and zesty and jump-started my taste buds. I don't know how those morgue people can do what they do and then turn around and eat, but I tried to drive the images from my mind. Before finishing my broth, I ordered chicken. When the food got to the table I looked it over with cold scrutiny, which is a habit you get into when you're traveling in a third-world country.

They'd presented me with something unrecognizable, with a glob of something else spooned on top of it. I studied it with the intensity of a scientist, rotated the plate several times, inclined my head to the right, inclined my head to the left, stuck my head directly over it, took a big whiff, and decided it looked sort of like it might be cheese. If I'd had a sheet of paper and a black marker, I'd have rated it a two-point-three for presentation, and held up the sign for others to see. It got an extra point for having flakes of color in it.

"I don't know what this is." Slumping back in my chair, I looked across the table at Amanda wolfing down her food. The more real estate I could put between this artistic creation and me, the better.

"I'll eat it."

I pushed it toward her. *"Mi queso es su queso."*

Amanda barked out a laugh. Then she pulled my dish over to her side of the table and caught the attention of our waiter.

As he sauntered over, she said, "What do you want?"

"A cheeseburger."

"They don't serve cheeseburgers."

"Do they have ground beef?"

"Probably."

"Okay, then tell them to fix me a ground meat patty, and bring me a roll, a couple of slices of tomatoes and a piece of cheese."

Over my objections, Amanda ordered me a plate with grilled pork, chopped avocado and chiles. When my food arrived, it looked like decayed body parts that should've come with a ransom note. And I got my Coca-Cola. The food turned out to be delicious.

Then Amanda said, "Uh-oh." Followed by, "Wish you hadn't done that."

I realized, too late, that out of habit I'd just poured my bottled Coke over ice. Ice that came from the same bacterial source as the tap water I'd been told not to drink. And before Amanda could warn me, I'd taken a hearty gulp. It was a real *"A-ha"* moment. My appetite dropped in inverse proportion to my climbing fear.

Mexico is crap. There is no remedy.

I pushed the glass away. There wasn't enough bottled Coca-Cola left to go with my meal, so I asked Amanda to summon the waiter and put in another order.

As the waiter added this to the tab, my eyes were drawn to a big, festively colored sombrero hanging on the wall. Apparently, whoever decorated this place considered it artwork to be featured among the black velvet matador paintings that were also proudly displayed. A velvet bull seemed to be snorting at me from out of the canvas. Then the sombrero moved. I blinked. For several seconds, I replayed this in my head, shaking off the event as an optical illusion, or worse, a delusion. Getting Amanda's attention wasn't easy. I sat there boring a hole in her while she flirted with our waiter. When she finally glanced my way, I did a quick eye cut to the sombrero on the wall.

She gave it a sidelong glance. Then it flew off the wall, propelled by a huge, honking rat.

That's it. I slapped my napkin on the table. *I've seen enough.*

We weren't the only ones who couldn't get out of there fast enough. After I paid the tab in American dollars, Amanda reminded me about converting my money to Mexican pesos.

Then she said, "We'd better find a place to stay before it gets any darker."

I wanted to shop around before committing to a hotel, but as we were about to walk out the front door of the café, Amanda grabbed my wrist and yanked me back inside.

"*El Mortero.*" She rattled off Spanish words like *patio* and *exito* and several other no-brainers to the maitre'd. Then she pulled me toward the back of the café and out a side door where others were dining on the patio. Thirty feet past the wrought-iron gate we fled through, we were on the side street running like our lives depended on it.

Chapter Fourteen

Out of desperation, we settled on the first hotel within walking distance from the café, a two-story building with wrought iron balconies and a sign hanging off the roof that read *Hotel*. I use the term "we" loosely, as Amanda was still calling the shots. The cook from the café must've laced my food with crack, because I'll never understand in a million years why I allowed her to talk me into staying at *Hotel Malamuerte*. That wasn't its real name, but in my mind, the English equivalent of a dive hotel fit this dilapidated building.

I should've figured this place would add a new dimension to my terror. Should've called Vegas and placed a humongous bet on it, in fact. So far, we'd dodged bullets meant for others and survived; didn't find Tiffany at the morgue; and the cryptic code that the doctor had spoken in led me to believe we'd get my sister back safely in a few more days.

So I should've known my happiness wouldn't last.

Twelve hours ago, I'd just spent the best night of my entire life with the greatest guy I'd ever met. Then an early morning phone call changed my life, and the trap door opened sending me right back to Daintyland. Now, here we stood inside the lobby of this so-called five-star hotel, and I should've known that the newfound sense of security I'd acquired while counting my blessings at dinner would tank.

At the front counter, Amanda spoke to the desk clerk through the arched opening. Light from the bar stole across the carpet of centavos—Mexican pennies—in the water fountain located prominently in the hotel lobby.

My eyes drifted over a pamphlet boasting that the Mexican people were as warm and friendly as the lovely desert sunshine, but I was thinking swarthy and deadly might be a better description. Just for fun, I glanced around to see if the front desk had postcards for sale like the irony section of Hallmark:

The scenery is here. Wish you were gorgeous; or,

I must admit this country brought religion into my life. I never believed in hell until I came here; or,

So your son is a drug lord, and this news spoiled your day; but look on the bright side, it's really good pay.

I let out an extended bray of a laugh, and the desk clerk's eyes slewed over to see if I belonged in an asylum. Sometimes I just crack me up. This happens when you're left alone too much.

The clerk manning the counter took customer service seriously by asking us, *"¿Quieren hombres?"* Which I found out from Amanda meant he wanted to know if we wanted any men sent to the room. When I stood stricken and grimacing, he nodded knowingly and told Amanda he understood and would send us a couple of hookers.

Amanda took pity on me. She lugged my hobo bag up the stairs to the room they gave us on the second floor. Then she unlocked the door, and *Welcome to traveler's hell.*

As soon as she slapped on the wall switch, things started moving across the floor and the table. That wasn't the part that made me suck air.

I saw it first. My eyes bulged like a young coed's in the sudden shadow of a slasher. Then Amanda saw it.

The room was supposed to have two beds.

It didn't.

And the missing second bed was the first thing I noticed.

Since I didn't think sharing a bed with a pygmy was on The

Rubanbleu "approved" list, I said, "No, absolutely not. This won't do. You have to go back downstairs and tell that imbecile we're not taking this."

"It's all they have."

"A little run-down" was a euphemism for the way our room looked. You'd need a scratch-and-sniff picture to fully appreciate how the room reeked of cigarette smoke and decay. The place was barely suitable for human occupancy.

"That can't be. Because it's not going to work for me." My scornful sniff traveled through the room and turned her around.

Dark brows slammed together. "It's not going to work for you?"

"No, it is not." I peeled back my scarf and re-fluffed my hair, and tried not to make eye contact. It's so much easier to hold my own with Amanda if I'm not looking directly at her.

Amanda had no reaction to my blistering mood. She seemed completely unfazed, so I called dibs on the bed. Apparently she had other ideas.

"I'm not sleeping on the floor, diva," she said in that exaggerated, huffy cadence.

"I'm not a diva." I started to explain why sharing didn't come easily to me. "You know how I'm a debutante?"

"You know how I'm a cop?" She drew a deep, bracing breath. "Maybe I'll just commandeer this bed, and you can sleep on the floor or in that chair." She gestured to a rickety chair with a lumpy cushion that had seen its heyday back in the sixties.

"You could try to be a little more understanding, Amanda. I've never had a roommate." I took a moment to meditate over this statement, then instantly revised it. "Well . . . except for that one time, when I first enrolled in TCU. But that only lasted about a week. She took a header off a clock tower . . . what are you looking at? It wasn't me. She was obsessively neat. And pre-law."

"If you want another room with another bed, feel free to meander on down and negotiate it yourself," she said in a cold, dispassionate voice. "And good luck climbing over the language barrier. Me? I'm staying right here. On my bed." Her body folded onto it like an origami penguin. "And if you're nice to me, I might even let you pick which side you want."

I swear that's about the time I saw her medication stop working. I wanted to flip to the weather channel on our rabbit-ear television to see if hell had frozen over, but I already knew the answer to that one.

A cockroach skittered across the tile floor—I swear I could hear it clicking along as it hurried toward a thin space beneath the baseboard and terra cotta. Then it squeezed beneath the baseboard and tile and disappeared from view. These insects were so big you'd need a twelve-gauge shotgun loaded with scattershot to dispose of them. I'd never seen *cucarachas* the size of rifle shells before. Roaches are like rats. For every one you see, there are fifty you don't see. They prefer the dark and scatter when the lights are turned on. While channel surfing recently, I heard an entomologist on one of those science shows say that if you have to have bugs, roaches are the cleanest—an obvious lie spread by communists and terrorists and people who live in Africa.

That's like saying "Oh, goodie—carbon monoxide—the most non-violent way to die!"

Okay, now I'm wondering if the gas heater has a leak.

Mother of God.

When does it all end?

"This isn't going well," Amanda said. Unnecessarily, I might add.

"It's a disgrace, I tell you."

Our room had a broken mirror hanging on one wall, and a huge red stain on the carpet. If forced to describe the size and shape of the stain, I'd say it was probably about four feet in length, and shaped like a body curled up in the fetal position. Suffice it to say, it needed yellow Day-Glo crime scene tape and scaffolding around it. It looked about two days old, not quite the chocolate brown shade of dried blood, but not the crimson red of an arterial spurt, either. Morbid curiosity got the better of me: I tested the edge with my toe. At least it was dry when I twisted my shoe and looked down at the bottom of my sole. Then I tested the middle. The carpet was dark, wet and squishy like a sponge against the toe of my Ferragamo.

I called Amanda over to witness this.

"Once again," I said, "I'm not staying here."

I must've gotten more worked up than I thought, because Amanda brought her hands down on my shoulders, stilling me.

"*Ay,* Dainty, you're such a P.I.T.A." She informed me this stood for pain in the ass. She rattled off a bunch of Spanish that didn't sound very nice, ending with, "I'll go down and talk to the guy."

As soon as she left, I hopped across the spot on the floor to keep from stepping on it. It seemed sacrilegious to walk on it, but I didn't want to have to look at it either. I moved to the other side of the bed and yanked back the coverlet. Lint danced on a slant of light from a part in the curtain. When I sat heavily on the bed, dust shimmered up from the mattress.

At home, I slept on thousand-thread-count silk sheets. These felt like burlap.

The air quality in this room would've violated the ozone standards for the metroplex. Had the room actually been located in the metroplex, it'd fall into the orange-alert category. Because of the humidity, the ventilation system was an incubator for bacteria and viruses. If we stayed here, we'd need that tropical medicine doctor the girl at the car rental agency told me about.

I pulled back the curtain, exposing a 12-pane door that

opened onto a balcony. Moonlight blued the room. In an effort to air out the place by the time Amanda returned, I stepped outside and fanned air into the room with a plastic menu I picked up off the table. Husks of dead bugs had stuck to the outdoor light. And I didn't like the way the railing on our rickety balcony shook when I rested my hand on it.

Contemplating my future, I wondered what tomorrow would hold. And whether we'd get Teensy and Tiffany safely back home. Things were so different here. Even the city lights were different at night. In the distance, the lights of El Paso glowed with a distinct yellow halo; in Mexico, they shone bright white.

From my place near the door, I studied the largest mountain on the outskirts of the city. People had piled white rocks against the side that spelled out: *Juárez—Biblia es la verdad. Léalo.*

"Hey—" I called out when Amanda returned "—be careful if you come out here. The hand rail's not stable."

"Yeah, that's where the last occupant hung himself. At least that's the front desk guy's version."

"You'd better be kidding."

"Hey, I've got an idea. Don't ask me questions until you're ready to hear the worst possible answer."

"Yeah? Well what does that say?" I pointed to the white rocks.

She joined me on the balcony long enough to translate the message. " 'Juárez. The Bible is the truth. Read it.' "

"Ha," I said. "These people are amateurs. Where I live is the buckle on the Bible belt. People are insane for religion. Last time I went to the fitness center, I saw people reading the Bible while riding the stationery bicycles and walking on the treadmills. I don't see how they do it. I can barely stay on those machines listening to my iPod."

Amanda jerked her chin toward the room. "Come back inside. You're a sitting duck for whatever's out there."

"Who does that? Reads the Bible while exercising on the

treadmill? I mean, you're walking along with your machine programmed to automatically increase speed and incline, reading the Good Book, and—*oh wait!*—no joke, the speed increases as your treadmill angles up, and the next thing you know, you're face down on the floor wondering what the hell just happened and why the trainer you won't go out with is trying to roll you over and give you mouth-to-mouth. No thanks, I'll just listen to Lady Gaga. At home. In bed. Reading a magazine."

"I mean it, diva, get your ass back inside."

"Drama queen."

For no good reason, I had the skin-crawling sensation we were being watched. Amanda knew the cause of my breathless entrance; she distrusted the darkness beyond the windowpanes as much as I did. As soon as I followed her back into the room, she pulled the drapes.

The air quality in Mexico was horrible. They burned their garbage in open fires, and ran their vehicles with a cheaper grade of gasoline. Which reminded me of a story WBFD-TV recently covered . . . a college kid in Laredo, Texas, drove his dad's new SUV over the border to *Nuevo Laredo* to gas it up before he went out later that evening for a night on the town. The *policía* arrested him and confiscated the new car. The boy's father wasn't upset with him, and why not? Because he had bigger problems. Like how to get his son out of a Mexican prison for no damned reason.

Mexico is crap. There is no remedy.

Back to the suffocating air quality.

Even if they had emissions testing—which I seriously doubted—none of the vehicles I'd seen since I'd been here would pass inspection on the other side of the border . . . not to mention Juárez's sewage problem. I imagined on gusty days when the wind blew northward, the stench in El Paso turned unbearable.

In an attempt to relax, I sat on the bed and kicked off my shoes before I noticed the strip of light between the threshold and the bottom of our door. "What's that?" When Amanda didn't answer, I wagged my finger at the breach. "See that?"

She gave me a slitty-eyed look. "What about it?"

"Know what that is?" I demanded.

"The obvious answer is 'a two-inch gap under the door' so I'm going to take a wild guess and say 'mail chute.' "

"It's a snake door," I yelled, drawing my feet up off the floor and curling my legs underneath me. "What kind of snakes do they have here?"

"Coral snakes. Rattlesnakes. Chihuahuan night snakes."

"There's something called a Chihuahuan night snake? Are you kidding me?" I yelled. "And I'm expected to sleep in here? That freakin' gap's big enough for a Gila monster to wander in."

"Gila monster," she scoffed. "The only monsters in this town that you have to worry about are the ones who masquerade as cops and businessmen . . . and the drug cartel. If I were you, I'd be more worried about scorpions."

"They have scorpions?" I shrieked. Scorpions give a jolt like a cattle prod. The antivenom tastes like transmission fluid. Scorpion stings have killed people.

"About this big." She held up her index fingers, measured twelve inches and narrowed the gap to six.

"I'm not sleeping in a room with scorpions. Or snakes," I said in a fractured voice. "Or freakin' Gila monsters."

"Well then, don't go to sleep, or get a damned towel and plug up the hole."

"We only have two towels."

"Use yours if it bothers you that much. I'm using mine for something else."

"What?" I shouted. "What's more important than plugging

up a snake door?"

"If you don't stop bitching, I'm going to shove it in your mouth."

I was about to send her downstairs for more towels when the din of reverberating sound vibrated the windowpanes. I shook out my shoes, giving each a quick inspection before I eased my feet into them, then moved toward the door leading out onto the balcony to see what on Earth would make such a noise. For no reason other than instinct, I shifted my attention to Amanda.

"Don't open the curtains," she said.

"Why?"

"Get away from those windows—now." She took a hectoring tone with me. "*Ay, idiota,* don't stand in front; stay behind the walls."

I'll take "Bad Roommates" for a hundred, Alex.

"You know, you really shouldn't call me names." Irritation mounted. I sliced her a smile. "After all, I'm the one bank-rolling this little shindig—"

Jim's cell phone rang while I was listening to her ramble on about why I'd better start paying attention to her, and about how I'd bucked her on every damned thing since we'd been here. Well, *hello,* it's my sister and my money, and Amanda's my employee, and even though this isn't Burger King, I *am* going to have it my way.

"Give me my phone back."

Without warning, what sounded like a drum roll echoed through the night—gun blasts from an automatic weapon.

The rest of my posturing slid back down my throat.

The thunderous amount of noise made it seem like the Earth had cracked open. Then . . . nothing but the hum of traffic swishing up and down the street in front of our hotel.

Blood pounded in my ears.

It's like I'm living in a parallel universe.

The 32ⁿᵈ parallel.

Fleet of foot, Amanda extinguished the light. For several minutes, we waited in the gloom with only the moonlight slanting through a break in the curtain, watching each other's silhouettes. Crime and fear had made this place surreal, and we were like puppets, waiting for our destiny to be determined by someone we didn't know and couldn't see.

"Do you think—"

"Don't talk," Amanda said. "I'm trying to listen."

To what? I couldn't hear a thing. Then slowly . . . surely . . . the scream of sirens closed in on the neighborhood. In no time, rotating beams of red and blue light from emergency vehicles leaked through the slit in the curtain.

In the hallway outside our door, I heard someone's face slapped hard. A couple of patrons involved in a dispute took their argument upstairs, each yelling as their voices faded, until a door in the distance slammed shut.

"We should've gone back home before it got dark," I said grimly.

"Two steps forward, one step back. It's better this way. At least we can hit the ground running tomorrow morning."

Amanda's bravery turned out to be superficial, because when she pushed her hair behind her ears, her fingers shook.

"So what's the status on our room change?" Hated to beat a dead horse, but hey, I had to know.

"Not going to happen. But they gave us extra *papel higiénica.*" She held up a consolation prize—a roll of toilet paper—and gave me a gap-toothed grin, which triggered a heavy eye roll on my part.

I moved closer to the window. It was killing me not to know what'd happened out there.

The crime scene was at the far end of an intersecting street. Steam or smoke coming off a wrecked SUV obscured my ability to see clearly. Within the cowl of smoke, flames died out.

Curiosity satisfied, I started to unhand the curtain and step backward. Invasive red and blue lights still flashed beyond our room. I'd convinced myself that whatever was going on outside didn't concern us . . . had nothing to do with us . . . was merely a coincidence that it happened outside our hotel. I even considered we might get a good night's sleep. But then the smoke abruptly cleared, and the silhouette of a cowboy hat on the head of a man wearing a longcoat materialized at the end of the street.

Snakes, Gila monsters, and scorpions react. They don't reason or plot or make plans to do you in. They just react. Disturb the ground, and the pit viper's rattle warns you to back off. Forget to shake out your shoes, and the lightning strike of a scorpion's barb will get your attention. Come too close, you'll hear the Gila monster's breathy hiss.

Given the choice between reptiles and scorpions or *El Mort-ero,* I'd take reptiles and scorpions hands down.

Amanda turned off the television. In the time it took her to turn around, the sucking pull of this International quicksand we'd waded into tugged me deeper. I struggled against this suffocating force as strongly as if I'd been swept beneath the Rio Bravo's treacherous undertow. Amanda'd been right, Teensy was the smart one. And if Teensy could be blindsided, who was I to think I could outmaneuver these cutthroats and orchestrate a successful recovery?

For no good reason, my earliest childhood memory rose like an apparition. Standing beside my mother's hospital bed, taking in the sight and smell of a new baby, I could almost hear the dulcet tone of my mother's voice.

"What do you think of your new sister, Dainty?"

"I don't like her."

"I don't like her either. Can you keep a secret? I didn't want

another girl because I already have the most perfect little girl in the whole wide world, and that's you, Dainty. Know what I think? I think we should just throw this baby in the trash. What do you think, princess? Should we throw the baby in the trash and get us another one? No? Oh, wait—did you want her?"

"Can I have her?"

"If you'll take care of her. Will you take care of her?"

"Uh-huh." Big head bob.

"It's a big job, Dainty, taking care of a new baby. Sure you're up to it?"

"Uh-huh."

"Then it's settled. I'll give her to you and you can take care of her and love her and watch out for her. Won't that be wonderful? Here you go. Hold out your hands. She's your baby now."

Daddy sat me on the bed. My mother gently placed my sister in my arms, cautioning me not to drop her. Then she sank back into a stack of plumped pillows and caressed my hair through threaded fingers.

"What'll you name your new baby, Dainty?"

"Teensy. 'Cause she's so tiny."

Slapped into reality by the promise I'd made my mother, the grisly residue of the day's events overwhelmed me. I mashed my face into my hands and felt the burn of hot tears against my palms. I wanted to go home. I wanted to talk to Bruckman. And I desperately wanted my mother. Nothing had gone right since she left us.

"Knock it off." Amanda, arms braced, stood inches away. "We don't have time for a mental disorder."

"I need to talk to my boyfriend." Tears sluiced down my cheeks.

"No. He'll insist you come home, and we can't go back tonight. Too dangerous."

"He could come here," I said through a sniffle. Safety in

numbers and all that.

She gave me a slow headshake of the *Poor little idiot* variety. "Dainty, why the hell would you want to involve anyone else in this mess—especially someone you love?"

She was right, of course. Amanda's spin on our predicament made me feel worse than ever.

"You don't understand." My chest burned with longing. "I need to hear his voice."

Amanda meditated on this disclosure for several seconds. "Do you need it like a jelly donut, or do you need it like a kidney? Because you'll just feel worse if you talk to him."

Point taken. Composing myself, I swiped the back of my hand across my eyes and pulled it together. "I hate this hotel."

"Yeah? Well I have low expectations." She took in the room with a cursory glance. "Unfortunately, they're being met." Then she said, "Dibs on the can," and angled past the stain on the carpet toward the bathroom.

CHAPTER FIFTEEN

Sharing a bathroom with Amanda was terrible, especially when she started making the same noises as my coffeemaker. I tapped on the bathroom door to see if I could help.

"Don't come in."

Believe me, it never crossed my mind, but the devil on my shoulder goaded me. "Why not?"

She farted at the same time the lights flickered. There was probably no connection between the two incidents, but I wondered. Not to mention that methane cloud problem hanging in the air . . .

"Do you think they serve free Continental breakfasts here?" No point in mentioning who made that comment.

"Ha!" exploded from Amanda's mouth like a cannon blast.

I walked away. As I did, I heard the whoosh of a flushing commode, at the same time water came out of our sink. I didn't know what to make of that, but I decided not to investigate because every time I did, things took a turn for the worse.

It didn't take long before the mystery solved itself. It quickly became apparent that every time someone flushed in the room above ours, water came out of our sink. Never mind that the faucets were turned off. It was enough to make me forego bathing. And I didn't need a case of trench mouth, either.

Note to self: *Do not brush your teeth with water from the sink.*

I started to think in terms of bottled water, and did some quick calculations in my head. At five feet four inches, I'd need, oh, say, three cases of bottled water hauled up here to bathe with, and, oh, say, another three to get my hair super clean. That's seventy-two bottles of drinking water.

My eyes slewed over to Amanda. Guilt set in.

Make that eighty-four bottles of water.

She gave me a funny look, accompanied by a huge eye roll. It occurred to me she'd read my mind.

What? I telepathically protested. *You're black. It's not like anybody can see the dirt and grime.*

She stomped back into the bathroom and slammed the door in a huff.

I *knew* she could tell what I was thinking. She *did* have a mind that could bend spoons.

"I have an idea, Amanda," I said to the door, "why don't you go out and get us a few cases of bottled water?"

Oh, all right, ten cases. A little more for her, plus a few extra bottles for us to drink.

Because of the water running from the faucet, I'm not exactly certain about this next part, but it sounded like she said, "Why don't you jump up my ass?"

The door swung open.

"Did you hear me?" I backed away, figuring she'd been in there contributing to the greenhouse effect again.

"Sorry. I have a tendency to drift in and out when you start talking." Amanda had removed her sweater, skirt and shoes, and padded into the room wearing only her shirt. She neatly folded her clothes over the back of the only chair at the table. The powder blue dress that'd earlier served as either a hump or lumbar support hung on the only clothes hanger, in a cubby hole that was supposed to pass for a closet.

Before I could repeat my bottled water suggestion, Bruckman's phone rang again. I ran toward the sound, and located it at the bottom of the glowing pocket of Amanda's sweater.

"Ohmygod, Jim, you won't believe what just happened."

"This isn't Jim."

I sucked air, holding the phone at arm's length as if it were a tumor that needed excising. No number came up on the digital readout, but I knew the caller.

Nerissa.

Tears welled. Which underscored my desperation to speak to another American.

She lit into me like there was no tomorrow. In her corrosive tone, she chastised me for upsetting Daddy. Apparently Teensy's and my little globetrotting expedition put him in the hospital. She wound down with a real butt kicker. "So if he dies, I'm holding you and that idiot sister of yours personally responsible."

News of my father stretched my frayed nerves as tight as banjo strings. I swallowed the lump in my throat. Daddy and I may not be on the best terms at the moment, but he's still my father, and I love him. And in Texas, the only thing stronger than blood is oil. I have both.

"Where's Daddy?" I said in a raw voice.

My stepmother got her second wind. "You're the most spoiled, selfish, inconsiderate little b—*rat* I ever met."

"Brat" is not what she wanted to call me.

"I am *not* inconsiderate," I said defiantly.

Amanda darted a glance at me.

I muted the phone with my hand. "Don't start." Then I unmuted it, but Nerissa was still haranguing. I pictured her wearing a spray-painted-on white cocktail dress (read: no white after Labor Day, or before Easter), with a plunging neckline (read: hooker), strutting up and down the hospital corridor with gouge-your-eyes-out stilettos (read: streetwalker) and her long, silky platinum hair (read: top half from a bottle; bottom half, extensions) cascading down a backless frock (read: harlot), dripping in jewels (read: "I'll take Deviant Sex Acts for five hundred, Alex") and wanted to jump through the phone and throttle her. "I hate you."

The call dropped. Or not. Imagine that.

I looked at Amanda. "Guess you figured out I'm estranged from my family. I'm sort of the black sheep."

"Didn't your parents believe in second chances?"

I gave a derisive sniff. "Yeah—that's why they had Teensy."

I thumbed the number to Bruckman's phone and remembered I was holding it, so I re-dialed my own cell phone number and waited for him to pick up. The phone routed to voicemail.

After that blistering exchange with my stepmother, I got a renewed urge to look for Tiffany. I continued to operate under the assumption that she was alive. I'm all for tunnel vision when the need arises.

"Get dressed," I told Amanda. "We're scoping out cantinas."

"I don't think that's such a hot idea."

This time, I didn't argue with her. "I don't think it's such a hot idea, either." But the cockroaches were conducting warlike attacks on us, and I'd had my fill of that. "You don't have to go if you'd rather not. I'll just get the desk clerk to get me a cab, and I'll see you when I get back."

She gave me a look of the *If you get back* variety.

I'd taken off my clothes and dressed for bed. Now, I slipped out of my shorty pajama bottoms and stepped back into my bright blue slacks. My heart started doing the rapid beat thing.

Several hours had passed since we checked into *Hotel Mala-muerte*. The crime scene down the street had been cleared, and everything appeared to be business as usual. The right side of my brain, the part that wanted to get my sister back, nagged my conscience. If we were going to venture out, this would be the time. Now that I'd gotten myself oriented, I realized we were not only close enough to the border, but on a direct route from the bridge. Teensy may have taken such a route, stopping in at the closest places, before burrowing deeper into the city.

Bar hopping.

As little as I drank, my sister made up for it.

Amanda sighed. "All right."

"What? No back-talk?"

She blew out a slow, resigned stream of air. "If I don't go with you, I'll probably never see you again. And to tell you the truth, I'm starting to like you." She reached for her skirt, stuffing a toe into it while balancing on one foot. Then she shrugged into the frumpy sweater.

I opened my purse and searched for my wallet. "How much do you think the cantinas charge for drinks? I figure we should each get one, but I don't think we ought to—" I was going to say, "drink them." But since every bloody thing about this situation had to turn into a big eff-ing problem, my life went to hell in a handcart. I sucked air. "My passport's gone."

After the Twin Towers fell to terrorist attacks, Homeland Security cracked down on people entering the U.S. I had horrible visions of spending the rest of my natural life in this God-awful place.

"How could I lose my passport?" My voice corkscrewed upward.

My purse was with me the whole time. As I mentally retraced my steps, my gut sank. I'd opened my handbag to give that beggar-child an American dollar, and his little co-conspirator ploughed into me. He'd stolen it.

But why?

My next thought sickened me: That little pickpocket had come out of the police department.

I admit it. I cracked. "Ohmygod, how will I get back across the border without it?"

"Thousands of wetbacks do it everyday. Swim."

"Ohmygod, Jim said these people drain their sewage into the

Rio Bravo." I couldn't help it. Tears beaded along the rims of my eyes. One spilled over onto my cheek.

"There's a spot near Ysleta and Socorro on the east side of El Paso where the river's about thirty or forty yards wide. It's a good spot to cross because those towns aren't monitored that closely by Border Patrol—"

"I'm not breast-stroking across a river of human waste."

"—of course, there's still the problem that you could drown. But we could find you an inner tube over here so you could tube across it."

"How do you think up this stuff?" I stared, stricken, as whitewater crashed in my head. My sister was injured. How was I supposed to help her swim across? Amanda stood, amphibian-eyed, doing a slow blink while I sorted this out in my head. "You cannot possibly be serious."

"Then pay me five hundred dollars. I'll get it to my cousin. He'll get a message to a man I know who'll make you a new one. A thousand if you want it by tomorrow afternoon."

"I'm not giving you a thousand dollars for a piece of paper."

To which Amanda breast-stroked over to the bed, and collapsed onto the mattress without removing her shoes.

Well, hell.

"We may need one for Teensy, too," I said dully. I didn't even barter. I already knew how it'd turn out. If I bitched to high heaven, she'd probably raise the price due to my failing P.I.T.A. score. Or worse, she'd ditch me. Didn't want to entertain that idea at all.

"Add another five hundred."

I couldn't help it. After listening to Amanda talking about numbers and costs, I must've zoned out because she said, "Did you hear me?"

I stayed mime quiet.

"Did you hear anything I said?"

143

"No. But I do remember hearing 'Sunday, Monday, happy days . . . Tuesday, Wednesday, happy days . . .' "

"Do you not understand simple addition?"

"No, but I'm a debutante, so I don't understand why you're not dressed to the nines."

"Didn't you learn math in school?"

"No, and after all these years, the math file's too large to store on my internal hard drive, so I'll just fill up the last little space in my head with directions back to this roach hotel."

Amanda had placed the extra roll of toilet paper on the table, so I unfurled a length as long as my arm, and folded it at its precut squares before stuffing it into my purse.

So . . . *ha!*

On our way out, we stopped by the front counter to ask the clerk to call us a cab. He considered me through his horn-rims, then wagged his finger in front of my face.

"No. I no call taxi," he said in his broken English. "You blonde. You pretty. If you leave without man, we never see no more time."

Amanda shrugged. "It's your call."

"We'll walk." I pulled my scarf tighter over my hair, and the two of us stepped out into the night.

CHAPTER SIXTEEN

We passed up the first two cantinas that were closest to the hotel, figuring we'd stop in the one that was farthest away and catch the others on the way back. Altogether, I'd say we walked about a mile and a half by the time we reached the third bar. Its name translated as "The Sure Thing."

Imagine, naming a bar after my stepmother. She must be very proud.

I paused at the entrance and took stock of the room. Trapped inside this dingy place with *No fumar*—No Smoking—signs posted on the walls was a smoke haze so thick that we seemed to walk through blue gauze. Loud music blasted above the reverberating din of voices, laughter and coughing. I'd probably leave this country with tuberculosis and have to go live in one of those TB sanitariums until I got cured, but it was the lesser evil, assuming I made it out of this swill pit. And it'd mean I'd found Teensy and brought her home, because I wasn't leaving Mexico without Teensy.

The bar had a creepy feel, including the mural painted on the wall in trompe l'oiel style that made the room appear much larger in the dim lighting, since it depicted the same tables with similarly dressed patrons lounging around in various poses. As for the real girls propped against stools, pressed against walls and draped over men, they could've ranged anywhere between fifteen and fifty. Or they could've been younger. Mexico is a harsh country where people lead bleak lives. Point being, they could've looked a lot older than they were due to environmental stress.

As I scanned the faces in the room, the term "lot lizards" popped into mind. Women wearing too much makeup and tight dresses that were out of style as far back as the sixties fawned over swarthy, paunchy men puffing on cigars and cigarettes. One particularly drunk male lost his balance and careened into a Pancho Villa type on his way out the back door, and for a few tedious seconds, I thought a fight would break out.

At the bar, Amanda ordered a couple of tequila shots and slid one over to me. I knew better than to drink mine.

"Check out those girls over there in the corner," I said. "They're minors. Why would anyone allow girls that young in a bar?" Not to mention they were making a big to-do over men three or four times their ages.

"I've got news for you—they're whores."

They did look busier than a prostitute at the Fraternal Order of the Stag convention, but I was trying to be nice, and didn't want to jump to conclusions.

"You don't have proof." Actually, what I had was 100-proof. I stared at my drink before pushing it aside. I needed my wits about me, and I didn't trust these people. Not even the bartender slinging our drinks.

Especially him.

Amanda finished her drink and then belted back mine, wiping her mouth with the back of her hand and wincing at the burn.

I quickly made the connection between trouble and tequila. The young females were all drunk, and the men pawing at them were taking advantage by copping cheap feels. Then one of them broke into song. Amanda joined in when everybody but me started singing *Cielito Lindo*. That's when I realized there's a huge difference between singing together and singing at the same time.

I returned my shot glass to the bartender and gave him a tight smile. "Coca-Cola, *por favor.*" I'm nothing if not well mannered. He returned the smile, exposing a couple of missing molars.

Then a *très, très* bad thing happened. Amanda apparently liked the look of this young drunk Mexican, because she excused herself from the bar with a "Be right back." As she pushed her way through the crowd to shine up to the locals, I felt empty, lost and alone. I sat on a stool, my back to the bar, and watched her across the room. The soda pop was just a prop, but it rented my seat for as long as I needed to stay. I'd be as safe here as anywhere, and yet I didn't want her to leave my side.

If water seeks its own level, Amanda was ebbing over to a wall of obvious unsavory characters, propped against the mural, striking various poses. I inclined my head past a person who was obstructing my view, and lost sight of her. When she popped up on my radar again, she'd cornered the young Mexican and was pulling him toward an unoccupied table for two.

Uncomfortable in my surroundings, I glanced around. An older woman with long dark hair too youthful for her years slid off her bar stool. With a drink in one hand and a lit cigarette in the other, she teetered toward me on stiletto heels with an exaggerated sway of the hips. She staked out the bar stool next to mine, concentrating on her cigarette as the ash grew longer. Her legs were a trellis of varicose veins, but that didn't discourage her from wearing a short, tight skirt.

Casting a glance at me, she spoke in a whiskey voice. "You berry pretty. I like."

"Thanks. You're nice, too."

Her eyes thinned. Mascara thickened her lashes, and she wore heavy blue shadow. Black liner meant to enhance her eyes had given her a harsh, sinister look.

"No . . . I like." She dragged out the word, then puckered her full, voluptuous lips, and air kissed me an arm's length away. "We go my house?"

Realization dawned.

I wanted to say, *Over my dead body*, but since that was such a highly likely possibility, I resisted putting that thought out into the universe, even in jest.

"Buy drink for you?" She lifted her glass to indicate a highball.

I didn't dare take her up on the offer, but wanted to thank her in a way that didn't leave us both avoiding eye contact in the morning. So I settled on "Thanks, but no, thanks." I slid off my barstool and moved to another one a few seats down. By the time I relocated, she was already so oiled and lubed she was practically slipping off the seat.

A girl nearer my age sidled up beside me. She gave me a wan smile, and then looked me over from head to toe. I did the only thing I knew to do—pulled out the picture of Teensy.

"Mi hermana," I ventured, using choppy Spanish phrases I'd picked up from Amanda along the way, *"¿la conoce?"* I was asking if she knew Teensy.

At first, she just stared at me through flat, impenetrable eyes. But I saw a flash of recognition when she looked at the photograph.

I sensed she'd talk to me. "My sister, in this bar? *¿Aquí, en este cantina?*" I probably used the wrong verb tenses and noun modifiers, but I knew I'd gotten my point across when she touched my hand and answered me in broken English.

"You. *¿Americana?*"

Knowing this could go either way, I did an almost imperceptible head bob.

"Yes, she here. She come with *amiga*—friend—*con el pelo*—with, how you say? Brown hair?"

"Yes. Tiffany." My voice cracked saying her name.

Then several things went wrong. First, a man jostled between us, and tried what I gathered was a pick-up line on one or both of us. Since I didn't know what he said, I let her answer.

"Would you ladies be interested in a threesome with me? Or perhaps a foursome with my friend Pancho Villa, who wants to keep his true identity as the Juárez Ripper a secret?"

"Of course, we'd love to. But only after you get us tickets to the red light district donkey show."

I imagined all kinds of crazy things—which were actually *not* so crazy—but the overriding thought remained, *What in the hell did you get yourself into?* Something Amanda and everyone else had been saying all along.

Which made me an *idiota*, because now I had the sudden urge to find the restroom—probably out of fear—but just because you know what triggers the urge doesn't mean it'll evaporate once you figure it out.

My new acquaintance scolded the man until he left us alone. She looked me over with soft brown eyes.

"I see you today. With the *mujeres*—the women—to look for, how you say? Bodies in the desert."

A head bob.

"You sister she missing?"

A headshake. "Her friend. Her friend is missing."

I had a pretty good idea we'd be getting Teensy back in a few days. Hoped so, anyway.

"I sorry."

I squeezed her hand. I'm sure people back home would think we were a lesbian couple, but it's different here. I'd seen lots of girls holding hands as they strolled through the market, or park, or down the street. I didn't think anything about it. In fact, it was endearing. But here? In a bar? Well, except for that drunk lady, I didn't exactly know how a hand squeeze would go over, and to tell you the truth, I didn't much care. I'd found someone who'd seen Teensy and Tiffer. Or claimed to.

My neurosis was showing.

"Can you show me where the bathroom is—*el cuarto de baño?*"

Her laughter sounded like musical chimes. "*No hay cuarto de baño. Ven conmigo.* Come with me. I show where you go." She tugged me by the hand through the crowd.

I balked when we reached the back door.

"It's okay," she said gently, kindly. So I went with her.

The road to hell is paved with good intentions.

"What's your name?"

"Maria del Carmen. You?"

Since the Catholic Church had a huge influence over these people, and everyone seemed to be named after saints, the Virgin Mary or the baby Jesus, I claimed my name was Maria, too.

"No, no, no, you Danny Prescott," she said, drawing out her discovery with each shake of the head to prolong the agony.

Chills froze me in place.

Deny, deny, deny.

"How do you know who I am?" I reasoned that perhaps Amanda had dropped my name in conversation with Maribel Espinoza earlier, when the females at the town hall meeting were searching for missing women. But there could've been a more sinister explanation.

"I come here every night for three years, Danny Prescott—" she flashed three fingers "—and look for my friend, Isabel. Sixteen years old. Gone."

"I'm sorry." For the record, I *was* sorry. I glanced around for an outhouse, and found myself standing in air noxious with the smell of human waste and auto exhaust. "Where's the bathroom?"

"Here." She opened her hand and sliced the air in a *Pick your spot* gesture.

150

"What?" This came out more sharply than I'd intended. But hey, I was slipping into shock at the realization that, instead of the privacy of a structure, I was standing in the middle of the world's biggest open-air outhouse.

What am I thinking? The whole country's an outhouse.

Amanda had warned me how many restaurants and bars had no indoor plumbing, but I hardly anticipated having to relieve myself behind a building, in the dark.

I stepped on something squishy. The strong odor of excrement wafted up from the ground. I thought of my beautiful Ferragamos, and wondered if I could persuade Amanda to clean them. For a fee, of course.

Then, the girl said, "I like your chirt," in a tone that bordered on something beyond admiration. Like if a member of the Gambino crime family complimented your shirt, you'd peel it off and gladly hand it over. To be fair, the longer I stayed here, the more paranoid I got, so it could've gone either way. But I sensed where this was headed and I didn't like it one bit.

"You give me chirt."

"No, I'm keeping 'chirt.' But thank you so much. You're very sweet."

"No," she said, "you give to me."

"Don't even think about it," I said, but she refused to walk away and give me my privacy. Before I could lower my slacks and take care of business, she pulled at my sleeve. "I'm fine. I can do this myself."

Light from the bar stole across the patio. I noticed movement in my peripheral vision, and could hardly believe my eyes. Amanda was doing a bit of sexual off-roading with that drunken stranger. He'd propped himself up against the tall, cinder block fence, while she'd dropped to her knees to sing karaoke into his microphone.

When I couldn't wait any longer, the girl stood guard over

me. After I finished, I called out to the lieutenant.

She hurried over, covered up in estrogen, in various stages of readjusting her clothing, and rattled off something in Spanish. Lively hand gestures made up a huge part of this conversation.

Then Amanda turned to me. "Give her your shirt."

The girl began unbuttoning her blouse.

"I will not."

"She's the only thing standing between you and the cops. Now take it off."

"What am I supposed to wear?"

She rattled off something else in Spanish before turning to me a second time. "She'll take your shoes instead. She thinks they'll fit her sister."

"I'm not—"

"Just fucking do it so we can get out of here in one piece."

The girl pulled off her right sneaker and handed it over. One at a time, I slid out of my Italian pumps, gripping Amanda's shoulder with one hand to stabilize me as I put on each of the shoes we exchanged.

Here's the "lemonade rationale" that I squeezed out of this particular sour lemon: I could always buy a new pair of Ferragamos; or my grandmother, the bluehair, would give me a pair for Christmas. But here, on the black market, my shoes might bring enough money for this girl and her family to eat for a month.

I'd barely tied the second shoelace when sickening screams from the crowd erupted inside the building. What sounded like a deafening drum roll carried out the back door and shattered the night. Instinct told me it wasn't really a drum roll, not with the ping of metal and broken glass that accompanied it. The karaoke machine abruptly went silent.

My mouth formed the word, "Oh," but my mind shrieked, *Run for your life!* My muscles had somehow short-circuited the signals coming from my brain, and I stood petrified instead of taking flight.

Amanda grabbed my arm and pulled me toward the man she'd left standing next to the wall. He'd dragged up a chair and motioned us over. We ran hell bent for leather. I'd learned to excel at the fifty-yard dash.

While Lover Boy gave Amanda a leg up and over, I climbed onto the chair. The sneakers gave me a certain amount of traction, but I still struggled to clear the wall. I couldn't even hoist myself up the rest of the way until he gave my rump a solid heave-ho. I sat on top of the wall with my hands bloodied from the broken bottles incorporated into the top of the cinder blocks to discourage burglars.

Amanda climbed onto an overhanging tree limb in the courtyard of the next building. I followed her lead.

We needed to get down. To locate an escape route and get the hell out of here. I expected she'd insist on me dropping to the ground, but I'd made it a fetish to cut back on activities that cause broken bones.

While I clung to the tree trunk, our window of opportunity to jump slammed shut. Men dressed in dark clothing stormed the patio shouting things I couldn't understand. My heart pounded.

Now we needed to remain hidden in the tree for the duration of this ordeal.

Amanda moved to the backside of the tree and out onto another limb in order to make room for me. I squeezed in front of her and grabbed hold of the trunk.

"Put your hands down," she hissed.

"I'll fall."

"I'll hold you steady."

"No."

"My hands are dark. They'll blend in. Let go and be still. I'll hold you."

In the nick of time, I unhanded the tree. Amanda slid her arms around my waist, and braced her palms against the trunk.

Until this moment, I hadn't noticed what big hands she had.

"They'll see us."

"Nobody ever looks up."

Morbid curiosity made me incline my head until I could see around the tree.

Amanda's lips brushed against my ear. "No matter what you see, don't react."

In the time it took to sneak a quick peek, Lover Boy had moved aside. It was enough to draw the eye away. From my vantage point, I watched a lone gunman talking to the girl. She was shaking her head in response to something he'd said, and I eased back into place. As I sat with my legs wrapped around the limb we were sitting on, my brain did a funny thing. It tried to re-write history, and turn this into a game of hide-and-go-seek.

For maybe a minute, I pretended I was seven and had found the greatest hiding place ever. One where Teensy and her friends would never find me.

Then a gunshot exploded, and something hit the ground with a sickening thud. Everything went quiet, or maybe it was the tinny, distant hum in my ears that blocked out the noise.

Amanda's new boyfriend screamed, *"Ya se fueron, ya se fueron."*

Footfalls stampeded into the cantina's courtyard—more gunmen. I've never in my life been so happy to hear the echo of sirens in the distance.

The gunmen cleared out, leaving only weak cries of the wounded in their wake.

"We have to go. Now," Amanda said.

Fine by me.

When confronted with the choice between a broken leg or death, I settled on injury. Amanda got down first. I didn't want to compare her amazing agility to a monkey in a mango tree, so let's say she made it look easy. She dragged over a chair, but when I swung down, I still couldn't touch it with my toes. She pulled it out of the way and said, "Let go, I'm right here."

"No." I was barely holding on by the tips of my French manicure when I felt her hands grip my calves.

"Let go."

I closed my eyes and released my grip. On the way down I remembered—stop, drop and roll doesn't work in hell.

I hit the ground like a sack of flour, with Amanda banging down beside me. Miraculously, the only thing broken was my fall. I'd give us a 9.9 in the Olympic tree-falling event.

"Now what?" I said in a hushed voice. Next door, authorities were rattling off rapid-fire Spanish and taking charge.

There didn't seem to be any way out other than to go over another wall and find out what was on the other side. I sure didn't want to do that, and I told her so.

Amanda stood in the middle of the courtyard and made a 360-degree turn. Then she pointed to the opposite corner.

"We climb that other tree and drop out onto the street."

My heart sank. I'd already gouged my hands and banged up my entire left side. Now that the adrenaline rush had worn off, pain set in. I offered up my palms so Amanda could see my scuffs and scrapes.

"What doesn't kill you makes you stronger . . ." she mumbled.

"Yeah, well, not everyone makes it into that category."

It sounded like total anarchy next door. I followed Amanda to the corner of the courtyard to scope out the other tree. For now, we were safe. Once we dropped over that wall and onto the street, who knew? Part of me wanted to stay put until morning when the owners came in to open up.

The caged animal part of me wanted out. "Okay, I'm game. But what about my hands?"

"I'll help you," was all she said.

We exchanged eyebrow-encrypted messages and settled on a small table. It was taller than any of the chairs and would serve as a good base.

"You should go first. Then pull me up," I said. It wasn't an altogether altruistic suggestion. That part hurt to admit. Truth was, I had no idea who or what we'd find on the other side. I had to face facts—so far, I haven't been very good at this recovery specialist thing.

"Unless . . ." Lost in thought, she gnawed at her bottom lip. "If we put a chair on top of the table, it'd get us closer."

We weren't Chinese acrobats. Even I could see there wasn't enough room to climb onto the table once we stacked a chair on it. "We need a stool or something so we can step up."

We scoured the patio with a glance. Light from the cantina stole across terra cotta containers bushy with plants. We said, "Flower pot," in unison.

The terra cotta pot was much heavier than it looked. It took both of us to drag it across the stone walkway. If either of us feared discovery, we didn't let on.

"That girl didn't rat us off," I said numbly.

"Don't think about it now. We can talk about it later."

I closed my eyes tight, forcing the girl's face from my mind. Instead of vaporizing, the image popped up behind my eyelids.

We climbed our obstacle course in relative silence, scooting along the branch until we could drop onto the side street undetected. But like Lot's wife, as we walked away from the crime scene, I looked back.

What I saw electrified my skin.

Near the corner, with his back to us, was the outline of a man in a cowboy hat and longcoat, backlit by the strobe of red and blue emergency lights.

El Mortero.

CHAPTER SEVENTEEN

During the night, pain knifed through me. *Oh, dear Lord, I've been stabbed.*

I came fully awake believing that someone had entered our room and filleted my guts. When I realized I hadn't been eviscerated, I decided I was having an appendicitis attack.

"Montezuma's revenge." Amanda fisted sleep from her eyes. She reminded me I'd poured soda pop over ice at the restaurant the previous night.

But I'd only had one sip. How can one sip of soda water over contaminated ice make a person feel like she had razor blades in her stomach? I washed down the rest of my food with the second bottled drink. Which left me with visions of food handlers using the nasty bathroom without washing their hands. Or field hands urinating on unwashed produce. I'd heard of that happening in backward countries where bathrooms weren't the norm. Mexico is crap.

Amanda offered to go down to the front desk to see if they had an anti-diarrheal, while I fell back moaning into the tangle of sheets. When she returned an hour later, I dragged myself from the bathroom, where I'd been almost the entire time she was gone. Then I flopped back into bed.

She tossed a small sack on top of the covers. "Drink this. You may be the best-looking car in the neighborhood, but if your transmission's messed up, you can't get it in gear."

She explained what it was and how much to take. Two capfuls didn't sound like it'd do the trick. I consumed a quarter of the bottle.

I awakened at dawn with Amanda's arm looped over me. We'd fallen into bed the previous night and slept in our shirts. Now, the full impact of our sleazy hotel hit me full force.

A rattling doorknob spurred me into action. I flung off her arm and jumped out of bed. The housekeeper came in, flipped on the light, yanked open the drapes, and turned to me with her arms braced across her chest.

"*Buenos dias,*" she said in a vitriolic tone, so I knew which one of us wasn't having a good morning. She stared with disapproval at the lump on the bed.

"Amanda, get up." I snatched my slacks off the back of the chair and toed my way into the legs as fast as I could, then hopped over the red stain on the carpet and turned on the rabbit-ear television. Our black and white model had poor reception, but it got one of the El Paso channels so I left the TV volume low until the news came on.

Although nobody had the bad manners to remark on the subject, I'm pretty sure I stank. Desperate for a shower, I retreated to the bathroom and left a drowsy roommate to deal with the maid.

That's when I noticed the "curlies" in the drain trap.

I felt the onset of my fourth gastro-intestinal attack and locked the bathroom door. I knew it didn't really lock, but this simple act made me feel better just the same. When I finally came out, weak and exhausted, I encountered the domestic wiping the lone table with a rag, and studying the rest of yesterday's ensemble that I'd draped over the chair.

She said, "Pretty," and jutted her chin at my pants.

"No." Hands on hips, I gave her a vehement headshake.

The early news broadcast had come on so I hopped over the stain and turned up the sound. With respect to looks and

159

temperament, the weather girl wasn't much different than WBFD's Misty Knight, informing viewers about the weather and wooing the camera with witty asides.

She said, "There's nothing like a big sausage to fill you up on a cold morning like this." I figured she was referring to the hot dog she was holding, but I gave the TV a resounding, "Amen, sister," anyway.

Amanda came out of the bathroom fully dressed about the same time that I watched the maid blow her nose into the same rag she'd cleaned off the table with, and shake it out onto the balcony. This was housekeeping.

In a low voice, I discussed the bottled water issue with Amanda. "I'm in no position to go out at the moment, so I think you should do it."

"I'm not your slave, Dainty. You hired me to be your interpreter and guide. I've more than done that," she complained in that sassy, exaggerated tone.

"But you brought me medicine last night. So I just thought . . ."

"Just thought what? That you could whip me like a rented mule? I brought you medicine because you were in pain. It's not my nature to walk the streets at two in the morning. Well, not in Mexico, anyway."

The housekeeper said something I didn't understand. Amanda responded, which touched off a lively conversation complete with hand gestures.

Then Amanda said, "It's settled. The housekeeper will get it."

"Really?" I almost smiled, victorious, until an internal voice reminded me that I'm Dainty Prescott, and I'm in Mexico. And since nothing so far had turned out the way I thought it would, this wouldn't either. Suspicion compelled me to ask, "What's the catch?"

"No catch. You just have to give her your trousers."

Who knew when I memorized all those Spanish curse words how handy they'd come in? I peppered my protests with most of them. It felt great to vent. I had no intention of parting with my slacks. None whatsoever.

So, *ha!* Keeping the pants.

But as the maid shuffled toward the door, my amphibian survival brain engaged. I called out for her to wait.

"Listen up, Amanda, I have to wear something. So she brings ten cases of bottled water and leaves her skirt." It was a frumpy, threadbare thing, but I eyeballed it, and it looked like it'd fit, and I only needed to wear it until we reached the market. Then I could buy something better. Besides, I told myself, the silk pants needed to be cleaned, not to mention I'd snagged them shimmying across tree limbs.

As far as I was concerned, I'd negotiated the better deal.

An hour into our morning, a knock sounded at the door.

"You get it," I said.

Amanda scowled. We'd started evaluating even the simplest items as things that could be converted into weapons, so I wasn't surprised when she dragged the chair closer to the door. When she opened it, the housekeeper was standing there with a Mexican man.

Age had stooped him. Two dollies loaded with purified water stood out on the landing. He off-loaded several cases and waited for Amanda to permit him inside. He nodded politely, and probably would've tipped his sombrero if he'd had a free hand.

The housekeeper slipped into the bathroom and came out wearing my slacks. I didn't even want to handle her skirt when she thrust it at me, but Amanda warned me to be nice, so I took it. After they left, I debated washing it.

Then Amanda said, "While you're figuring it out, I'm taking a shower. But remember, if you wash it, you'll have to dry it. So if you want to get a move on, just wear it." She hauled two

161

cases of bottled water into the bathroom and shut the door.

Meanwhile, I swigged another quarter bottle of anti-diarrheal.

By the time I'd thoroughly washed my hair and rinsed it by splashing purified water over me, I was good to go. We were ready to strike out, and we were both dressed like vagabonds.

Life was good.

Hotel Malamuerte had a small café. Actually, it was more along the order of an indoor taco stand, but I was hungry and feeling lightheaded, and when had Amanda ever refused food? I ordered an American breakfast; Amanda got something I was unable to pronounce and couldn't identify. As we sat in a remote corner of the lobby watching the foot traffic out on the sidewalk, Amanda and I planned our day.

"First, we go to the *mercado*," she said.

Not what I wanted to hear, now that I'd thought about it. That place was big, and noisy, and—*oh, wait!*—El Mortero might show up to kill me. "Do we have to? I mean, aren't there other places to buy clothes?"

"Yes, but that woman had something important to tell us. We should find out what it is."

She was right, of course. Maybe the old woman knew where to find Teensy. Or Tiffany.

"We need to go to the bank and change your money. If you keep spreading American money around, you'll get a reputation. Blend in. That's what I've been harping about. Then we need to go to *la tienda de pelucas* . . . the wig store. And the drug store. A little dark pancake makeup ought to 'Meskin' you up."

"Then we'll go back to that hospital and pay that doctor a visit."

Amanda drew in a deep breath. "You're not going to like this next part." I inwardly braced for bad news. "I'll be leaving you alone for a couple of hours. Lock yourself in the room; you'll be fine."

Alarm bells went off in my head. "You're not leaving me."

"It'll be fine."

Now that was a stretch. If we got lucky, it might just turn out to only be horrible.

My mind went berserk. I envisioned her abandoning me. "I'll go with you. What do you think?"

From her expression, it wasn't hard to tell.

"I'll make better time without you."

My stomach roiled. Panic set in. "You're ditching me."

"I need a thousand dollars."

"You need a thousand dollars, or you're ditching me?"

"For the two passports, diva. Also, I could use an extra five hundred."

"What for?"

She gave the room a furtive glance, as if she were a special agent, especially dispatched to clear the room of bugging devices. "Gun."

Silence shuddered up to the troweled-on ceiling.

A vision of us locked up in a Mexican prison lodged in my mind, where we'd be buried so deep inside that they'd have to pipe in sunshine. Or maybe, on a good day, we'd be taken to the desert and allowed to bust rocks until we dropped from heat stroke or exhaustion. And on a bad day . . . well, let's just say we'd be expected to pay attention to a guard named Euse-bio who wasn't getting enough attention at home.

To get to the market, we walked two blocks and assimilated into a small crowd where husks of people, numb and downtrodden, lingered near a dusty intersection, waiting to board what passed for a city bus. Mexico has no middle class. Its citizens are either wealthy or impoverished. Guess which class we were marinating in noxious, exhaust-smelling air with?

The bus rolled up on bald tires and screamed to a stop.

Amanda climbed aboard first, leaving me standing in a boiling cloud of toxic gray smoke. I climbed on, choking and sputtering, only to find there weren't seats available for us to sit together. She'd claimed the empty seat behind the driver. I shot her a wicked glare and clumsily traversed the aisle, gripping the back rail of each seat as I worked my way to the rear of this lame excuse for public transportation.

Driving in Mexico is insane. People drive like maniacs, and the driver of this bus fit right in. He slammed on the brakes and leaned on the horn, sending me reeling into the lap of an elderly man wrapped in a loose weave poncho. The old man had brilliant eyes in an unusual shade of green, and body odor so vile it whipped my breath away.

Normally, old people like me and think I'm cute. But I keep forgetting, I'm Dainty Prescott and Mexico isn't normal. This guy unleashed a unique tapestry of curses on me, words I'd mastered on the plane ride to El Paso.

I muttered, *"Lo siento,"* even though I wasn't sorry, because I don't do sorry, and it wasn't my fault.

I moved as far away from this old codger as I could without actually tumbling into the seat next to him, where a withered old man leered at me as he stroked a small tan animal on his lap and chanted, "You want some? You want some?"

I realized what I'd taken to be a skin-diseased pet wasn't an animal at all, but an appendage, and a small, wrinkled one at that. The woman seated behind him hauled off and slapped him upside the head. She screamed *"Tonto, tonto."* Which I found out later from Amanda meant "fool," and did not mean the Lone Ranger's faithful companion.

I hate Mexico.

Even though it had to be forty degrees outside, it had to be one hundred ten degrees inside the bus. The windows were shut, sealing in all the vile body odors of the people who'd ridden this route ahead of us. You could tell which maturing females were having their time of the month just by the scent trapped beneath their clothes. These wretched smells escaped with each exaggerated movement, like when the bus hit a pothole. When compared to the nasty odors in our hotel room, I was secretly appreciative now that I probably smelled the same way.

This wasn't exactly a robust, expensive, purpose-built vehicle. We bumped and rocked and lurched along, and whenever the driver braked to a stop, the wake of toxic fumes spewed out by this Dachau-on-wheels abruptly infiltrated the floorboard. By the time we'd gone a couple of blocks, I was nauseous and about to experience a violent bout of projectile vomiting. This hideous contraption reminded me of the old dilapidated bus my mother and I used to ride back and forth from the Prada to our hotel the summer we went to Spain—oh, wait—this *was* the bus my mother and I used to ride back and forth from the Prada. They bought a new bus and sold this one to their poor Latin American stepsister.

I looked toward the front of the bus, at Amanda chatting up the driver, and took a dim view of her blatant flirtation. People were starting to elbow each other and do chin-juts in her direction. Then a heavyset woman in a *serape* yanked the tattered overhead cable tied with frayed lengths of rope knotted together that connected to a toy bell above the driver's head. The dull clink flatly echoed as we screeched halfway through the intersection before the bus came to a complete stop.

The din of reverberating screams filled this tin can on wheels.

A bunch of Mexicans, traveling in generational hordes, climbed aboard bringing the kinds of foul body odor capable of melting eyebrows. Others carried small children, most of them dirty or sick with runny noses, or desperately in need of a diaper change. By the time we'd gone several blocks I wanted to retch.

Apparently I wasn't the only one. Someone in the back was experiencing violent vomiting. That triggered a chain reaction of dry heaves onto the floorboard.

The driver stomped the foot feed. While others had braced for this, my neck immediately snapped back. When I looked at the front where Amanda had sat, she was no longer there. A skinny teenager cradling an infant had slid into her seat. Next thing I knew, Amanda shoved through a bottleneck of riders and stood in front of me, burning a hole into the man sitting next to me with her laser-eyed stare until he gave up his seat.

The bus made a stop across the street from a school. In a low voice, Amanda translated the hand-lettered signs that'd been posted on chain link fences. "It warns teachers to hand over their Christmas bonuses or die."

"Think they'll do it?"

"If the cartel's behind it, you give them what they want," she said between clenched teeth. "If they want something you have and they get hold of you, they'll skin you alive and wear you around like last year's Prada slingbacks."

We rode the bus route for a long time, mostly because I wouldn't get off until we arrived in front of the market. Even though I could see it on the street that ran parallel to the one we were traveling, I saw no point in straying off the beaten path. The sheer size of this city made me realize if we couldn't locate Tiffany here in Ciudad Juárez, I was virtually certain we wouldn't find her in some flyspeck dot on the map that couldn't even handle civilized tourism.

"Get up." Amanda elbowed me. "Start toward the front of the bus."

"What?"

"Just do it."

She was already prodding me up the aisle. Next thing I knew, we were out on the sidewalk, heading back in the direction from which we'd just come.

"What the hell?"

"Look."

I tracked her pointed finger. The modest sign overhanging a storefront had a stylish picture of a woman's cascading hair.

Amanda had spotted a wig shop.

Even better, it was five doors down from the bank.

CHAPTER EIGHTEEN

After I exchanged a large portion of my U.S. dollars for Mexican pesos, we went inside the wig shop and I bought a wig made of natural hair in a dark brown shade. We stopped in at a drugstore for makeup and a bottle of pills that were not only strong enough to stop intestinal disturbances, but threatened to lock up a person's bowels for a week. We were barely out of the drugstore before Amanda applied a dark powder crème foundation to my face and neck.

Then she looked at my hands. "You need gloves."

The morning frost had yet to burn off, and my fingers had gone numb from the chill. Amanda swiped the backs of my hands with the same powder crème finish and pronounced me acceptable. To me, I just looked dirtier and grimier than ever.

The dark makeup and hair raised my comfort level now that I didn't stick out like a sore thumb. I still wore the scarf Amanda'd bartered away my jacket for the previous day, but this time I tied it loosely around my neck. We both needed a coat, and the market seemed as good a place as any to buy one.

Fresh sides of beef were being wheeled in on gurneys, and the smells of the market were already starting to ripen. There were good scents, too, like the ones coming off the fresh flowers being unwrapped and stuffed into large plastic buckets, and stands that offered brand name perfume for sale. I knew this was either bootleg perfume, or perfume that had been watered down, so the bottles probably weren't worth their price, even with the haggling.

The moment we entered *el mercado,* I scanned the crowd in search of *El Mortero.* Since I now knew this ghoulish figure was at least a head taller than the rest of the people lurking around, he'd be easy to spot. And now that Amanda had "Meskined" me up, I'd be much harder to spot.

Halfway to our destination, we found a booth with coats. We both tried on a few, but I'm the only one who bought one. Amanda said it'd be better to find one somewhere else for her, since it wasn't a smart idea to be throwing a lot of money around in one place. If we spread it around, there'd be less chance for gossip.

"We still have a problem," she said as we walked past a display of piñatas hanging overhead. "Your eyes are so blue they jump out of your head."

She'd probably blame an ostrich for having a long neck.

"The first place we come to that has eyeglasses, you're buying a pair."

When we reached the little stand where we'd gotten my scarf, the lady manning the booth was nowhere in sight. But the old lady with paper-thin skin, that had the pale blue dress Amanda made off with, was watching over her neighbor's place. She regarded me through scornful eyes, but Amanda seemed to have developed a rapport with her, which led me to believe she'd bought the pretty dress, not stolen it. She easily struck up a conversation, and in no time at all, the woman lifted a gnarled finger and pointed to some distant place beyond my field of vision.

Then Amanda respectfully thanked her, took me by the elbow and steered me hurriedly up the walkway.

"Where are we going?"

When she failed to answer, I repeated my question with more force.

"We need to check something out. Then we're leaving."

Leaving the marketplace? Leaving the city? Leaving this earth?

"What're we checking out?" I asked, low and under my breath. It was a real effort to keep up with her. For someone with short legs, she took long, rapid strides, moving quickly through the beehive of activity.

Amanda came to a halt in front of a wall filled with postings. At first it looked like a cheesy collage. Then I saw a poster with a picture of *moi*, Dainty Prescott. As I moved closer, I recognized this likeness as an enlarged copy of my passport photo. Beneath my picture, in crude lettering, read: Danny Prescott.

My heart drummed. "I don't understand."

"It's a public hit list. You're on it."

"Why would I be on a hit list?" I said with my voice crescendoing, as if by unraveling at the seams in a public place, Amanda would realize the extent of my terror and make this go away.

I knew I'd gotten loud but, *hello,* I hadn't done anything, yet someone wanted me dead.

Amanda urged me to leave.

"No. I need to understand."

"No," she said sharply, "we need to get out of here."

I reached for my *Wanted: Dead or Alive* poster, but she slapped down my hand before I could tear it off the wall.

"Let's go, Dainty."

"But—"

She jerked me hard so that the rest of my protest, the *I'm taking this with me* part, slid back down my throat. "*El Mortero.* He's right behind us."

CHAPTER NINETEEN

I wanted to run. Wanted to take off like the lead wildebeest in the migration across the Serengeti. But Amanda held me back.

"Don't run," she said, hanging onto my arm and pulling me back. "Do not run. Do not call attention to us."

"I'm sorry," I whispered nastily, "but you'd run, too, if your picture'd been up there with mine."

"It was."

I stopped dead in my tracks. She could've slapped me across the face and it wouldn't have stunned me more. Amanda loosened her grip, but continued to push me forward until we assimilated into the crowd. For once, I was happy—no, thrilled—to look like a peasant. I didn't have time to think. When you're swimming against the current, sometimes it's best just to stop struggling and let the rushing water take you where it wants you to go, until it washes you up onto the bank and you can catch your breath.

Amanda turned out to be my rushing water.

When the crowd emptied out of the marketplace, she pulled me off to the side. People were boarding two tour buses, so our cover had thinned considerably.

Then I looked over at the marketplace entrance and saw *El Mortero* looking around confused.

"Get on the bus," Amanda said, forcing me forward and up the bus steps. These weren't dilapidated city buses. They were charters. But I couldn't tell where they were from or where they were going. I just followed instructions and climbed aboard. As the last passenger got on, the levered doors slammed shut, effectively closing us off from view.

From the back of the bus, I watched *El Mortero* recede as we pulled away. He looked around, as if bewildered. By the time he realized we'd slipped through his fingers, we'd already entered the flow of traffic. He ran toward the buses, pursuing us into the next block. As he overtook our bus, we ducked down in the seat.

"Do you think they'll stop?" I asked, even though I already knew the answer.

The bus ahead of us slowly ground to a halt. A domino effect took place, and ours subsequently rolled to a stop.

"What do we do?"

But Amanda wasn't paying attention to me. She was staring straight ahead as *El Mortero* boarded the first bus. Then she called out to the driver in Spanish. I realized she didn't like the answer because she became loud and animated when she called back out to him.

The next thing I knew, the levered rear doors swung open, and she forced me down the steps and out onto the sidewalk. Then she dragged me behind the bus, where we waited until she saw a taxi letting people off at the market.

"What just happened?" I said, all breathless and frightened.

"Nothing," she said, disoriented. "You were having a baby in the back of the bus." Then she mentally re-grouped. "Run toward that cab."

She took off like a puma, frequently casting looks over her shoulder to make sure I was keeping up.

When we reached the taxi, we recognized our old driver from the queue. I'm still not sure how we did it, but we managed to pile into the back seat at the same time.

Amanda barked out instructions. He laid on the horn, cut

someone off and whipped out into the flow of traffic with such vigor that I felt the pull of gravitational force against my cheeks.

"You owe him an extra twenty," Amanda said as we huddled together.

She could've promised him an extra twenty, fifty, or hundred-fifty, for all I cared. The main thing was that we were safely ensconced in vehicle with our very own NASCAR driver, the *Antonio Stewart-o* of *Meh-hee-co*. Fully realizing that I'd probably end up on the International Watch List before this ordeal was over, I decided to embrace the lawlessness. Forced to operate in a frontier *sin justicia*—without justice—I wanted Amanda and me to be the ones walking away once the smoke finally cleared.

"Did you really see your picture on the hit list?" I whispered.

She nodded.

"Do you still have your passport?"

She nodded again.

"Then how'd they get your photograph?"

"Not sure. Maybe at the restaurant, maybe walking into the cantina."

"I won't give you anymore trouble, Amanda. If you think we need a gun, get it."

She flashed a grin. Then her smile flatlined. "Just try and stop me."

Our driver stopped one street over from the hospital and let us out. I gave Amanda my scarf, which was long enough to wrap around her shoulders, and we angled over to the wrought-iron gate. Once inside, the doctor we'd spoken to walked toward us from the far end of the corridor. As soon as he noticed us, he did an about-face and picked up his pace.

Amanda yelled, "Wait," and broke into a dead run.

We intercepted him in a narrow stairwell, a gloomy, poorly lit area that echoed with staccato conversation, and was barely wide enough to accommodate the flapping of hands and arms that I'd become accustomed to seeing when Mexicans got excited. We took our act upstairs to his office. I was the last one in, and after the door sucked shut behind me, he toggled the deadbolt.

He apparently had no use for Amanda at that point, and spoke directly to me. "Your sister is better. If you come here tomorrow after the sun goes down, you can take her."

I gasped in relief. My whole body tingled. My muscles untensed, and I felt the weight of the world plucked from my shoulders.

The next part tightened them like a stringed instrument.

"You must figure out how to leave the country with her on your own. She cannot run. She is very weak. You will have many problems."

I didn't even realize I'd been shaking my head. I only knew that, come hell or high water, it would happen.

"You need more than the two of you. You need the help of others."

"I don't trust anyone." And by "anyone" I'd included him, as well.

Not to mention I'd had occasion to observe these people. Absent a middle class, there seemed to be—not two classes of people, like the rich and the poor—but three, which distilled into the following categories: "have," "have not," and "will take." I fleetingly wondered which group Teensy's doctor belonged to.

"Now you must go."

We must not have moved fast enough for him, because he clapped his hands to hurry us along.

"After you left, they came. The only reason they didn't shoot everyone here is because we convinced them we did not know you, and that you must be crazy. And that we would not help you if you returned. That someone would call to let them know you are here. So you must leave now, and not return before tomorrow night. Do you understand?"

We nodded.

"Thank you," I said almost breathlessly.

"Follow me. I will take you to the tunnel."

Tunnel?

"It will put you across the back street, to the room where our generator is kept. When you return tomorrow night, you will come back to that room. Someone will be waiting for you. Should something happen—" and by this, he meant something bad "—you must find another place to seek shelter. You must not bring a massacre to this hospital. Like last night."

My eyes riveted on Amanda. What was he talking about? Was he blaming last night's shootout on us?

"You must remember, Danny Prescott, that the things you do here affect others. Now go."

We'd reached the end of the tunnel and ended up in a mini-power station. Writing in red letters appeared on the only door. Even though I had little command over the Spanish language, I knew that it spelled out warnings of danger.

"Tomorrow night, then." He opened the door a sliver, touching the small of my back as I made my way out. *"Vaya con Dios."*

Go with God.

Chapter Twenty

We didn't arrive back at the hotel until shortly after noon. I didn't have much of an appetite, but knew Amanda's tapeworm needed to be fed, so I suggested we try a café that I'd seen a half block down.

Surprisingly, Amanda declined. "I'll grab a taco on the way to meet my cousin. We still have a problem. We don't have a picture of you or your sister to put in the passports."

"Don't worry, if we can get two of me, we can use one for her. We look so much alike we could be sisters," I deadpanned.

She didn't want to smile. I could see the tension in her jaw as she clenched her teeth and tightened her lips until they became a thin, dark thread. Then her eyes crinkled, and the corners of her mouth tipped up.

"Get room service and wait until I come back. Don't open the door for anyone. Wait. Forget room service. Get something from the hotel café and take it upstairs. Then shove the table in front of the door and stack the chair on top to give it extra weight. Don't come out until I get back. And don't open the curtains to the balcony. Are you listening to me? Because you look like you're about to drool into a cup."

I couldn't help it. I said, "I'm sorry, I have a tendency to drift in and out when you start talking." Then I smiled to show I still had a sense of humor.

"You're not going to like this next part," she said. "I need to take your phone."

It was as if she'd asked to cut out my beating heart and wear it as a talisman. "It's my only connection to Jim. I can't."

"You don't have any choice. Without it, I can't pin down my cousin once he gets across. You'll just have to tough it out until I return."

"But Amanda, it doesn't have much battery life left. Why do you think I haven't used it? I'm trying to save what's left for an emergency."

"I've got news for you, girlfriend, this whole damned trip has turned into one continuous emergency."

I squeezed my eyes together so tightly that blue spots danced behind my lids. "It'd be better if you didn't answer any calls," I said, grudgingly opening my eyes as I handed it over. Then I opened my purse and pulled out a piece of paper. I wrote down the number for my own cell phone, the one Jim had traded me for, and gave it to her. "Tell your cousin to call this number. Give him the name of our hotel and pass on that information. My boyfriend's name is Jim. Tell him to have Jim call the hotel and ask for you."

She gave a slight nod.

We went upstairs and I counted out the money. "Are you certain you can do this without getting caught?"

"Sure. You roamed around for twenty-four hours with your blonde hair functioning as, more or less, a strobe light, and dressed like a fashion model with constipation of the brain and diarrhea of the mouth, so it's not like you set the bar real high."

I studied her face for a long time, memorizing her features as if this might be the last time I saw her alive. Or in case she ditched me and I needed to find her again someday, and beat her head against the car bumper until the air bags deployed. In an uncharacteristic move, she hugged me like her life depended on it. Then she left without so much as a backward look.

Frozen in place, I waited by the door for what seemed like an hour. In fact, it was probably less than a minute. I heard a noise out in the hall. The ensuing silence took on an ominous quality. I opened the door for a quick peek and saw Amanda standing in front of me.

"What the hell's the matter with you?" This was a question guaranteed to turn the conversation antagonistic. She pushed past me and back-kicked the door with her foot. Then she spun around and locked it. "What, exactly, do you hear when I speak to you? White noise? The fashion channel? Birds of the jungle? What?"

"Why're you yelling at me?"

"Because I told you not to open the fucking door for anybody except me."

"*Pardonez moi,* but I just did what you told me to, and oh, wait . . . look. You're standing right in front of me."

"You didn't know it was me. I didn't identify myself to you. We don't have a code word."

And the red cow moos at sunset.

My demeanor went frosty. "Excuse me, but aren't you supposed to be somewhere?"

"Girl, what'd I tell you when we were walking across the bridge?"

"To stick to you like a two-year old special needs child." My cheeks blazed.

"We need a code word," she said.

"I agree. I think it should be *pygmy.*"

"The code word is *diva.*"

My face burned. "You made your point. The code for access to this room is *Mexico is crap.*"

Amanda smiled. "I'm leaving now, and when I walk out that door, we may never see each other again. I suggest you do what I say."

"Be careful."

She marginally relented with the meanness. "You, too."

Then she was gone. I dragged the table over to the door and wedged it beneath the lock. Next, I stacked the chair on top of it. After skirting the red stain to flip on the TV, I turned the volume down low and retreated to the bulletproof spread on the bed. I missed having another heartbeat in the room, even if it did belong to Amanda. And once, I thought I heard a noise outside my door. It scared me so badly I turned off the television. I talked myself into believing the housekeeper had stopped by, but since the room looked pretty much the way we'd left it, and since this was a crappy hotel, she'd probably already been here.

The only thing that'd brought me comfort was the TV, and now I didn't even have that.

My mind played tricks on me.

What if Amanda didn't return? The pulse in my throat thudded.

What if the women from the town hall meeting found her decomposing body in the desert? Scary thoughts amped up my blood pressure. I experienced an enormous temperature spike wondering what'd become of me if Amanda ran off with my money and left me here, helpless and defenseless, with nothing but my wits to save me?

Or half-wits, as the case may be.

I'd been crazy to allow her to separate herself from me. She was supposed to be my guide. Bad thoughts continued to bombard me, raising my panic level to a new extreme. We had no deadbolts or alarms to stop the people who were looking for us from crashing in. This place wasn't safe.

What if someone smashed in the door? How would I elude them? The idea of a quick getaway was an engineering mystery to me.

I began to think in terms of escape, and plotted my next

move as though it would happen.

If an intruder tried to break in, I'd take the bed sheet and tie it to the balcony. I'd go over the handrail and drop to the street. And if the railing, which was loose, tore away from its holdings, well, I'd probably have plummeted to my death anyway. What I needed was to be able to shimmy down to the sidewalk without making the drop in the first place.

Once I'd formulated an exit strategy, I stripped off the bedsheet and ripped it into thirds, tying the ends together and knotting it at approximately three-foot intervals. Satisfied, I lashed the makeshift rope to the bed frame. Then I pulled back the curtain and cracked open the door leading out to the balcony. Sunshine made a latticework of light coming through the little square panes. I threaded the rope past the door, coiling it so it'd be ready to fling over the iron bars if the need arose.

Then I sat back on the bed and waited.

And waited.

And waited some more.

It only took two hours to develop severe cabin fever. I needed to keep my mind occupied, but the noise from the street kept leaking through the crack in the balcony door. I finally gave up and shut out the city, but I left the rope coiled inside the door, at the portal to my escape route.

I was starting to go stir crazy, and wished I'd brought a fistful of those propaganda pamphlets on beautiful Mexico up from the front desk to short-circuit my paranoia. Then I remembered having *The Ladies' Guide to Homicide* to distract me.

I pawed through my hobo sack and pulled it out. I flopped onto the bed with my back propped against the wall, and stuffed both of the degenerating pillows behind my head. Then I began to read.

The opening sentence chilled me to the bone.

So you want to kill off your rival and make it look like natural causes, or an accident . . .

CHAPTER TWENTY-ONE

Around six o'clock, I glanced up from reading my stepmother's how-to manual on murder and saw movement beneath the gap under our door. With my breath caught in my throat, I sat bolt upright, alerted like a drug dog, and set aside the book. Then came a soft knock. The headrail of the festively painted ladder-back chair jiggled against the knob. Recent events reminded me that passive posture invited attack. I rose from the bed and tiptoed over to fortify my barricade. While I carefully forced the chair back into place, the muted *tap, tap, tap* sounded again. My heart thudded like unshod horses on a dirt racetrack.

My mind shrieked, *Get out, get out, get out.* Galvanized into action, I scrambled across the carpet, flung open the door to the balcony, and tossed out the rope.

This was it. This was the ambush Amanda'd warned me about.

The doorknob moved back and forth. Someone was rattling the handle to test it.

I sensed my life was in mortal danger. I made a cursory glance to see what I could salvage, then grabbed my purse and stuffed the book in at the last second. Then I pulled the balcony door wide open and slipped my purse over my shoulder. Just as I grabbed hold of the rope, the table moved and the chair crashed to the floor.

"Sayonara, sons-of-bitches!" Oops, I might've said that out loud.

I swung a leg over the iron railing. Then I heard Amanda call out my name. Immediately after that, I heard a sickening crack. I dove toward the room as a section of handrail broke away. It teetered precariously above the sidewalk as I low-crawled across the landing enough to get my footing. I stumbled back inside, ready to noose my roommate's neck with my bed-sheet rope.

If I hadn't been so relieved to see her, I probably would have.

"I think my stepmother murdered my mother." I threw myself into her arms. Amanda seemed smaller and more frail than she appeared in her clothes, but she emanated a kind of quiet strength, and I felt it in her embrace. "And I think she's trying to do the same thing to my daddy."

It didn't matter that I might be having a psychotic break, or that Amanda had almost done me in by pretending to be an intruder. She walked quietly to the balcony, saw what I'd done, and reeled in the sheet. Then she studied my handiwork and nodded in approval. We sat for the better part of a half hour before she interrupted my ramblings.

"There's a little kiosk my cousin told me about, where you can get your picture made." She showed me the fake passports. They looked pretty authentic from what I could tell. And she had laminate to cover the photographs once they were in place. "Like it's a little booth with a curtain over it, and you drop in coins and it snaps your picture. He said he used to take his girlfriends there for cheap photos. I think we should go now. And maybe while we're out, we can get something to eat?"

"Sure. Whatever you want."

I was so happy to see her that I'd completely abandoned the idea of killing her.

We found the kiosk and I paid for a four-pack of photos. I picked out the best one of myself, and saved the others for Teensy to choose from. Then we headed for Señor Pepe's, which turned out to be eight blocks down from our hotel, and had a reputation among college kids as the place to go to be seen in Mexico. Part of me didn't want to go in. The other part figured they'd have better restroom facilities. And they served American food, which is what I wanted. Amanda, of course, didn't care since quantity trumped quality, hands down.

We walked in and took our chances.

I stood my ground, insisting that we get a corner table, where I could watch the door. The waiter apologized for seating us near the kitchen, and even offered to give us complimentary drinks for having to endure the flurry of activity. I opted for water, and told him not to open the bottle. I didn't trust anyone not to put something in my drink, or to refill the plastic container with bacterial tap water. Amazingly, Amanda followed my lead.

With an eye trained on the door, I continued my story about *The Ladies' Guide to Homicide,* and outlined my reasons for suspecting my gold-digging stepmother had murdered my mother. When I started to fret over my daddy being in the hospital, Amanda covered my hand with hers.

"You can only do what you can do, girlfriend." Then she gave me a squeeze and pulled away. Our food had come, and people thought we were biracial lesbians.

Midway through dinner, I said, "I'd like my phone back."

"And that's another thing." She swallowed a mouthful of her double-meat, double-cheese burger and washed it down with purified H2O. "I talked to Jim."

My eyes instantly watered. "You did? What'd he say?"

"Before or after he called me every name in the book? I don't like him. You can do a lot better." She took another ravenous bite.

While waiting for her to finish chewing so I could pump her for more information, my eyes strayed to the front door. A looming figure strode the length of the glass windows, moving toward the entrance. I grabbed my purse and threw down enough pesos to cover the tab, as Amanda's eyes went wide from this sudden outbreak of activity.

"He's here," I said, sucking air.

We'd already decided to head out through the kitchen if *El Mortero* showed up. Now, I was out the door with Amanda hot on my heels. All the other diners' heads moved in a collective shift, their eyes riveted on a couple of grimy ladies from the barrio, trying to fit in with the American college kids. The place had one back door, and Amanda found it. When we burst through it, the screen slapped shut behind us. We'd made it as far as a dimly lit courtyard. A couple of young guys were back near the gate, loading food scraps into a mini-dumpster. Several more were huddled in a dark corner, smoking weed.

"Buenas noches," said Amanda.

"Bon soir." No need to admit who said that.

We made our way down the back alley, walking briskly until we came to the corner. A police car that resembled the ones driven by El Paso police officers sped by with lights strobing and siren blaring.

"That looks like . . ." I didn't get to finish. Amanda grabbed my hand and shouted, "Rogelio," and pulled me through the bottleneck of traffic.

It was our cab driver, the NASCAR wannabe.

We piled into the back seat of the taxi. As soon as the door slammed shut, he sped away from the curb and merged with the rest of the traffic.

"Did you see that police car?" I asked.

She nodded.

"It looked like it came from across the border."

"It did."

"Why would the El Paso police be here in a patrol car?"

"They're not."

Then she told me about a recent situation that had turned into an international incident. An El Paso officer in hot pursuit of an auto theft suspect chased the culprit across the International Bridge. When he got halfway across, he realized he couldn't catch the thief and broke off the pursuit. But other cars had him boxed in, so he did the logical thing—meaning logical in his mind—and continued across the bridge into Mexico. His intention was to turn around at the border crossing. Only instead of letting him through, Mexican police arrested him.

"Why?"

"Because he brought a gun into the country."

It took a few moments for this thought to gel. "What happened?"

"They seized the patrol car, which was new, by the way, and all the equipment inside it. They took his uniform and gun, and that black belt with his gear on it, and threw him in prison for four months before the two countries entered into some kind of agreement to release him. It was in all the papers. Now some Juárez city official's driving around in it."

There were two things wrong with Amanda's story. First, even I knew "that black belt with his gear on it" was called a Sam Browne; and second, Amanda would've known what kind of agreement officials had entered into to get the officer released.

The creepiest feeling crawled over my skin. Part of me wanted to ask the officer's name. The other part warned me to leave it alone. Because if I pulled at that thread, there might be nothing left of my protective sweater. And God knew I needed to believe Amanda was one of El Paso's finest.

Ohmygod, I'm totally paranoid.

"Did you get it?" When Amanda didn't pick up on what I'd asked, I formed my hand into a gun. When I was sure Rogelio had his eyes on the road and not on the rearview mirror, I put my finger to my head and pulled the trigger.

She gave a slow head bob, and I fell back against the seat, wondering if this was a good thing or a bad thing.

By the time our taxi driver pulled up in front of *Hotel Mala-muerte,* I was never so happy to return to that dive as I was on this night.

CHAPTER TWENTY-TWO

We returned to our motel room to find it had been ransacked. I found this violation of our space appalling.

"Has anyone seen the bed?" I asked, standing in the doorway. Caustic humor made me feel better.

"What's missing?" Amanda moved around the room, taking a quick visual inventory.

"My clothes. The extra ones I brought for Teensy and me." Apparently they'd taken my dirty lingerie, too, because it wasn't in the bathroom drying out after I'd hand-washed it. "You?"

"Nothing important. Rule of thumb is keep what's dearest to you near you at all times. Anyone could've taken it. Probably hotel staff," she ventured, "but we'll never really know."

At that moment, Jim's cell phone rang. I looked at the digital display and didn't recognize the number. For no good reason, I pressed the speaker button so Amanda could listen in. When I answered, Nerissa went all Enola Gay on me.

This time, I was ready for her. A homicidal rage that I didn't realize I was capable of focused me. "I'm onto you." I spoke with lethal calm, in a voice so deadly that Amanda stopped in mid-stride on the walk over to her side of the bed. She dropped onto the mattress and watched me deal with the unfolding drama. "Better nothing happen to my daddy or I'll hunt you down—"

"And what?"

"I'll . . ." What? Kill her like I suspected she'd done my

mother? "I'll turn you over to *El Mortero*—the Undertaker."

Shock of my life, she cackled with laughter. "Like he'd ever come gunning for me . . ."

"What?" I may have shrieked. She *knew* him. How could she know him . . . unless . . . they were in cahoots? No, couldn't be.

"You think you can hurt me? Not down there you can't. You're so naive. Nobody's gonna save you and your sister. You may think you're special up here, but down there you're nobody. You'll find out soon enough you're on your own. And you know what else, bitch? I'm well on the way to controlling the Prescott family fortune."

The sound of her voice was a cruelty to the ear. I felt a brick of ice where my heart should've been. "Even if I don't make it back, Gran will do you in."

"Don't count on it."

The cell phone's low battery warning chirped. I made an emboldened stance. "Yeah? Well, don't *you* count on getting your sleazy mitts on one crying dime of *our* money. Have you checked the attic for your suitcase lately?"

Dead silence.

Instead of nasty taunts, she injected a syringe of syrupy sweetness into the next part of her message. "Then I guess I'd better hope you don't make it back. I know people, too, Dainty."

After Nerissa hung up on me, Amanda shot me a smile. "You know how you're a debutante?"

While Amanda stood in the shower stall, drenching herself in bottled water, I contemplated the phone call from Nerissa.

The cell phone chirped again and I looked at the digital display. My personal number appeared and I knew it was Bruckman. I had no idea how long the battery would last, but even if I talked fast and told him I loved him, it'd be worth it.

The second I heard his voice, the dam to my tear ducts burst.

"Something bad happened to Daddy." My shoulders wracked with sobs.

"Dainty, where the hell are you?"

"Jim, I love you." I admit it. I fell completely apart, drooling like a derelict at a detox center. "Where do I start? I'm in so much trouble, and I don't know how to get out of it. You were right about everything."

"Where are you?"

"In the colostomy section of *Juárez*, on the corner of rectum and butt crack. I call it *Hotel Malamuerte* but it doesn't really have a name, just this big red sign that says 'hotel' on *Avenida Juárez* and—" Three beeps and the call dropped.

Amanda came out of the bathroom, rubbing her head with a towel. "What's wrong?"

"Battery's going dead . . . can't get a signal . . . Mexico is crap . . . pick one." I unhanded the lifeless cell phone and it dropped onto the bed.

"We have a lot to do tomorrow, so we need all the sleep we can get. For now, be thinking about how to get your sister across the border."

"What's to think about? We get a ride to the border crossing and walk across."

"Girlfriend, you're so naive."

Amanda had the uncanny ability to cut to the chase. We couldn't just assume we'd get to the hospital tomorrow and Teensy'd be there. And even if she was, people who'd come there looking for her had threatened the doctor and the staff. If she hadn't posed a threat, it wouldn't have been necessary to move her in the first place. We had to assume people were still after her.

And we had people after us.

In the grand scheme of things, I didn't know what diabolical part in this my stepmother played—maybe none—but having

Teensy and me dead would certainly work to her advantage. I didn't want to think about it.

I also didn't want to think about having to kill these freakishly large and virtually indestructible cockroaches using only my ratty sneakers and a swizzle stick Amanda had smuggled out of the cantina in her sweater pocket. To spare the grisly details, suffice it to say that I've never encountered cockroaches the size of sparrows before.

While Amanda jammed the table against the door, I retreated to the shower with my bottles of water. We'd taken to running scalding water into the sink and submerging our bottles to warm them. The hairpiece I'd worn earlier had matted my hair; I'd sleep better if I washed it. And since we were staying at Poverty Central, I'd have to dry it over the little space heater recessed in the wall.

When I finally walked out of the bathroom, the light had been switched off. A thin snore came from Amanda's side of the bed. I saw the knotted sheet sections near the balcony door and was secretly thrilled that Amanda didn't chew me out over it. When I drew back the covers, we had a set of clean linens with hospital corners tucked tightly over the mattress. I knew they'd still feel like burlap, but there's nothing like freshly laundered sheets to disguise a lumpy mattress.

Propped against the wall with a half-disintegrated pillow shoved behind my neck, my thoughts vacillated between longing to be with Bruckman, my recovering sorority sisters and the rest of my TCU mafia, and trying to divine what would prompt my sister to come to this place. Rich people have rich friends. Teensy and Tiffany could've chartered a flight and traveled anywhere. So why here? Why this place?

In time, I dozed.

Pulled from sleep by instinct, I sensed a shift in the bed and realized Amanda had gotten up. I rolled over and slitted my eyes open. She padded toward the bathroom and pushed the door to. A bar of light appeared below the door.

Apparently the door wasn't plumb, because it eased open when the lock didn't click shut.

Amanda lifted the lid to the commode. I rolled away from the glare of the incandescent bulb.

With my head lying on my outstretched arm, I saw her at this lopsided angle, reflected from the waist down in the cracked mosaic of mirror.

You know you shouldn't watch, but there's a certain fascination, so you do.

Amanda was standing close to the toilet, holding what appeared to be one of those long, slim, purple Japanese eggplants. I love those things, especially sliced and tempuraed.

My *weird-ar* kicked in.

I sucked in a sharp intake of air.

Oh, wait.

That's not a Japanese eggplant.

She's peeing standing up.

CHAPTER TWENTY-THREE

Amanda must've felt my blue laser stare boring a hole through her, because her eyes shifted to the crack in the door and just beyond. We locked gazes in the fractured mirror. With an expression of abject horror etched on her face, her eyes riveted on me as her stream arced into the bowl.

She was a *he.*

Do not for one second think I made this up.

I did what any blueblood worth her salt would do—screamed bloody murder.

He emerged from the bathroom with shock in his eyes, and was on me like a cheetah on a springbok. Straddling me, he pinned me to the bed and pressed his unwashed hand over my mouth. I figured I could safely assume his real name was not Amanda, but that's the only name I knew to call him besides "dirty, filthy, nasty, rat bastard piece of crap." And since he still had his hand over my mouth, I couldn't speak.

Amanda's voiced dropped an octave. His expression turned dark and forbidding. The intense, black-eyed stare curdled my blood. "Stop struggling, I can explain."

I blinked in horror, because no, he could not explain. There was no explanation whatsoever to go along with what I'd just seen.

"I'm going to remove my hand, Dainty, and you don't want to scream, okay?"

He had a formidable voice with a resonant timbre that made

him seem like a giant. I tried to nod under the force of his palm. The full weight of my situation came crashing down around me. I'd been sharing a bed with this . . . this . . . this . . . transvestite, hermaphrodite, whatever. And a scandalous act such as this could never make it onto the list of approved behavior for ladies of The Rubanbleu, no matter how dire the circumstance.

Oh, and one other thing—I was starting to think coming to Mexico was a bad idea.

"Calm down." He slowly let off the pressure, locking gazes with me in an effort to evaluate the full measure of my terror. "Calm down, okay?"

"I am calm." Or not. Everything was fine except for my pesky little hyperventilation problem. I admit it. The room spun.

This incident had become a soundtrack-worthy moment. Now I ask you—would it be too much trouble for someone to tell me why I didn't figure out Amanda was a transvestite until now?

My poise deserted me. "I'm not a violent person, but if you ever do that again, I'll fatten your lip 'til you look like a Ubangi."

"Let me explain."

I stuttered in search of my enormous vocabulary, and came up with, "Yeah?" *And holding on Line One, listeners, we have "sexually maladjusted weird-o." Go ahead, caller . . .*

He confessed to being a transvestite—a cross-dresser—and said that he went by the T-girl name Amanda C. Morof. *Quelle surprise.*

I'm a firm believer that harsh truths should be accompanied by expensive gifts, and I didn't see a Ferrari anywhere around here.

I took a stroll on the blunt side. "Are your boobs real?" Then I felt more words working their way to the surface, until I bit out, "I suppose you're not a police lieutenant, either, are you?"

Regaining a patina of respectability eluded me, but, *hello*, I'd been rooming with Satan's sidekick.

"I guess you want to slap me," Amanda said.

Actually, I wanted to take a sharp instrument to his gonads. Then I decided applying tin snips to the testicles would be my weapon of choice.

What sounded like a cop knock rattled the walls. Our eyes shifted to the door.

I couldn't get *A man to see more of,* or whatever his real name was, out of my mind. The lieutenant—my guide—spat out a stream of Spanish. A man on the other side of the door yelled back. Then the doorknob shook and the lock popped open. I can only imagine what went through the hotel clerk's mind when he forced the table aside.

I didn't think it could get any worse.

I was wrong.

Not only did the proprietor order us out of the hotel, he demanded that we leave immediately.

In the middle of the night.

I admit it, I pretty much went totally blank.

Where would I go? I'd been pretty much bled dry of funds, give or take the emergency cash I always carried in a secret compartment in my wallet. But the night clerk was standing there yelling at us, so I dressed quickly, slapped on my brown hair, grabbed my purse and hobo bag and headed for the door. He stepped aside to let me pass.

I bolted down the stairs like a scalded ape, struggling with the decision to stick to the main route and risk getting mugged or gunned down in mid-stride, or worse, to take the back streets to the part of downtown that was still alive with music and festivities.

Executive decision. I picked the more congested route.

Experience told me the "safety in numbers" theory didn't exist in Mexico. It just made for more massacres. But I figured I'd be more likely to find people climbing out of a cab from the queue by sticking close to the more popular cantinas, and I'd seen a decent-looking hotel closer to the border as well. If I could rent a room with a telephone, I'd call Jim Bruckman and figure a way out of here.

The scent of rain hung heavy in the air. The closer I came to the cantinas, the more guys started making hissing sounds as I walked by, *"Pst, pst."* Since I wasn't the Pied Piper, I didn't understand this custom where strange men tried to fall into step with me and chat me up.

Ahead, I spotted a cab disgorging a middle-aged, well-dressed Mexican couple in front of a restaurant. I sprinted their way with my hand on top of my head to keep my hairpiece from slipping off. In my haste to leave, I'd forgotten to anchor it to my scalp with hairpins.

Apparently I wasn't the only one needing a cab ride. Three of us haggled with the driver, but I was louder, more desperate, and had a wad of cash in my hand. In the end, I won out.

Safely ensconced in the back seat, I locked gazes with the driver. "Do you speak English?"

"Leetle beet" (translation: little bit).

"I need a hotel on this street. I saw it when I came across the border."

"Slowly." He clamped his fingers and thumb together several times in the universal hand gesture for "talking."

I repeated my request, slowing my excited 45-rpm speech down to 33 and 1/3.

"There meeny (translation: many). What it look like?"

"A . . . ho . . . tel." I volumed up my Texas drawl to help him understand me better. Then I drew a little box in the air, and finger-walked a little hand-person into it. "Something *nice-o. Clean-o. Understand-o?*" I'd picked up on the idea that adding

"O" to the end of an English word might turn it into a Spanish word. He just stared at me with a blank, scary expression.

Which made me *wrong-o.*

The driver turned right onto a side street, cutting the corner too sharply and bouncing over the curb.

My heart lodged in my throat. He veered off in a different direction.

"Hey, Magellan—where do you think you're going?" I tried the door handle, but the back seat had child locks. "Pull over, pull over. I want out." Visceral panic set in. This must've been how Teensy felt.

For all the haggling I'd done to get a taxi to the new hotel, my victory earned me a joyride through the city in a cab with no shocks, with me frantically clinging to the seat as we sped through the crowded, honking streets. In my unusually savvy defense, I took the bull by the horns, sliding into the middle of the back seat where I could pummel him better. He recoiled from shock at the first insipid punch, so I grabbed him by the collar and drew back my fist. The cab drifted into the oncoming lane, and he swerved hard right to avoid traffic.

"*Ay, señorita, no, no.* You the *Americana* they look for. I see the men coming close."

Recoiling, I unhanded his shirt and flopped against the seat back.

He'd protected me. Winded, I took deep breaths.

My eyes misted. "I'm so sorry. So very sorry. *Lo siento. Lo siento mucho.*" I couldn't remember how to say "I'm scared" in Spanish, so I told him in English. "Please help me."

"I have the picture. Is you?" He pointed toward the dashboard, where a copy of my hit list photo had been taped.

I didn't answer. I saw the sign for the hotel and pointed it out to him as I scooched up close and hung my arms over the front seat.

He rolled up to the curb, wrenched the gearshift into park, and waited for his fare. While I was separating my colorful Mexican Monopoly money, he removed the Wanted poster and handed me a pen. "You sign for me?"

That took a second to soak in. "You want my autograph?"

Huge head bob. "Worth money."

I wasn't at all certain I should do this. After all, signing my Wanted poster could be tantamount to signing his death warrant—or my own—especially if he bragged about it to his friends. If word leaked out, whoever was after me might torture him until he told them where he'd dropped me off.

He went on to say that over the past two days, *moi*, Danny Prescott, had skyrocketed to the status of a cult figure. To hear him tell it, one of the garment factories had already started turning out T-shirts with my passport picture on them that read: *¡Viva Danny Prescott!*

This sounded like a crock.

Any other time, rising to the level of a celebutante would've tickled me pink. But a political icon? Not a chance. And especially not now. A sudden, unwelcome visual of hundreds of thousands of Mexicans wandering the city wearing Long Live Danny Prescott T-shirts in Easter colors with my grinning face plastered across the front flashed into mind.

I came to the conclusion that my face on a T-shirt was a bad thing. What other commercial atrocity would they initiate? Construct a Plexiglas coffin and put my cold, dead corpse on display like Evita Peron, to use as a political tool to rally the populace? Parade tens of thousands of mourners past with candles?

Until now, I'd gone virtually unnoticed except for the people who wanted to kill me. Before you knew it, this'd be like having my face broadcast on "America's Most Wanted," with watchers phoning in from all parts of the country. Natives who'd claimed to see me in Mexico City driving a taxi; country people who'd report me waiting tables at an out-of-the-way café. Drug lords who'd placed a bounty on my head.

That part sobered me. My self-importance came to a quick end.

"Tell you what—if you'll give me your address, I'll send you a signed picture when I get home," I said with an enthusiasm I didn't feel. "It'll be much better than this. A professional photo."

While pawing through my handbag, I realized I'd left *Hotel Malamuerte* in such a hurry that I'd forgotten to get my book— or, as I liked to think of it, another nail in Nerissa's legal coffin. Without *The Ladies' Guide to Homicide,* the authorities might not have enough information to get a conviction on that cow. Assuming, of course, that she'd hastened my mother's death, which I firmly believed she had.

Dizzy with the promise of incriminating evidence, I shut my handbag. "I'm sorry. I left something back at the other hotel. You'll have to drive me back there."

He didn't complain, merely whipped out into traffic and fishtailed in a 180-degree turn, then careened down Juárez Avenue without regard for red lights or stop signs. For no good reason, I thought of that scene in *Gone With the Wind* where Big Sam rescues Miss Scarlett in shantytown, when he took the horses by the reins and bellowed, "Hoss make tracks."

In the luck of the draw, I'd found Big Sam's Mexican counterpart.

We returned to the hotel I'd been thrown out of an hour earlier, just in time to see people running from the arched entryways. I paid Big Sam the fare and asked him to wait while I sneaked in the side entrance before the night clerk spied me and called the police. Only instead of the night clerk being an obstacle that needed surmounting, a frightened teenage girl was screaming into the telephone, pleading for help. The small red canals filling up the grouted space between the terra cotta floor tiles had spread past the counter and were running into the lobby. I had to hurry before this entire hotel was roped off with crime scene tape.

I took the stairs in twos. When I reached the top of the landing and turned toward our former room, Amanda C. Morof was standing in the partially opened doorway, frazzled and unkempt.

"She lives," said my ex-guide, heralding my arrival with sarcasm, "and the villagers rejoice!" Then her expression hardened into petulance. "You never call. You never write."

"Hello, Amanda." Head down, keep walking.

"Looking for this?" She held up *The Ladies' Guide to Homicide*.

"As a matter of fact, I am."

"You're ungrateful, Dainty."

"Give me my book."

"When you left in a hurry, I took it. I knew you'd want it, so I saved it because I knew you'd come back looking for it."

"Fine. Thank you." Which was more of a formality than based on true appreciation. I am, after all, well bred. "Now give it."

"I don't care what you think of me, but for now, we need to stick together."

"I'm doing just fine without you. We're done. You've more than been paid. I have no reason to think you can't make it back across the border, so I'll just be on my way. Ta-ta."

"Dainty, they killed the desk clerk."

The room temporarily blurred. I wasn't having a stroke and the blue-eyed Americana looking back at me in the cracked mirror hadn't drained of all color. These people just needed to point me to a chair and get me some fresh air.

Muted sirens pealed in the distance. In a moment of disorientation, I wondered who the "they" were that Amanda was talking about, but I wasn't going to stick around to find out.

"You'll never make it out of here without me," she said.

"Already did."

"No, I mean out of Mexico. You need me."

"My cab's waiting." Overwhelming urgency hurried my speech. "For the last time, give me my book before the police get here and we're both screwed."

She handed it over and I stuffed it in my bag. "Have a nice life."

Then Amanda said the magic words: "Stick with me, Dainty. I still have the map to the safehouse."

CHAPTER TWENTY-FOUR

At the same time the two white crime scene vans wheeled up to the hotel, Amanda and I slipped out the side door expecting to find Big Sam waiting for us in the queue cab. But this was Mexico, and I'm Dainty Prescott, last year's debutante, this year's intern at WBFD-TV, and black sheep heiress to the Prescott fortune—maybe—so I'm not sure why I thought escaping from a crime scene without detection would be simple.

As best I could tell, we had no place to run besides a dark dirt road, or back into the hotel. Then things picked up. A cab rounded the corner and slowly rolled our way.

"That's him." Although I couldn't see anything beyond a featureless human form behind the wheel, I figured Big Sam had probably been told by authorities to keep moving.

It had started to mist. Amanda had already piled into the back seat before I realized our driver wasn't Big Sam.

Tires screamed as he pulled away from the curb with both of us ensconced in the back. Momentum slammed the door shut. We zoomed past the crime scene vans with Amanda and I folded over each other like origami lobsters to keep from being seen by the authorities.

"This wasn't my driver," I hissed.

Amanda tried to read the directions to the safehouse from the occasional glow of a street lamp. The driver's confrontational response raised the hair on the back of my neck.

Amanda turned to me. "He says it's not a safehouse. That

those women lied."

"They had no reason to lie to us."

"He says he knows a better place."

"No. Tell him to take us to the hotel I found back on Juárez."

All he had to do was make a U-turn and go back the way we'd come. Straight down Juárez Avenue, near the border. Even I, who am often directionally challenged, knew we were headed the wrong way.

A car whipped in front of us off a side street. Taillights flashed. Our driver braked sharply before slowing to a crawl. Headlights popped up behind us, closing in at a rapid pace. We'd been boxed in like trapped animals.

Rain fell past the windshield like glitter in the headlights. Windshield wipers thumped in rhythmic cadence.

Wide-eyed, Amanda and I shared a simultaneous thought: *Gypsy cab.*

She soaked in our surroundings like a formidable black sponge.

I formed my hand into the shape of a gun. "Pull it."

"Not gonna happen. Too many of them."

Men piled out of the car in front of us as well as the one behind, yanking at the back passenger door handles, shouting orders peppered with obscenities while Amanda and I tried to hold the doors closed. Petrified with terror, I got a fresh, unpleasant taste of what my sister had felt.

Headlights on two more cars popped up in the distance. Then gunfire exploded all around us. I dove to the floorboards, too numb to make a peep, as the staccato ping of bullet-scored metal echoed all around us. Amanda piled on top of me. Time crawled forward.

Gunpowder and smoke hung heavy in the air. When I lifted my head above the back seat, the windshield was full of fractures and bullet holes, and our driver lay slumped and bleeding behind the wheel.

I sucked in a deep breath, pulling in the acrid, foul remnants of cordite still hanging in the air. Bullet holes, stitched into our taxi, made my stomach roll over. Metallic odors of death and decay snaked up my nostrils and back out again as blood leaked out of the cabbie. Then I whiffed human excrement and the pungent smell of urine coming from the front seat, and wanted to retch.

All four doors opened in a domino effect.

A swarthy Mexican yanked our driver out and dropped him onto the road. Then he toed the motionless body. For no good reason, he hauled off and kicked the corpse in the ribs. Blood shot out of our driver's mouth, sending whitewater crashing between my ears. I did my best not to faint.

We couldn't have been more than five miles from El Paso, but the distance might as well have been a light-year away.

Amanda appealed to these men in Spanish. They ignored her. One of them gave me a onceover that left its filthy residue on me minutes after he stopped pointing his rifle in my face.

Realization dawned. We were being overtaken in the same way that Teensy and Tiffany had been. "I won't have sex with him."

The cutting look Amanda gave me said, *You will if he wants.*

Gripping my hobo pouch and purse, I fought the man trying to pull me from the cab. In the end, I lost.

Amanda and this man had a heated exchange. Some words I picked up led me to believe that whatever this man wanted had to do with police, our taxi and hurrying up.

My traitorous guide became my unofficial handler. "Get back into the cab, Dainty."

"No. There's blood in there." This said as one of the men pinned my arms behind my back.

"He wants us to get into the cab."

As Amanda slid into the driver's seat, a man brandishing a machine gun tried to coax me into the front passenger seat. Having a gun in your face can lead a person to make bad decisions.

"*Ándele.*"

Oh.

Right.

Yes.

Because who wouldn't want to end up with only the fingertips of one hand protruding up from the hard dirt of a shallow grave like the thousand female textile workers who'd been murdered and dumped in the desert over the past ten years? With nothing but a little pink *descanso*—wooden cross—to mark where my mummified body eventually turned up.

"I'm not going anywhere. You'll have to kill me first."

I didn't expect my last stand to penetrate the language barrier. But I did hope a guts-out scream would spotlight our predicament for anyone within earshot. Not to mention commanding the attention of everybody else within a two-block radius, including investigators back at the hotel crime scene.

I felt the smack of a gun butt upside the head.

Ow, ow, ow.

Sorry, sorry, sorry.

I'm going, I'm going. Lay off me, will ya?

I'm unclear as to how long I faded in and out of the conversation, but I picked up a few tidbits in my struggle to remain clear-headed and functioning.

According to our kidnapper, the neighborhood we'd entered, Riviera del Bravo, was located in a really bad part of town. Which was like saying Death Row is a really bad part of prison.

The length of our ride seemed to grow in inverse proportion to the declining property values, until we finally arrived at a

my head and it came away bloody.

"Think they'll just go ahead and kill us?" Which wasn't the real question, since I figured they had something else in mind first.

"They're going to help us."

"He whacked me in the head." I touched the goose egg above my ear.

"Because you wouldn't stop screaming."

"He hit me," I repeated, even angrier the second time around. Gathering my strength, I pushed myself fully upright. "Is that food I smell?"

I knew the scent of chili beans, and wanted to be offered a bowl. They had meat, too. I could see chunks of it left on Amanda's plate.

"*Cabrito* and *frijoles*. Barbequed goat and beans. Want some?"

I wondered how it'd taste, but *hello*, it really didn't matter. I was starving, so I nodded.

She called out to the men. A moment later, a wiry old man in a faded plaid shirt and three days' growth of whiskers popped out of what I took to be a kitchen, carrying a tin plate heaped with chow. He said something I didn't understand, and I shrugged. But when he thrust the plate at me in the universal gesture that said *Here*, I practically snatched it from his grasp.

"Coca-Cola," Amanda said. She turned to me as he wandered off in a bow-legged shuffle. "It was either Coke, beer, coffee or water."

I knew better than to drink the water. I had a knot on my head. I wasn't brain dead. "Where are we?"

"Dainty, you're not going to believe this." Amanda spoke with an enthusiasm I didn't feel. "They said they'd help us."

I must've misheard. Five scary-looking men I didn't know— one of whom bashed the side of my head in—were going to help us find my sister?

"Wait. First they tried to kill us and now they're going to help us?" The elderly man returned with a green hoop-skirt glass bottle in his clutch. "Thank you. *Muchas gracias señor.*" That pretty much exhausted my Spanish repertoire.

He gave me a toothy smile wide enough for me to see all the gaps left by missing molars.

As he backed away, I took in the room in stages: concrete floor, once-bright yellow walls that showed the patina of neglect, a small black-and-white television, the plain dining table surrounded by mismatched chairs, and a homemade banner overhanging an open doorway that the little old man had entered. The wall hanging had been put together in three vertical panels of green, white and red, similar to the flag of Mexico, but without the coat of arms. The writing read *Los Commandos,* in flouncy black script, and had a coiled, ready-to-strike diamondback rattlesnake with crossed sabers on it.

For no good reason, I thought: Patty Hearst and the Symbionese Liberation Army.

"Where are we?" Disoriented, my eyes flickered over my surroundings, all the way up to the single bare bulb screwed into a socket in the ceiling.

"It's the safehouse they told us about," Amanda said. She meant the town hall women.

"These people killed our cab driver."

"That was a gypsy cab. The kind that took your sister and her friend." She ran it down for me in quick, abbreviated strokes, the way it'd been explained to her by the men milling around the table.

"Paco—" she pointed to a nondescript man whose fingers were traveling up and down the neck of his guitar "—saw us get into the cab outside the hotel. He called the others. They were close by because the hotel owner was a member of *Los Commandos.*"

Our hosts turned out to be a group of businessmen, mostly shopkeepers and restaurateurs, but some were doctors and lawyers, and even a few progressive-thinking preachers who'd grown tired of *mordida*—these shakedowns. When members of the group heard the hotel owner had been killed, they came to ferret out information. *Los Commandos* had learned to implement their own brand of frontier justice. For every innocent person killed by crooked cops, the *sicaros* and the cartel, *Los Commandos* would kill one of them. In our gypsy cab fiasco alone, they did away with our cab driver, as well as the four men in the other two cars who were part of the Kidnapping Express.

Our musician strummed a beautiful melody while the others ate. I didn't understand a word of this song, but he sang it like a love ballad. Occasionally, he'd pause long enough to tap the guitar with his fingertips before resuming his catchy tune. I considered this an interesting technique until Amanda said, "That represents the gunfire."

Then he sang my name in the chorus.

"Danny Prescott, Danny Prescott.¡Viva la güera brava!"

According to Amanda, it meant blonde, brave "gringa," or white girl. "You're famous."

Or infamous. "He wrote a song about me?"

"No, Dainty, he's singing the song they've been playing on Mexican radio."

She addressed one of the men at the table. Nodding like one of those Chihuahuas with the spring-loaded heads in the back dash of a low rider, he got up from the table.

Amanda said, "You made the news. Picture and all."

"I'm in the newspaper?"

" 'Fraid so, girlfriend. Front page."

"What does it look like?"

"Couple of columns." She gave a little hand flip. "Headline

210

about that tall." She measured an inch. "A few quotes."

"No. What'd the picture look like? It wasn't my driver's license photo, was it? Because that's not very good. My eyes are half closed and I look like a drunk. But that lady told me she'd count to three before she took it, and she just said, 'Three,' and then snapped it. Like some sort of cruel joke. They're like that, you know? She didn't say one, or two . . . why're you looking at me that way? It's important."

Amanda chuckled. "Of course it's important. We girls should always try to look our very best."

When I saw the article, my mouth gaped. They'd taken a photo of my passport picture, so the resolution was grainy. But when I held it at arms' length, it was enough where anyone could've recognized me.

"What does it say?"

"This is the part you won't like."

Chapter Twenty-Five

As Amanda read me the newspaper article, I studied the shadows cast by candles resting on a small altar or shrine. They danced across oil paintings of Jesus and the Virgin Mary hanging on pale frescoed walls. Lulled by the conversational buzz coming from another room, I momentarily closed my eyes.

"Are we safe?" I murmured.

Distress puckered her lips. "As safe as we can be in Mexico." Amanda returned her attention to the news story. "Here's the part you won't like. Your bounty went sky high."

Somewhere in the back of the house, a door opened with a rusty-hinge squeak, the kind like those special effects used in cheesy horror flicks just before the hand comes out of nowhere and claps across the Homecoming Queen's mouth and the butcher knife to the neck ends her reign. In walked an old white-haired man with a face that looked like a dried-up riverbed.

He stopped directly in front of me and extended a gnarled hand. "*Buenos días,* Danny Prescott. Welcome to Mexico's murder capital." Then, he excused himself long enough to gather a sheet, a small pillow and several blankets, while I slumped over onto my side.

"Do you have the . . . well, you know . . ." Molding my hand into a gun shape again, I looked up at Amanda from my lopsided angle.

"Yes."

"Good. Because I can hardly keep my eyes open." I yawned,

Dracula-like, into my sleeve. "Where will you sleep?"

"Over there."

My eyes slewed to an overstuffed chair several feet away. "Good."

My heavy eyelids fell to half-mast. I floated in and out of the background conversation until the room blurred and went dark.

In time, I slept a fairly fitful sleep.

I awakened to the white-haired man telling a story to his *compadres.* By way of words interlaced with pantomime, he described, with his hand formed into scissors and snipping the air in front of him, how kidnappers chopped off their hostage's fingers. Then he molded his scissor-fingers into a syringe. Even with my fractured Spanish, I understood that the kidnappers injected the victim with anesthetic, but didn't wait for it to take effect.

I came fully awake. Amanda was still asleep in the chair, curled up like a cocktail shrimp with a blanket pulled up to her chin.

The old man pushed back from the table and shuffled over. "Danny Prescott, you want soup?"

I nodded. *Starve a cold, feed a head injury.*

"Bread?"

"Yes, thank you. And a steak. Some kind of meat." So sue me. Fright made me ravenous, and these guys had a good cook. I decided to go for it.

While I waited, a cat burst into the room like the point man on a DEA no-knock warrant. It looked like it had on a tuxedo, and when it hopped onto the sofa and drilled me with its paws, I was happy to have another heartbeat sitting next to me.

The old man assisted me to the table, while the others—there were five of them—gave up their seats, lingering nearby to watch me make a pig of myself. I felt like I was being studied, like Dian Fossey and *Gorillas in the Mist.* Not that I cared. For the first time since I'd been here, I'd adjusted to my environment, and felt safe.

The old man puttered around, waiting on me like I was an invalid. He brought me an orange soda, and a bowl of white bean soup with huge chunks of ham in it, and warm tortillas to sop up what appeared to be *carne guisada*. I stuck my nose into the steam coming off the soup and inhaled deeply.

Soon, he joined me at the table.

"This is delicious. Best meal I ever ate." Which probably echoed the sentiments of those Andes Mountain survivors-turned-cannibals when they got their first meager fare upon being rescued after that plane crash. Using manners unworthy of The Rubanbleu, I wolfed down the beans, mopping up the last of the broth with a hunk of tortilla. Then I spooned *carne guisada* onto a fresh one. "I'm so hungry."

"You want more?"

Grunting in the affirmative as I washed down my taco with orange soda, I craned my neck as he padded off to ladle more beans from a vat on the stove. When he returned with seconds, I said, "Who are you? And what do you do here?"

"My name is Julio Cordova." He gestured to a photograph on the small altar. "And that was my son, Dr. Hector Cordova, one of the original leaders of *Los Commandos*. He has been dead for many months. Now, I am a leader for things he stood for."

I blinked. The man was fluent in English. Maybe the others were, too?

"What does that mean?"

"We are a vigilante group, fighting for justice."

He told me about others like Teensy and Tiffany, young ladies and young men who'd met the same fate. When *Los Commandos* found them alive, simple injuries were treated, they were fed, and given a place to sleep until arrangements could be made to find them safe passage to the border crossing. According to Mr.

Cordova, everybody was on the take, and he warned me to be careful who Amanda and I asked questions of.

"So you help people," I said.

"Yes. And now you help the people too, Danny Prescott."

"I don't understand."

"The people, my people, they are afraid. They don't pay the extortion, their houses burn. Their family dies. Like my son Hector."

He told me about the small clinic Hector ran, a thirty-five bed ward for the insane. And about how extortionists demanded two thousand dollars a month in order for him to continue operating the hospital. When he didn't pay, they torched his house. The next time they paid him a visit, they lowered the amount to a thousand dollars. When he didn't pay, they shot up the clinic and killed one of his nurses. The third time they came around, they lowered the amount to five hundred dollars a month. When he still didn't pay, they murdered him in front of the patients.

"What happened to the clinic?" I said.

"It barely stays open. My son's fiancée helps. So do her friends. But it is hard to get nurses to come when they know these men could return when the hospital becomes profitable again."

I learned Dr. Hector Cordova's fiancée was Maribel Espinosa, the lady we'd met at the town hall meeting. As a consequence, Maribel had taken up his cause.

"There are a lot more of us than the ones in this room, Danny Prescott, but you have become a symbol to galvanize my people."

"Why me?"

"Because you have gone three whole days eluding them. You are *la rubia*—the blonde. *Con ojos como el cielo brillante*—with eyes like the bright blue sky. And yet you thwart them at every turn. You have changed your look. They do not know that, so for now you are safe. The song calls you *la quimera*—the, how you say? Chimera. A fantastic thing that changes shape."

"I don't want to be a symbol. I only want my sister back. And her friend."

He gave me a vague palms-up, shoulder shrug. "Sometimes we don't choose our destiny, Danny Prescott. It chooses us."

Yeah, well, pass me by, I wanted to say. *Just give me my sister and her friend, and I'll be out of your hair for good.*

"You look very much like I imagine your sister looked before . . . before they beat her."

Every muscle in my body rippled. I stopped eating. Grabbed my napkin and wiped my mouth. "You've seen my sister? When?"

He patted the air in a downward motion. "Calm yourself. I have seen her. She is much better."

"Was she here? In this house?"

"When they brought her, she was hurt very bad. We have a doctor. He came to see her, but she needed to be in a hospital. Maria Elena and Rosa put the blankets around her. They are two women you met at the town meeting. The ones who went looking for the dead girls. Raul and Joaquin, their husbands, they took your sister in the back of the truck. They are members of *Los Commandos.*"

"Where's my sister?"

"You do not need to know. It is—how you say?—compromising our operation."

"I swear I won't tell a soul." I made the sign of the cross—not that I'm Catholic, but I figured the odds were good Mr. Cordova was, so what could it hurt? And hey, at this point, I needed all the help I could get.

"You will return home with your sister. And you will think because you are in the United States, that it does not matter who you tell. But the cartels' tentacles stretch much farther than you imagine, even across the border and deep into your state. And if you give the newspaper an interview, or the television stations, or decide to write a book, you would be—how you say?—sealing our death warrant.

"So you cannot say. And the best way to not say," he wagged his finger "is not to know what to say. Your sister is in a safe place. Like this is a safe house. Tomorrow, Teensy Prescott will be delivered to the hospital, and you will be there to receive her. After that, you are on your own."

"No. There's one more girl. My sister's friend Tiffany. We can't leave—" I amended that statement—"I can't leave Mexico until we have her, too."

"No, Danny Prescott. It will take more than you to bring home this girl."

Chills swarmed over me. "But you know where she is, don't you?"

"*Sí.* You must be patient. We do not have what you call a 'plant'—an operative—in *la hacienda.* But we are watching for the moment we will take her back. It will happen." He paused, momentarily lost in thought. "If they let her live."

Overwhelmed by the reminder that my sister's friend might already be dead, I felt lightheaded and queasy in the stale, smoky room. I excused myself from the table and asked to step out onto the patio. He pointed me through the kitchen and out a side door.

"Not too much outside, Danny Prescott. You come back soon. Not safe. You are in Riviera del Bravo."

Though I'd just left plain and minimally adorned surroundings, I entered the polar extreme when I stepped out onto the uneven rock of the patio. This courtyard had bougainvilleas in hanging baskets and container plants that were lush and well cared for. Whoever owned this place had done what they could with what they had to work with, trying to make this one little spot an oasis of serenity.

I drew in a cleansing breath. Thinking I was alone, I whispered into the crisp night breeze, "Please help me get my sister and her friend home safely."

A lone sentinel rose like an apparition from a chair near an iron gate that had been covered with solid sheets of corrugated metal, and reinforced with thick metal panels like the ones you see covering large holes in the asphalt next to safety pylons and "Men Working" signs. From the street, this house probably appeared no different than the others on the block. But from inside the courtyard, it was easy to see that this extra measure of fortification made it necessary to move the gate with small roller wheels mounted at the bottom.

For no good reason, I thought: blowtorch.

And then my mind cast back to the huge metal barriers that'd replaced the old chain link and concertina wire fences that separated the two countries before Homeland Security stepped in. If someone would show me how to use one, maybe I could cut a hole in the fence so Teensy, Tiffany and I could slip through.

And Amanda.

There was always Amanda.

I wondered if she knew how to use a blowtorch. Then I laughed out loud. Blow dryer, yes. Blow torch? Doubtful.

Unless . . . I could get Bruckman to cut a hole from his side of the fence.

Mr. Straight Arrow himself. That'd be like sending in an Eagle Scout to pull a heist. What I needed was a man who didn't mind bending a few rules.

In the distance, popping sounds filled the night. It reminded me of the present my blue-haired grandmother gave me for my twenty-second birthday, that'd been covered in bubble wrap. I didn't care for the gift—she'd forgotten it was my birthday and hurriedly re-gifted a toiletry set with small soaps and cheap scents that her housekeeper had given her ten years ago. But I loved the bubble wrap, and spent the rest of my short visit with her popping it. The memory left me as quickly as it had flashed into mind, replaced by a horrible reality.

What I'd heard wasn't bubble wrap.

A series of gun bursts shredded the calm. Somewhere, someone was dying.

The man seated near the fortified gate had a rifle slung over his shoulder, held by a leather strap. He walked slowly toward me as if he didn't want to frighten me with sudden movement. I gasped, involuntarily raising my arm to ward off a blow. This was the man who'd hit me.

"Is time," he said.

"For what?"

"For you go inside." He jutted his chin toward the back door. "Is not safe."

"You hit me."

With eyes downcast, he said, "I sorry, Miss Danny Prescott."

For the record, he didn't look all that sorry. But on the off chance he really did regret trying to cave my head in, I didn't see any use in making an already bad experience worse. "It doesn't hurt much."

"I sorry."

I nodded so we wouldn't have to keep doing this.

As I glanced up at the breaking cloud cover, I was treated to a moment of clarity. Like Scarlett O'Hara standing beneath a tree on the family plantation, shaking her fist at the heavens and vowing never to go hungry again, I raised my open arms skyward, and inwardly put myself in those Southern belle shoes.

As God is my witness, I'll not leave here without my sister. Nor without her friend. If I have to lie, and cheat, and steal, I'll not leave this hellhole without them.

Then I did as I was told—walked back inside with my shoulders squared and the screen door sucking shut behind me—wondering how my life would ever be the same if I couldn't keep my promise.

CHAPTER TWENTY-SIX

Once or twice in the wee hours of the morning, I got up from the lumpy couch to check the front windows at the safehouse, not because I didn't believe we weren't safe—after all, the casement windows framed in metal had inside hand cranks that could be rolled out for ventilation. But I still hadn't shaken the haunting feeling that *El Mortero* might turn up here, and I longed for a sound sleep until Amanda woke me up at dawn. A full stomach had relaxed me, and a dying fire still occasionally crackled in the fireplace. But licking flames cast unusual shadows on the wall, and I needed to check one more time, to stave off the nightmares I'd collected on this trip.

After I padded back to the sofa, I crawled under the blanket and hugged my arms around myself before falling into a fitful, dreamless sleep.

Around five o'clock in the morning, for no reason other than instinct, I cracked open my eyes and shifted my attention to the casement windows. I have no idea what strange physical reflex drew me to the hand-loomed rug that had been fashioned into a curtain and fastened with clamps to a single rod mounted on the wall above the glass; or what primitive instinct compelled me to peer out from behind it. But since I already had the uneasy feeling of being watched, the fringe of moonglow at the edges of the blanket curtains drew me to the windows. I barely moved the rug aside.

The purple Mexican sky was dotted with diamond-like stars.

The stunning desert view of the mountains was no less spectacular than it was the first time I saw it. My gaze drifted down to the horizon, where giant saguaro cacti pushed up from the earth like tuning forks as far as the eye could see. This should've been pretty. Should've been a place where, under happier circumstances, I could've done a bit of exploring with Jim Bruckman.

Nah.

Mexico is the shits. Literally, figuratively, and any other way you'd think of. While such a description's hardly Rubanbleu appropriate, it's the unvarnished truth. You'd think the remedy would be to walk up to the first person you met and slap the fire out of him, thereby warding off problems with anyone else, so long as you remained in the same location for the duration of your stay. But leave the area, and you'd have to start all over again as soon as you reached the next town.

Bottom line: There's no remedy for Mexico.

My mind fired questions like a piston-driven engine. I thought of the two conversations with Nerissa and quickly blotted them out. In my current situation, I could do nothing to help my father from hundreds of miles away. I could do nothing to help my mother, either, except to guard that incriminating book like my life depended on it. And since I'd be reunited with my sister tomorrow, that left me to contemplate ideas that would put me closer to finding Tiffany.

As I stared past the part in the curtain, something moved in the periphery of my vision. For a moment I thought my mind was playing tricks on me. One of the giant saguaro cacti shifted.

Because everyone in the house was asleep, except for a lone guard posted outside in the courtyard, I didn't want to call out in alarm in case I was wrong. I squeezed my eyes closed until gold comets arced behind my lids. As soon as I opened them wide, everything looked the way it did when I first peeked out from behind the brightly colored curtain—nothing at all like the blurred, ferocious shape that I thought I'd seen emerging from the darkness, before it sharpened quickly into the form of a man dressed in a longcoat.

A cactus swayed from side to side. I rubbed my eyes hard until blue dots appeared. Again, the scenery remained unchanged.

For a second, I wondered if I'd ingested a hallucinogen. This made no sense. The stress of this adventure had finally done me in. Had I lost touch with reality? Was I having a psychotic break?

I closed my eyes and massaged my temples.

Then I heard movement.

My muscles tensed. My back stiffened like rebar. I heard shuffling from the kitchen and let go of the curtain, looking over my shoulder in time to glimpse the guard refreshing a tin cup with coffee. He nodded politely before self-consciously tucking his chin into his chest. I'd become a disruptive presence here at the safehouse, and knew they'd rest easier with me gone.

His footsteps receded until the door sucked shut behind him.

I returned my attention to the window and beyond. Only this time when I peeked out, I screamed bloody murder.

Separated by sheer millimeters, I stood on one side of those casement windowpanes expecting to see cacti, while a dark and substantial face looked down on me from the other side of the glass.

El Mortero.

CHAPTER TWENTY-SEVEN

Instead of charging in with their firearms at the ready, the safe-house members stormed into the living quarters in stockinged feet, with disheveled hair spiking up from their heads, shirts haphazardly buttoned and their pants hastily zipped but not fastened.

Amanda sat bolt upright in the chair, then stumbled over, looking like she didn't know what hit her. I told her I'd seen the Undertaker, and she passed on this information.

Then white-haired Julio shuffled in, slower than my incontinent great-uncle Maurice on his way to the toilet. Hearing the reason for the commotion, he adjourned to another part of the house.

He'd better be going after a bazooka.

The last one left to save me was the safehouse's lookout. He stepped into the room, minus the rifle, with a dark brown stain soaking the front of his shirt.

Even he couldn't save us.

With the kitchen light behind him, the Undertaker walked in larger than life. His arrival went beyond confidence—arrogance sprang to mind—but I had an inkling he could pull off whatever he wanted. Most anyone could, if they'd wandered in with a gun pressed against the back of our sentinel. Which I assumed he'd done.

This was the moment the needle on my day moved from simply horrible to completely sucking on the Suck-o-meter. My life flashed before my eyes.

The Undertaker unleashed a unique tapestry of curses, mostly ones I'd memorized back at DFW airport. He finally wound down his rant with, "Dainty Prescott, you almost got me killed."

Then everyone went about business as usual, which meant back to sleep, except for the guard, who adjourned to the kitchen and fired up the stove.

Was this for real?

Hello, you people left me in a room with the Undertaker.

I looked to Amanda, wondering why she hadn't gone for her gun, but she was as thunderstruck as me.

"I should take you over my knee." Laugh lines bracketed his lips, but he wasn't laughing now. "I'm Gus. I know your papa. We go way back."

He spoke flawless English, with the drawl of a Texan, sounding nothing like the dangerous, formidable Undertaker I'd worked up in my imagination. Polite in his manners and meticulous in his dress, his soft-spoken voice belied the ruthlessness that lay behind stunning eyes in a dazzling shade of icy gray.

And he had a finger-crippling handshake.

Agustín "Gus" Quintanilla stood well over six feet in his black lizard boots. Add the Stetson, and he measured closer to seven. Before relocating to Mexico after mandatory retirement at age fifty-seven, he'd worked for the U.S. Border Patrol, stationed in El Paso. As a former Border Patrol agent, and the mastermind of *Los Commandos,* he'd been an expert tracker until something went terribly wrong—*moi,* Dainty Prescott.

"I hope you won't let on how you stayed one step ahead of me," he said. "It'd be bad for my reputation." He winked as he smiled, and for a second I thought I detected a twinge of admiration that we'd eluded him. "I met your father fifteen years ago when he flew to west Texas to check on some oil wells. I won't go into specifics other than to say we became . . . not exactly friends . . . more like friendly acquaintances. When he learned your sister was missing, and that you'd come here to find her, he hired me to find you. And now that you found us, we'll see to it that you get home."

"I'm not leaving without my sister. And I'd rather not leave without her friend Tiffany."

"Don't worry about your little sis. We'll get her home once she's feeling better. As for her friend, well, that might take awhile."

"No. Don't you have any buddies left in Border Patrol? Aren't y'all supposed to help each other?"

"If a Border Patrol agent picks up the phone and calls another agent, he'll drop what he's doing and help. Customs and Border Protection has everything at their fingertips. State-of-the-art equipment, including choppers and what-have-you. If the military has it, CBP has it. But this is Mexico. The Rio Grande's the end of the line." He gave me a brittle smile.

"Don't you know anybody who'd help us?" My patience had worn thin, and he took too long to answer, so I prompted him with a hand smack to the tabletop. "Think."

"There is this one guy." He meditated long and hard on that thought. "We fought together in 'Nam. He flew choppers. A crazy som-bitch, that's for sure."

The man Quintanilla spoke of, the only one he knew who was insane enough to affect a rescue in Mexico, had been captured by the Viet Cong after crashing his helicopter in a three-canopy jungle. He'd started out a robust young man, but shrank to a hundred and seventeen pounds during captivity. The Viet Cong kept the POW in a cage and fed him rats and putrid rice for a year before the Screaming Eagles showed up.

Optimism quickened my pulse. "Could he fly in here and

take us out?"

Quintanilla hooted. "You have quite an imagination, Miss Prescott. Do you have any idea what'd happen to someone crazy enough to do that?"

I held my breath and remained perfectly still, waiting for him to fill me in.

"As soon he came across the border in that chopper, he'd have the Mexican equivalent of the Marines on his ass pointing guns in his face, or trying to shoot him down."

He explained about all the cameras, mounted on towers and pointed at the border. I'd seen them from the back seat of our taxi as we headed for the International Bridge. At the time, I thought they were traffic cameras, with which I have an alarming familiarity back home. But Quintanilla disabused me of that notion when he ran down the sophisticated measures the Border Patrol made use of when it came to tower cams, or remote video surveillance systems.

Quintanilla said, "Assuming he got off the ground with you and your sister aboard, the real Marines would be waiting to shoot him down on the U.S. side as soon as he entered U.S. airspace. And if he didn't make it and y'all got arrested, you'd be behind thick old iron bars, crouching over an open sewer pipe just to take a dump."

I was sick of people telling me what not to do. I wanted to know what I *could* do. "Then we should do this at night. There'd be fewer people around."

As soon as he heard "night," he started in with a big head-shake. "That's even worse. The fewer the people, the more you stand out. Listen to me, little girl. Border Patrol has FLIR: forward-looking infrared. Think night vision cameras. Your best bet," he went on, grim-faced, "is to stay here until the interest in you dies down, and these people move on to another victim. Your sister will be much improved, and we'll do our best to smuggle you out of here in a few weeks . . . probably no longer than a month, tops."

"Not gonna happen."

"Then your next best bet is to make a run for the border crossing and explain your situation once you get across. Sure, you'll have to go through a lot of red tape, but it's much more doable than what you just described."

I leveled my penetrating stare at him. "My sister's injured. You likely know what her condition is better than I do, Mr. Quintanilla. So tell me—can she run for the border crossing?"

"No." He sighed. "But there's something else we can do."

He hatched an elaborate plan that included crossing the Rio Grande between two towns east of El Paso—Socorro and Ysleta. The town of Socorro already had a reputation for harboring illegal aliens. Ysleta was home to the sixteen hundred documented Tigua Indians, and one of three reservations in Texas. Neither town's civilians would put much stock in another person coming across the river.

Quintanilla expected us to cross in inner tubes. Or at the very least, to put Teensy in an inner tube with Amanda and me holding onto the sides. He explained how we had enough time to cut a bottom out of plywood, and bore holes along the edges of the seat where lengths of rope could be threaded through to tie it onto the inner tube. I decided real fast that I shouldn't be hanging onto anything that I'd had a hand in constructing.

I also decided Quintanilla was insane.

"Are there snakes?"

"That's the least of your worries."

Not the answer I was looking for. "And in the meantime, how do we get these killers off our backs?" Visions of unidentified males firing on us like ducks in a carnival shooting gallery filled my head. I could see our assailants gunning for the biggest target—the inner tube that Quintanilla said he could pull out of an old tractor tire—and Teensy slipping away at the last minute. "How do we fight them off? Are you and your vigilantes prepared to exchange gunfire with these lunatics?"

While he mulled this part over, I dreaded the thought of crossing the river. Oh, sure, good swimmers might start out strong, but once they tired and their feet dipped below the surface, the powerful current would pull them into a raging undertow, never to be seen again until they popped up dead, and bobbing like fishing corks.

"You ask me—and you didn't—there are lots of ranches in west Texas." My words caught him off guard. I could almost see little cogs turning in his brain as he anticipated my next comment. "If this friend of yours could fly us out of here, why couldn't he land in some out-of-the-way place?"

"Ah, youth." Quintanilla expelled another wistful sigh. "To be so young and naive again. You think anything is possible." He shook his head, and not in a good way, but his eyes had a speculative gleam in them, so maybe he was starting to think my idea wasn't so far-fetched.

"Why couldn't that work?" I demanded.

"Dainty, Dainty, Dainty. You are your father's daughter." He cracked a smile—again, not in a good way. "All aircraft have transponders. That's how air flight controllers keep track of who flies where. The second Border Patrol gets wind of a rogue aircraft, they'd send up a UAV."

"Speak English."

"Unmanned aerial vehicle. A drone, if you will. A military-style plane that can look down on an aircraft from thirty thousand feet in the air. A Predator, painted in camouflage shades of blue and gray. Think video game. Think pilot in an office, watching a rogue aircraft through a screen. And you know why?"

It was a rhetorical question.

"Because the Predator has a little bubble near the nose with a camera mounted inside it. So the pilot at the controls, sitting in his comfy office chair, can see everything this bird's doing."

"Then my pilot would have to keep flying until it was safe to land."

Quintanilla gave a derisive snort. "Doesn't work that way. A chopper has to refuel every six hundred miles, more or less. The drone has enough fuel to stay airborne a lot longer than it'd take a chopper to run out of gas. It won't work."

"I want to hire your friend to rescue us."

"Let's get one thing straight: He's not a friend. He's someone I know from way back."

"He owes you a favor, though."

"When you're in the middle of a war, like 'Nam, and you save someone's life, they don't owe you a damned thing. You're both Americans, so you do it. He'd have done it for me if the situation had been reversed."

"Then do me a favor and ask him for me. For my sister. I know you don't know us, Mr. Quintanilla, and maybe you don't even like my father, or have any respect for him. But we're Americans." My eyes welled. "I'm asking you as an American."

"You don't have enough money."

"Daddy does."

"Even if they settled on a fee, this guy wouldn't do it. Hell, he probably hasn't climbed out of a bottle in years."

"But you said he was brave."

"No, I said he's crazy."

Potato, po-tah-to. One man's crazy was another woman's fearlessness. "Do you know how to contact him?"

"You aren't listening. Did you not hear me when I said his bird could be shot down? Even in the best-case scenario, he'd lose his pilot's license."

I heard what Quintanilla was saying, but I wasn't listening. In my mind, I saw this crazy chopper pilot willing to fly Teensy and me to freedom. Oh, yes, right . . . and Amanda. Whatever else happened, I figured my daddy'd make it worth his while. "Find him."

"We lost track. But I know someone in Border Patrol I can call who can probably locate him. Everybody thinks the Texas Rangers are hot shit. Funny thing about Border Patrol—nobody ever stops to think that anything the military has, Border Patrol has."

"My daddy can pay. You know he has the money."

"You don't understand, little girl. If this guy agrees to do this—assuming he's not doing time in the pen—I don't think it's money he'll want."

To be perfectly frank, I love my sister, but I draw the line at blowing the old geezer. To the retired Border Patrol agent, I said, "I'm not doling out sexual favors, if that's what you mean."

Quintanilla hooted. "You missed the point."

"Enlighten me." What other atrocities would this man demand in order for us to strike a deal to land that chopper and take us out of Mexico?

"He'd do it for the sheer excitement. To see if he could get away with it. He's crazy. He'd probably do it for fuel money."

"Call him." My mind automatically created a persona for the man who'd save us, and I gave him a superhero name. Winged Warrior Bill. The image of a tall, dark and handsome fellow rose like an apparition in my mind. But that wasn't fair. My superhero already had a name. Or a criminal ID number. "Who is this guy?"

"Deke Richter."

I nearly pitched over.

The guy who could save me was none other than WBFD-TV's very own helicopter pilot, Chopper Deke.

CHAPTER TWENTY-EIGHT

"Chopper A-ho?" I shrieked.

As soon as the words "crazy" and "helicopter pilot" came up in conversation, I should've snapped to the fact that I knew only one person in the world who fit the bill. Not to mention Chopper Deke and I had something of a tenuous relationship. Which is to say he enjoyed leering at the interns, and I found him revolting.

He stood about five feet eight or nine inches tall and had white-blonde hair that stuck straight out from his head like a curry comb, thanks to the liberal application of mousse he raked through it, which only made him look like everything you told him was a surprise. And he had the spookiest light blue eyes I'd ever seen. I'm not sure if I'd even heard Chopper Deke's last name until Quintanilla provided it; but the crazy man the retired Border Patrol officer mentioned was one and the same, I just knew it. How'd I know? Because I'm Dainty Prescott, and these things don't happen to other people, only to *moi*.

And we're not talking "crazy" in the sense of waxing psychotic, or babbling delusions, or making funny noises by strumming his bottom lip with his fingertips; but crazy in the thousand-yard stare sense. The kind that made the whites stand out from those spooky blue eyes—like the planet Saturn with the bulging white ring showing all the way around it. He spoke in a loud, raspy voice, and used double entendres when addressing women. The last time I saw him, he intercepted me in the parking lot of WBFD-TV and asked me if I'd like to suck on something big and hard. Never mind he was holding one of those giant colorful pinwheel lollipops. What Chopper Deke had in mind for me had nothing to do with candy.

But times change, and even though I wouldn't have given that maniac the time of day if I hadn't been in my current predicament, I needed the help of any American or Mexican willing to do what they could to get me, my sister and her friend out of here.

Oh, yes, right . . . Amanda, too.

The more Quintanilla talked about Chopper Deke, the more I realized I was destined to take a helicopter ride, something I'd fought tooth and toenail to keep from doing back at the TV station. The man was nuts. But he just might be able to pull off a rescue. And since nobody else volunteered to med-evac us out of here, the applause needle moved another jump in Chopper Deke's direction.

I activated Bruckman's cell phone. Assuming I could get a signal, I figured I had one or two quick calls, maybe three tops, before the phone totally died.

I placed the first call to WBFD-TV. Not surprisingly, one of Rochelle's multiple personalities answered.

"Rochelle, for the love of God, don't hang up. It's Dainty Prescott. I don't have much time, so I have to talk fast. I need to talk to Chopper Deke. It's a matter of life and death."

"Are you still locked up in a Mexican jail?" she asked, as if she were bored stiff inspecting a fresh manicure and couldn't care less.

"I'm not in jail. Just put Chopper Deke on the phone."

She must've picked up on the panic in my voice because she transferred me to his extension. I didn't expect him to answer. After all, he was supposed to be flying Traffic Monitor Joey over the metroplex, getting out the morning traffic report. I merely wanted to leave a message on his voice mail with the safehouse number, and a desperate plea for him to call me back.

"Yo."

"Chopper Deke?" My voice cracked under the stress of it all.

"Who wants to know?"

"Dainty Prescott."

"Doesn't ring a bell."

"Sure it does. You know me. I'm one of the interns at WBFD. I'm the one from TCU." My panic meter quickly moved from desperate to inconsolable. "You know . . . petite blonde?"

"Oh, right," he said in a tone filled with boredom. "Thirty-six C-cup, tight little ass, and a face like an angel. I remember now. You're next on my list of future ex-wives." If the barometer for indecency could be measured by chuckles, Deke had the nastiest laugh I'd ever heard.

"I'm not a thirty-six—wait—how do you know this?"

"I've seen you naked. Naked in my mind," he said playfully, which momentarily rendered me speechless.

"Deke, I need you to focus," I said in a voice tinged with sternness.

"Well, I'm all for that. I sure do want to focus. And since it's you calling me, I'm guessing you want to focus even more than I do. So I think we should both focus. How 'bout that? You free tonight?"

Hup! Didn't much care for the way the pervert put a nasty spin on my unfortunate word choice.

"Listen carefully, Deke. I'm not playing around."

I ran down the events that brought me to Mexico. I talked fast, told him I didn't have much cell battery left, gave him the telephone number to the safehouse in case we got cut off and wound down with my bottom line.

"My sister's badly injured. I don't think we can make it to any of the border checkpoints. There are too many people after us. I know I don't have the right to ask for your help. And Mr. Quintanilla says you'll probably lose your pilot's license if you do this. Actually, he says that's the least of your worries." I conveniently left out the part where he could be shot down. "But Mr. Quintanilla said you're the only one he knows who might actually pull off a rescue like this. So I'm asking. Will you help me?"

I held my breath. For several seconds, I thought I'd been talking to dead air. Through the long pause, my conscience got the better of me. I brazened out the worst-case-scenario of this unpleasant disclosure. "One more thing, Deke . . . Mr. Quintanilla said you could be shot down."

Roguish laughter filled my ear.

Then the phone went dead in my hand.

That siphoned the oxygen out of my lungs. I closed my eyes tightly, and grimaced to keep from breaking into sobs.

"He hung up on me," I announced to the room at large, then cracked open my eyes and shifted my gaze to Quintanilla. "New plan. Help me brainstorm." Rapid-fire thoughts popped into mind. "What if we paid a bunch of people to surround Teensy and me—"

Amanda shot me a sour look.

"—and Amanda, and we ran for the border all at once?"

Quintanilla gave a slow nod. "You're talking about what's known as a bonsai run, and it won't work. Border Patrol agents deal in volume. You've been watching too much Cheech and Chong."

I'd never seen Cheech Marin's movie about an American citizen rounded up with illegal aliens by mistake and deported south o' the border, but I'd heard about *Born in East L.A.* from my recovering sorority sisters, who dated frat brothers who enjoyed sitting around on lazy Sunday afternoons watching cult classics from our parents' generation.

"What you're suggesting is paying innocent people to form a human shield around you and your sister." He darted a quick look at Amanda and made a sweeping hand flourish. "And her. Haven't you learned anything since you've been here? Human life means nothing to the cartel, or the smugglers and the human traffickers. They gunned down forty people in a bar night before last, remember?" He fixed me with an accusatory stare.

My head suddenly hurt so badly I thought my brain had caught fire. Easy to see, he blamed me for the cantina shootings. Tears welled. I sealed my eyes shut and tried to block out the vivid image of that poor girl wearing my Ferragamos. Bless her heart. She probably thought she'd made the greatest trade of her life, when in fact it was me who'd been the lucky one. In those slick-soled Italian shoes, I'd have never gotten enough traction to scale that wall in time to keep from being gunned down with the rest of the bar patrons. And if that young girl hadn't taken my shoes, she might not have been shot trying to buy Amanda and me extra time to get over that same fence. A tear slipped out, tracking down my cheek.

They wanted me.

They'd come looking for me. The shooters had known in an instant that those beautiful Italian slippers weren't shoes a poor Mexican would buy. And the girl, with her shy smile and fathomless brown eyes, hadn't betrayed us by giving away our position. My chest clenched. There are five people I'd take a bullet for. Five. Teensy. My best friends, Venice Hanover and Salem Quincy. Daddy. And Bruckman. But this stranger . . . this sweet, gentle young woman . . . took a bullet for me.

The pressure became too much to bear.

I admit it—I cracked.

I fisted my eyes and wept, not only for the girl who wanted my shoes, but also for all of the innocents' names on all of those pink crosses, who'd met a similar fate just by wanting something better in life.

The house phone shrilled. My lids popped open like roller shades as Quintanilla strode over to answer it.

Actually, he didn't so much answer it as merely lift the receiver, put it to his ear and breathe into the mouthpiece like an obscene phone caller. His eyes slewed over to me, and he held out the receiver.

I sprinted across the room. "Hello?"

"Say, toots . . . where, exactly, am I supposed to put this bird down?"

I couldn't help it. I came completely unraveled, choking on my own sobs. Words tumbled out in a hyperventilating rush. "In the park in downtown Ciudad Juárez, not far from the International Bridge, between two-thirty and five o'clock. During *siesta*, when there are fewer people. If you can get here that fast."

We hammered out the rest of the details over the landline. After he finished the morning drive time show, he'd head for El Paso around nine o'clock metroplex time. Give or take three hours, he'd refuel before flying into Mexico. With the change in time zones, that'd put him in the area around eleven o'clock, El Paso time. We settled on three o'clock for the pickup. I knew I'd be jittery during the wait, but at least we'd have a margin for error in case anything went wrong. I let him know he'd have four passengers: Teensy, Tiffany, Amanda and me—assuming we could rescue Tiffany by the time Deke landed. In reality, I'd pretty much given up hope of finding Tiffany, but I'd vowed to return with her, so I had an obligation to stay until I tracked her down, even if it meant giving up my seat in Deke's chopper.

Deke was supposed to stand by until I'd found Teensy, and he gave me the number to his cell phone. He estimated he'd need fifteen minutes from the time I called until he touched down in the park.

"No margin for error, toots. Be there, or be left behind."

Ha! Cutting it close had been the story of my life down here. Before hanging up, I had a moral obligation to warn him about what he'd probably already figured out.

"Deke . . . just so you know what you're getting yourself into . . ." I swallowed hard, inwardly praying he wouldn't back out. "We could all die."

He let out a maniacal cackle. Then he asked if I knew what the President of Mexico's helicopter looked like. Then he muttered, "Never mind," and the last thing I heard before he smacked the phone down in my ear was, "You owe me big, blondie. And boy, am I gonna have fun collecting."

Around seven o'clock that morning, while the aroma of ham and eggs and tortillas warmed in a cast iron skillet filled up the safehouse, I fleetingly dreamed of a hot bath. Amanda and I were grimy and grungy, and starting to smell like swamp gas; and I knew with all the men sitting around the table, wolfing down breakfast, that we'd have enough time to clean up without inconveniencing the others by hogging the bathroom.

But as I folded my blanket and placed it neatly on the sofa, the place turned into Grand Central Station. Quintanilla charged in from a back room shouting orders. Footfalls thundered as others rushed in—men I didn't recall seeing before—armed to the teeth. Hand gestures turned like windmills as this posse of men figured out where to go.

Amanda sat up, wide-eyed, and drank in the chaos from her place on the chair. The commotion had nothing to do with lining up for chow.

Quintanilla grabbed his gray cowboy hat off a wall peg and adjusted the brim low over his forehead as he angled my way. "There's been a problem. Stay here until we get back. Do not leave. I'll take you to your sister later this afternoon."

"What's wrong?"

He ignored me, choosing instead to head out the back door onto the patio. I jumped up from my place on the sofa. Amanda left the comfort of her chair. We both went out the back door in time to see them leave through a rear gate. A light dusting of snow covered the flat patio rocks. With each new breeze, it shifted, changing directions and blowing back again. Pulling my sweater around me so tightly that I was hugging myself, I shivered.

Whatever happened, this was not good.

Engines to multiple vehicles turned over and we dashed back inside to see if we could pinpoint the direction they'd left in. Only the lone sentinel remained at his post.

And Julio Cordova, who shuffled down the hall on his way to the bathroom.

Amanda and I each parted a section of the curtain enough to look out. Instead of driving toward town, they seemed to be moving further into the desert. When the last vehicle disappeared in a cloud of dust, a loud thud came from another part of the house. We exchanged awkward glances.

"You think the old man fell?" Amanda said.

I shrugged. "We should check on him, don't you think?"

"I don't know. Those are private quarters. If they'd wanted us back there, they'd have given us a room."

"What if he's hurt?"

"You're right. Go check on him."

"You go check on him. You speak Spanish."

"He speaks English, too. You go check on him."

I said, "Rock, paper, scissors."

Amanda began the count. On three, she made a fist. I held out scissors-fingers.

Rock smashes scissors. I lose.

I wandered down the hallway, passing several closed doors that apparently went to bedrooms, until I saw a bar of light beneath a door. I gently tapped on the wood.

"Señor Cordova? It's me, Dainty Prescott. Are you all right?"

I could hear rooting around inside the bathroom. How embarrassing for us both for me to be lurking outside the door. But he hadn't said anything, and he was old. He could've slipped and fallen.

"Señor Cordova? Did you fall? Do you need help? Should I come in?" I stared at the doorknob like it was a callous that needed removing. I didn't want to go in there. "Señor Cordo—"

The door swung open. The rest of his name slid back down my throat.

The man who'd stood guard on the patio last night had his rifle slung behind his back, and a handgun pointed in my face.

Chapter Twenty-Nine

Amanda called out to me from the living room, "Is everything all right?"

"Careful what you say, Danny Prescott." The guard touched a finger to his head as a reminder of the knot he'd left me with last night.

My heart climbed into my throat. From what I could see on my side of the bathroom door, Mr. Cordova's *huarache*-clad feet were lying sideways on the floor. I assumed the rest of his body followed the curve of his knees and ended up at or near a bathtub or shower.

"Everything's fine," I called out in a strident voice. Then I slowly eased away with palms up and slightly raised, until my back touched the corridor wall. To the man, I said, "Why are you doing this? You're supposed to be helping us."

"You are worth a lot of money, Danny Prescott."

His words sickened me. Then he reached behind his back, pulled out a length of rope and shook it at me.

"No. No way. Not gonna happen." I gave him a vehement headshake. I'd been through a similar ordeal before and I credit still being here with not allowing myself to be bound and tethered. "I'll do what you want, but I won't be tied up."

Dark eyes smoldered. "I will kill your friend."

"No. She doesn't have anything to do with this."

Then Amanda rounded the corner and saw us. The man shouted to her in Spanish. She spoke calmly by way of an answer. This heated exchange went back and forth for what seemed an eternity. In fact, it probably lasted less than a minute. But when you're looking down a gun barrel the size of a cannon, waiting for an orange flash to end your life, you kind of lose track of time. Trust me on this.

"We're going for a drive," Amanda said.

"Uh-huh." What I meant was, *Like hell.*

"He wants me to drive and he's going to sit in back with you."

"Where are we going?"

"You're not going to like this part, girlfriend."

"Try me."

"The desert."

"Okay . . . well, I didn't pay you all that money for nothing." This was code, reminding her I'd given her my last five hundred dollars to buy a gun, and she'd by-God better still have it.

"Too much talk," the man said.

I went for my purse, but he stopped me.

"I want my book."

He shook his head and gestured for us to move toward the back door.

"It's just a book," I yelled, frantic.

Amanda spoke, and he let me get *The Ladies' Guide to Homicide.*

Then he said, *"Ándele,"* and we hurried out of the safehouse at gunpoint, loaded into a Jeep, and headed into the desert.

We arrived at a huge, dilapidated building with a dreary concrete exterior that still had enough sand-colored paint left on it after years of weathering to know what the original color had been. Next to a side entrance to this spooky old place with dozens of broken windowpanes running beneath the roof's overhang sat a huge cement water trough with a hand pump. The half-full trough had turned brackish and dark, and what water it did contain was contaminated with algae.

In self-defense, my mind initially rejected Amanda's explanation that we'd been brought to an abandoned slaughterhouse a few miles into the desert, on the outskirts of Ciudad Juárez. But after we were taken inside and herded into an open area where farm animals had once been prodded down a long, narrow chute to their deaths, I became an instant believer. Meat hooks dangled from angle-iron struts bracing the roof. The concrete floor slanted toward a drainage tunnel that collected blood from freshly slaughtered livestock.

A dozen men dressed in all types of fashions, and from all types of means, huddled in one corner like the underdog team in the Sunday night football lineup. Our kidnapper shouted to them from across the room, ending his exclamation with "Danny Prescott" and pointing his bony finger at me. Excited rumblings echoed through the empty warehouse; a flock of birds, nesting in the housing of old lighting, broke from their perches and fluttered out the shattered windowpanes near the ceiling. The smell of old blood hung heavy in the air.

While I looked around for a place to vomit, Amanda tuned in to the heated exchange between several well-dressed men and our kidnapper.

Amanda whispered, "It's an auction. They're here to buy us."

What?

She nodded, distressed. "Human traffickers."

"They can't do that," I hissed, but her expression said, *Wait and see.* I shook my head with such violence that it jarred my retinas. Then I looked around for the nearest exit and saw heavy chains securing the doors.

I'll spare you the indignity of having to go through, in words, what we went through in real time, other than to say we were prodded into a room at gunpoint where other young girls were waiting. The inside temperature was befitting a meat locker. What started out as a few unpleasant shivers became frightful shudders.

"Dainty? Dainty Prescott? Is it you?"

My eyes cut to the direction where the sound of my name had come from.

Tiffany.

In that instant, my entire world narrowed to a single focal point, and that was my sister's friend. Her long brown hair had become oily and matted. The expensive dress she had on was dirty and torn. She stood, barefoot and shivering, and the downy hairs on her arms stuck out like needles. Oddly, her face appeared freshly made up until I realized that she'd succumbed to the temptation to have her eyes and lips tattooed with permanent makeup. Despite the guard's instructions not to talk, we ran to each other and embraced.

"Get me out of here," Tiffany said under her breath.

"We have a plan," I mumbled, hugging her again, piping my message directly into her ear canal.

Then we were separated. The man spoke sharply, in a terrifying voice with a resonant timbre that made him seem like a giant, but I didn't care. Another man entered, well dressed and formidable in his presence, and exchanged eye-encrypted messages with the guard.

This was *El Jefe* . . . the man in charge, I thought. I'd seen him before . . . but the clothes were different.

Yes.

At the border crossing.

One of the uniformed men sitting in chairs, wanting to know if we had fruit or vegetables to declare.

My stomach flipped.

An eerie feeling overwhelmed me.

That's how they did it. Screened the people coming into the

country, picking out the pretty ones, the tipsy ones, or those otherwise not in complete control of their faculties. Easy prey, bypassing the rest. Teensy and Tiffer fell into the first category. These other girls were lovely, too. And it wasn't just Americans. I was pretty sure I remembered one of the Mexican girls' faces from a flyer taped on a wall along with other missing girls' pictures at the Mexican police station.

Struck by irony, I snorted in disgust. We were in a meat market.

Correction: We *were* the meat market.

The Mexican girl from the missing persons flyer had a large bruise on one cheek shaped like the butt of a gun. I immediately thought of the man who'd hit me in the head and torqued my jaw. She'd probably put up a struggle the way I had. Her bottom lip looked like it weighed eighty-eight pounds, and the split lip telegraphed she'd taken a blow to the mouth. But the look in her eyes bragged *spitfire*.

I hadn't been paying attention to our kidnapper. But the malignance in his tone snared my interest. Pure fright had settled on Amanda's face.

"What?" I said this on a whoosh of air.

"He wants us to take our clothes off. So they can see what they're bidding on."

Not gonna happen. I'm not getting naked for a bunch of scum buckets.

Then I realized Amanda had an even bigger problem than the rest of the females in this room.

We shared a simultaneous thought: What would they do when they realized she was a *he?* Probably kill her.

An unbidden image of how they'd do it sprang to mind, and I instantly wanted to projectile vomit all over the guard. Let's just say it had to do with julienning Amanda's Japanese eggplant and leave it at that.

There must've been ten or twelve girls, total, in the slaughter-house's dank anteroom. But even in close quarters, there was no way to enlist their help in creating a diversion without letting our kidnapper in on the deal.

Amanda said, "Do you remember how to get back to the door we came in?"

Big nod.

"Remember what I told you back at the bridge?"

Our kidnapper growled out an order that sounded filthy and vile. I knew we shouldn't be talking, but it really didn't matter. I didn't need words when I remembered Amanda's best advice.

"You'd better attach yourself to me like a two-year-old special needs child."

No problem-o, I thought.

With my book clutched tightly to my chest, I clasped Tiffany's palm with my free hand, and held on for dear life.

CHAPTER THIRTY

While our kidnapper looked on, Amanda put on a little impromptu peek-a-boo striptease for him, pulling back her blouse enough for him to see a hint of skin behind the bra, which I now knew to be stick-on, flesh-tone silicone. Then she hiked up her skirt and wiggled her tush. The guard cracked a smile, but his eyes were as hard as pebbles.

Her next move shocked me. She did a provocative little shimmy-shake with her shoulders and glided toward him with the grace and stealth of a panther. Then her hand went behind her back as she pretended to unfasten her skirt, and when it came back out, she screwed an evil-looking black semi-automatic up his snout. She relieved him of his handgun and pointed that at him, too.

"Keep them quiet," I urged Tiffany, and then pushed her toward the women.

Amanda growled out an order. Our kidnapper's shoulders sagged beneath the weight of his rifle.

"Dainty," Amanda said low and under her breath, "take off your scarf." I started to hand it over but she said, "Stuff it in his mouth."

I did as I was told.

"Now tear your shawl into strips."

I whipped it off from around my neck and quickly rent it into several lengths of fabric. Murderous fury had filled me with resolve to leave here intact, and fortified me with strength that felt almost super-human.

"Tie his hands." When I moved toward him, she said, "No, no. In back. Tie them behind him." To Tiffany, she said, "Go over near the door and keep a lookout for us. Don't make noise."

Girls who'd started to strip immediately grabbed their clothes and re-dressed. By the time I looked up from binding our gunman's hands, Tiffany had moved across the room without me even hearing her.

Amanda rattled off something in Spanish, and the Mexican girl with the fat lip nodded. She took the man's handgun from Amanda and handed it to me. Then she relieved him of his rifle. She peppered her conversation with Amanda by inserting locations like Colombia and Belize, Bolivia and Mexico City into her phrases. I assumed these were places where we'd either become wives to troll-like drug lords, or be pressed into indentured servitude as prostitutes.

Amanda continued in Spanish. To me, she said, "Short firearms course," and I assumed she was instructing this girl with the spitfire gleam in her eye on how to reload. The girl took the trussed-up guard's bullet strap and slung it around her neck like Pancho Villa while Amanda studied him with a stare so blank that it bordered on autism. "See, Dainty," she said with detachment, "the way to a man's heart isn't necessarily through his stomach unless you're talking about a knife or a bullet."

I wedged the book into the waistband of my skirt and jammed the gun underneath the guard's chin. "Where's my sister?"

He moaned. Of course he couldn't answer with my scarf stuffed in his mouth, so I reached up and pinched the tip of it. "I'm going to pull this out of your mouth. If you yell, I'll shoot you in the nuts, do you understand?"

In case he didn't, Amanda's translation coaxed out a head bob.

"Where's my sister?"

He answered in his native tongue. In a quick exchange, Amanda ferreted out that Teensy had been taken to the insane asylum, Hector Cordova's clinic, to convalesce. I had an idea that once she recuperated she'd be in as much danger as she'd been in the night she climbed into that gypsy cab. I stuffed the scarf back into the guard's mouth, careful not to touch any decaying teeth.

"Okay, Dainty, take down his pants."

"What? No. Let's just get out of here."

"Take down his pants."

I called Tiffany over and delegated instructions. I figured she knew what was coming because she didn't seem the least bit upset about yanking down his cheaply manufactured khakis.

"Pull them all the way off. Now his skivvies."

Tiffany did as she was told. The guy's family jewels and his jeweler's loupe popped out for all of us to inspect. The Mexican girl spit on his incredible shrinking gonads.

Then she lowered the rifle to his groin and said, "Kiss my ass, *cabrón.*"

I swear he squeezed out a couple of tears.

While Tiffany and I bound his ankles, Amanda took off her skirt and swapped it for the guard's pants. They were too long, and she huffed and puffed as she rolled up the cuffs, still talking as every girl hung onto her every word.

"We're all making a break for it. When we get to the Jeep, you'll have to pile on and sit in each other's laps. Some of you may have to climb on top." She pulled the man's belt out of the loops and threaded it into a noose. "Nobody gets on the hood. Because when I hit the gas, we're going. And if you fall off, I'm keeping on going. Understand?"

Everyone nodded as she worked in a crouch, looping the belt around the guard's neck with precision before cinching it to a rusty, uninsulated water pipe that ran the length of the room.

Project completed, she dusted off her hands and stood.

Now she wore what looked like Depression-era clothing and was dressed no better than a tramp. All she needed was a newsboy cap resting jauntily on her head and a copy of the *El Paso Times* tucked under one arm to complete the picture. The baggy, nondescript trousers and black orthopedic shoes did nothing to enhance her ensemble.

Then she turned to me. "Dainty, as soon as I open the door, shoot him in the *cojónes.*"

CHAPTER THIRTY-ONE

Amanda carefully opened the door that led out into the main auction area. I went first, pulling Tiffany behind me. For maybe thirty seconds, our prospective buyers were too engrossed in their own conversations to notice us moving stealthily toward the exit.

But before the last girl filed through our holding tank, one of the men shouted and pointed at us. We ran. The report of a rifle made a deafening sound as the simultaneous, guts out scream of the guard reverberated through the slaughterhouse.

I'm a nonviolent person by nature, except for the time I smashed a Coke bottle against a brick wall and held Ricky Huff at bay after he tried to pull down my underpants in fourth grade. I didn't shoot the guard in the nuts like Amanda wanted me to. The Mexican girl from the missing persons flyer did it for me. Amanda's warning shots zinged off the walls and chilled me to the core.

While Tiffany and I piled into the front passenger seat of the Jeep, the rest of the girls were jockeying for position in the back. They sat three deep on each other's laps, and two of them clung to the roll bar. I looked in the ignition and didn't see the key. For a few seconds, I could only blink in despair.

Did Amanda have the key? Or the guard?

I was halfway to hyperventilating when Amanda fired off a volley of shots and barged out the door. She emptied her pockets, tossing the contents into the water trough, before running hell bent for leather toward the Jeep.

"Dainty, help me with the cars."

There were six or seven cars parked near the slaughterhouse. She wanted my help to disable them. I know nothing about cars except how to start them and how to drive fast.

I said, "Shoot the tires." It seemed like the right thing to do.

"Only works in movies."

She ran to the first vehicle, opened the door and popped open the hood. The side door to the warehouse cracked open a sliver, and she eyed it with ferocity as she fired off a couple of shots.

It slammed shut.

She showed me a weird octopus-thingy near the engine and told me to yank it out and throw it as far as I could. Following her lead, I went to the next car and removed this contraption. When I went to the third vehicle, the keys were inside, so I removed them. Amanda was working on the last car—she moved quickly—and then we were done.

We got into the Jeep and I offered the second set of keys to the girl in the missing persons flyer. She snatched them out of my hand and called to a couple of the Mexican girls. They jumped out of the Jeep and ran for the pickup. Amanda and I had Tiffany and four other girls with us—all Americans—when she cranked up the Jeep and churned up a cloud of baked earth.

I don't think she planned to retrace our steps; she simply pointed the nose of the Jeep toward Ciudad Juárez and floored the accelerator.

She bounced over a pothole, rocking the vehicle.

"Hey—*Auntie Maim*," I hollered, "watch where you're going."

Amanda kept a death grip on the steering wheel. "Think you can do better, diva?"

"*Ha.* I was born to race."

"Yeah? Well, you can show me one of these days . . . if we make it out of here."

For no good reason, I felt energized. There's something magically useful about adrenaline dumps to get your duff in gear when someone wants to kill you. Or force you into prostitution. Soon, we mowed down our last tumbleweed and splattered our last cactus. Amanda wheeled the Jeep onto the highway with a jolt, with the Mexican girls closing the gap behind us.

A sense of calm spread over me. I looked over at Tiffany, and studied the contours of her pretty face. She wore the distant stare of someone slipping into shock.

"Are you all right?"

"Not really." Then she said, airily and childlike, "Are we going home now?"

Now that I'd figured she'd live, irritation set in. "Okay, I'm going to try not to be too hard on you, but what in the hell did you think you were doing, coming down to this godforsaken hellhole?"

She gave a slow headshake and stared straight through the windshield. Whether her lack of explanation was due to an unwillingness to answer, or the inability to respond, her silence unleashed the snarling Doberman inside me.

"Whose brain-dead idea was this?" I asked in a way that would've made the doyennes of The Rubanbleu clutch their bosoms while reaching for the smelling salts.

"Your stepmom said we should come to Juárez," she answered, zombie-like, as if she'd been tranquilized and had to think long and hard in order to navigate her way through a simple sentence. "Called it a rite of passage. After the debutante ball, she even chartered a private plane for us and handed us a boatload of spending money. She told us to live it up. Said life was short, and you never knew when you'd die."

Poor, gullible girls. Especially my sister, who'd tried to get along with Nerissa from the get-go. That wretched, vile woman must've known if Teensy went missing she could kill two birds with one stone, because I'd go looking for her. And my dumb-bunny sister walked right down the primrose trap.

And dumb-bunny me followed her down the *Alice in Wonderland* rabbit hole.

Since we were no longer sure who to trust at the safehouse other than poor Julio Cordova and Mr. Quintanilla—and let me just say, I was starting to have my doubts about him again—we decided against returning there. But the police would be looking for this Jeep and the pickup, and it was imperative that we ditch our transportation as soon as possible.

I turned to Amanda. "We have to get rid of these vehicles."

She nodded.

I twisted in my seat and looked over the Americans crowded into the back compartments of our vehicle. They looked young and frightened and traumatized.

I cupped my hand around my mouth to amplify the sound. "Where do you want to go?"

They looked at me through haunted eyes, and collectively chorused, "Home."

CHAPTER THIRTY-TWO

By finding Tiffany, we'd picked up four extra American girls, all kidnap victims, all wanting to go back home. We couldn't leave them behind if they wanted our help, but this posed a huge problem for Amanda and me. We couldn't have this entourage following us around while trying to sneak Teensy, Tiffany and me . . . and Amanda . . . out of the country, and I didn't know what else to do with them now that the safehouse no longer seemed safe.

So after we ditched the cars, Amanda got directions from a crazy guy on the street who was drooling into a cup, and we took the girls to the asylum with us.

I'd already started thinking of the place as Club Med.

Imagine . . . 1915 to 1920. East Henscratch, Kansas. With linoleum floors in vomit-colored tiles, cheap WWI surplus mattresses on the floor; walls painted a pale shade of blue that had dulled to gray over the years; a single bare light bulb screwed into a ceiling socket; thick iron bars over the windows; uncontrollable screams echoing off the walls . . . then you have an idea what a Mexican insane asylum is like.

The building's brick exterior was in various stages of turning to powder. The place needed a new roof and the windows needed a good cleaning. But inside, all of the nurses and attendants remained in relatively good spirits, which I attributed to the ability to get good psychotropic drugs, of which I could use a few mood elevators myself . . . and they were all running around in *¡Viva Danny Prescott!* T-shirts in Easter egg colors pulled over their smocks. So were the patients I could see from my place near the receptionist's desk.

Amanda told the young lady we were looking for Maribel. She tapped on a door several yards away and stood there until the door swung open and Maribel came out.

The moment Maribel saw us, she clapped a hand over her mouth. Then she spoke to the girl, who gave my face a quick study and then pulled at the front of her T-shirt and stared at the picture upside down. As the young girl ran to tell the others, Maribel took my hand and pulled me down the hall. Amanda followed.

We ended up in what appeared to be a parody of a conference room, with the table and chairs a mishmash of eras, and the projection equipment either vintage or dismantled. The bars on the windows added a creepy touch to the already dismal facility, and served as a reminder that what was locked up inside here to keep outsiders safe was also keeping the occupants safe from outsiders. Had the building's exterior not been crumbling, Dr. Hector Cordova's enemies would've needed a military tank to get in.

Again, my head took a stroll over to the irony aisle of Hallmark:

I'm here at Club Med, I'm locked up inside;

But it's not so bad, considering you thought I died.

I said, "We came to get Teensy. I know she's here."

Maribel shook her head.

Amanda took over and translated. "She *was* here. But they had to move her. The coyotes figured out they were trying to nurse her back to health."

"Where is she?"

"Back at the hospital."

"Fine. We'll go there." I looked at Maribel. "Thanks for all you've done. I'll send you a check when we get back home." I grabbed her hand and pumped it hard. We needed to get over to that hospital, the sooner the better.

Amanda said, "Not so fast. Maribel says all the cab drivers and public transportation people are on the lookout for you. The coyotes put a bounty on your head. Now you not only have them to worry about, but all the other scuzzballs who want in on the reward. They'll kill you if they get the chance, Dainty."

"Then we'll walk. You don't even have to come with me, Amanda. I'm starting to know my way around this town."

"We came together, we're leaving together."

I turned to Maribel. "Can you give us a ride in your car?"

She smiled, and Amanda translated. "She doesn't think you'll want to ride in it. It's what you might call 'conspicuous.' "

"Why? What does she drive? The Oscar Mayer wiener car?"

"It's full of bullet holes. Because they suspected Maribel was harboring your sister."

"I'm sorry." For the record, I was starting to do sorry very well.

"She's got a better idea, though. But she doesn't think you'll go along with it."

I didn't think I'd go along with it either, but I said, "Try me," on the off chance it might work.

Talk about hiding in plain sight . . .

And that's how we shuffled past the military, the cartel, the coyotes and the smugglers on our way to the hospital, a dozen drooling or raving mental patients mixed in with seven Americans—all wearing *¡Viva Danny Prescott!* T-shirts that Maribel gave us, all bound in straitjackets, our heads covered with towels and our chins tucked into our chests—out for a bit of fresh air on a bitter cold day, chaperoned by the asylum staff.

CHAPTER THIRTY-THREE

When we arrived at the hospital, Maribel stopped the group in front of the iron gates while one of the chaperones unbuckled Amanda's straitjacket. While Amanda finagled the lock on the gate, the chaperone helped me shrug out of mine.

Funny thing about crazy people . . . not funny-funny, but funny-strange . . . regular people—which is to say people who believe themselves to be sane—tend to look right through them.

Note to self: If ever you plan to do something on the sketchy side of society, take a handful of mental patients with you.

Once Amanda and I were free of our restraints, we slipped through the gates and into the building while the rest of the Americans loitered outside with the patients. As soon as we stepped into the lobby, the receptionist went wide-eyed and motioned us back outside. Something was happening down the hall, and the danger quotient had just spiked. Amanda gave her the A-okay sign, but I shook my head no. I'd come to retrieve my sister, and I wasn't leaving without her.

At the far end of the hall, angry voices grew louder. The doctor began to shout. Footfalls echoed down the corridor.

We'd lost the opportunity to bolt out the front doors. But we were close to the elevator, so I pushed the button. The door slid back like a gaping mouth, and as we stepped inside, it closed us off from view.

Amanda hit the stop button and the elevator gave a dying shudder. We waited inside like a couple of caged animals.

258

Just beyond the door, I heard the doctor use the words *muerto* and Teensy Prescott in the same sentence. Then he mentioned the morgue.

My heart broke.

Amanda grabbed my hand and put a finger to her lips. She thought I was going to lose control.

A lot of things went through my head, but the overpowering thought was that my life had irreparably changed for the worse. Before I knew it, the voices in the corridor fell silent, and the people who were looking for my sister were gone.

I didn't trust myself to speak, but I croaked out a request. "Please tell me I didn't hear what I think I heard. Please tell me I misunderstood. That I'm wrong."

Amanda shook her head, *You're not wrong.* "I'm sorry, Dainty. She's dead."

The words, *"She's dead,"* were simply too large to force down my ear canal.

The truth was, I couldn't have cried if I'd wanted to. The moment I heard the news that my sister was dead, I simply went numb inside.

Amanda whispered, "She's at the morgue."

I didn't say anything. I didn't cry. I only blinked.

"I think it's safe to leave." Amanda pulled out the stop button; the elevator took a jarring dip. When the door peeled back, we were six inches below our level. It wasn't a huge drop, but since I didn't have the energy to move in the first place, Amanda got out first, then grabbed my arm and hoisted me up.

We left the way we'd come in. Maribel, the chaperones, the mental patients and the Americans were now congregating inside the gates, waiting for us to reappear.

I descended the front steps and walked over to Maribel with Amanda beside me.

I said, "Tell her," and she did.

"We need to get to the morgue before the coyotes," I said stunned and in a monotone. "I have to claim her body before they take her away." I didn't want to think about those evil men turning my sister over to the Cook, to be disposed of in a vat of acid, as if she'd never lived, never dreamed or set goals and never touched the lives of the people she met. I experienced a sense of urgency that was so completely ingrained, it hijacked my sorrow and dominated my common sense. "We have to beat them there."

I didn't want to slip back into the straitjacket, but Maribel's argument that we would endanger the lives of the Americans and the patients if we didn't blend in convinced me. Then we filed out of the gates and walked down the street at a brisk, determined clip.

At the morgue, Maribel kept our entourage busy by tying up the restrooms, while Amanda and I shed our straitjackets and struck out to find the chief coroner.

As soon as he saw me, he did a double take. "Go back, they are coming."

"I want my sister's body."

"You must leave. The hospital called to warn us. Men are on the way."

"Don't give her to them," I pleaded. "My family will pay."

"*Ay, Dios mío,*" he cried, "must I put you in a body bag, too?"

The front door banged open and thundering footfalls echoed through the lobby. The coroner grabbed a couple of blue smocks, hair covers and face shields, and told us to put them on. Then he directed us to several bodies in various stages of autopsy. He'd lost his mind trying to pass us off as coroners, but we'd run out of time as the men pushed their way through the doors.

A heated exchange took place between the doc and the

coyotes. As much as I wanted to burn their images into my mind so that I could find them and make them pay for what they'd done, I didn't dare turn around. The coroner I'd been paired with handed me a scalpel and pointed to a place I should cut.

I couldn't do it.

As hostility crackled all around me, I pretended to assist, even going so far as to pick up the Stryker saw. At least I had a formidable weapon in my grip. And if those men came anywhere near Amanda or me, I wouldn't hesitate to fire it up and use it.

The chief coroner seemed to have everything under control, right up until he used *"crematorio"* and "Teensy Prescott" in the same sentence. I almost passed out from shock. Halfway to hyperventilating, I placed the Stryker saw back where I got it, and braced both hands against the steel table. The repulsive stench of stomach gasses from a freshly autopsied corpse closed in on us from across the room. Choking back their gorge, the men couldn't get out of there fast enough.

With my back to the nearest wall, I slumped to the floor near a collapsed wheelchair, and pulled off my face shield. The revolting smell hit me full force.

The chief coroner came over to check on me, but I didn't need or want his help. The fury within me continued to mount, and when he tried to help me to my feet, I lashed out with what venom I had left. "How could you?" I shrieked.

He recoiled as if I'd sunk fangs into him. I got to my feet under my own steam, ripped off the smock and the sanitary hair cover and shoved them at him as I pushed past.

Amanda gawked.

As I headed for the door, the coroner called me back. "Danny Prescott, your sister is here."

I halted in my tracks, did something like a military pivot, and gave him a dedicated eye blink. "What?"

"She is here. I only told the coyotes so they would not take her."

Tears welled. "Where is she?"

He pointed to the refrigerated cooler.

"Show her to me." I could barely breathe in any more of this putrid, suffocating air. He led me to the walk-in cooler and opened the door. Then he pointed to a white body bag.

A hairdresser who used to cut my hair, before I changed to the gay guy I use now, once told me about being asked to style a dead client's hair for the funeral. She said she completely rejected the idea until the deceased's daughter offered her a thousand dollars. It was in her mother's will, she'd said. After a considerable amount of schmoozing and a cashier's check, my hairdresser went to the funeral parlor with her little hair kit. When she got there, nobody told her about the gasses that collected in people's stomachs after they die, or about cadaveric spasms. They simply pointed her to a room with a bunch of bodies inside and flipped back the sheet on old Mrs. Weinstein. My hairdresser said she was halfway through when the body on the next gurney rose halfway up and groaned. She dropped her shears, high-tailed it out of there without her kit, and never looked back.

I can't emphasize the words "cadaveric spasms" enough.

Before the coroner could unzip it and peel back the plastic so I could make identification as next-of-kin, the body in the body bag sneezed.

I admit it. I jumped back and let out a guts-out scream.

This must've gone on for some time, because Amanda hauled off and slapped me. Then it was over. Huge purple-black bruises ringed Teensy's eyes like a sleep mask. Her face was battered and swollen. The rest of her skin was as white as chalk, and her lips were puffy and blue.

As I took all this in, my sister's eyes popped open and her

head flopped toward me.

"Hi, Dainty," Teensy said, through groggy, sluggish speech. "I knew you'd come. It's freezing in here. Would you mind if I took your sweater?"

CHAPTER THIRTY-FOUR

With our straitjackets back in Maribel's hands, and the group of mental patients considerably downsized, we said our good-byes and made promises to stay in touch that no one really believed we'd keep. The chief coroner helped us get Teensy into the wheelchair I'd seen propped up against the autopsy room wall, while the rest of us—me, Amanda and the American girls—slipped into white physician's smocks that concealed the *¡Viva Danny Prescott!* T-shirts Maribel made us put on at the asylum. Accompanied by one of the assistant coroners who'd been hand-selected by the chief coroner to escort us, we were driven to a hotel across the street from the park in the coroner's van.

When the assistant pulled up in front of the hotel to let us out, we looked like a bunch of medical students attending a convention. I paid for two rooms, which earned us a severely arched eyebrow from the female hotel clerk, even though we'd made a pact to stick together in one room until it was time to leave. Amanda and I couldn't afford to have these girls wander off while we were arranging their escape. None of them had passports or ID, so Amanda and I were the best shot they had to get out of here.

The time was two o'clock. We'd cut it too close for comfort.

After arranging to leave our smocks at the front desk—we let the clerk think the coroner's office was sending someone by later to pick them up so they could be laundered and returned to us—we went upstairs to our room and locked ourselves inside. The only time anyone ventured across the hall to the bathroom was when the staging area bathroom was in use.

At two-fifteen, as the girls settled in and synchronized their watches, Amanda and I left my sister and the rest of the Americans and went downstairs to make a long-distance call from the house phone. At first, the lady working the desk declined until Amanda pulled a wad of cash out of her bra and slapped a ten-dollar bill, American money, onto the counter. It looked sweaty and unsanitary, and I felt my nose wrinkle in disgust. But the lady behind the counter snatched it up like one of those motorized coin banks designed to entertain children, the kind with the little hand that darts out and snatches a coin placed strategically on its perch. She held up three fingers, which I gathered meant she expected me to conduct my business in three minutes. Since I no longer had Chopper Deke's cell phone number, and had only managed to commit part of it to memory, I called WBFD-TV.

As usual, Rochelle answered. Even though she usually faked a cheery lilt, she often vented her frustration behind the scenes with the enactment of rude pantomimes, heavy eye rolling, or by raising a stiff middle finger to the mouthpiece secure in the knowledge that the caller couldn't see her. Most people phoning in assumed Rochelle was sweet and helpful. Those of us who had to work with her knew she was not. On this particular afternoon, her tone telegraphed an openly filthy mood. Hostility sparked at the other end of the line.

I announced myself, explaining that I needed the number to Chopper Deke's cell phone.

Her demeanor instantly changed. One of the more vicious personalities in attendance at the Board of Directors meeting being routinely conducted inside Rochelle's head turned the reins to the telephone over to one of the nicer members. Rochelle instantly became the caring, nurturing person that I knew lurked deep inside her. Very deep. Excavate down to bedrock deep.

I made a little finger motion to the desk clerk, scrawling across the air with an invisible pen, to show I needed something to write with, and she handed me a scrap of paper. I wrote the number down and thanked Rochelle. At that moment, I felt a lance of love in my heart for her, the by-product of knowing I might never see her again.

"Dainty, is there anything we can do here?"

"No." My voice cracked. A tear leaked out of one corner of my eye. "But thanks." Then a jarring thought occurred to me—the kind of sensation you get when the plumber opens the cabinet beneath the sink and a rat dashes out. "Are you absolutely, positively, a hundred percent certain this is the right number?"

"Don't you trust me?" she said with a reproachful sniff.

I could feel Nice Rochelle slipping from my grasp, and knew that I had to get her back before Cruella Rochelle moved into the CEO's chair.

"Rochelle, the lives of eight people depend on getting this right."

She asked me to read it back. When I did, she pronounced it to be correct, and I profusely thanked her.

"Gordon sent a crew."

"What?"

"Gordon sent a crew out to report your situation. Haven't you been watching the news?"

I shook my head, then realized she couldn't see me. "No." I looked up and met the no-nonsense gaze of the desk clerk. "I have to go now. Bye."

Then she took my breath away by saying something I swear I'd never heard her say before, and probably would never hear again. "I've been praying for you."

"Thanks, Rochelle." Thoroughly touched, a desperate giggle escaped my lips. Then I recovered. "Just so you know, if I make it back alive, I won't tell anybody you said that."

"You'd by-God better not."

The phone went dead, severed by the desk clerk's finger depressing the switch hook.

"I have to make another call."

She didn't say anything, merely stared through beady onyx eyes. Keeping her finger on the switch hook, she cut her gaze to Amanda.

"Girlfriend, when we get done, you owe me twenty dollars." Amanda pulled out her wad of cash and peeled off another ten. The woman behind the desk plucked it from her hand and toddled off to a small office.

The time was two-thirty.

I dialed the number to Chopper Deke's cell phone. On the fourth ring, I got antsy. Why wasn't he answering? I met Amanda's expectant gaze and knew we were thinking the same thing: *Oh, shit.*

Then a gravelly voice said, "You owe me big time, toots."

The relieved giggle I emitted sounded more like a whimper. "We're in a hotel across from the park. But there's a problem. We have more girls. You have to take them all. There are eight of us."

"No can do. Too much weight."

"They're built like me; most of them, anyway. They probably average a hundred-fifteen pounds each. More or less." An understatement, at best.

He muttered a few numbers—quick calculations I didn't understand the meaning of.

"Thanks for tossing in the monkey wrench. Boils down to fuel or load. Less fuel, more passengers. Don't like that. Can't go as far. The more fuel, the farther we go. You pick. Sacrifice fuel, or sacrifice load. End of story. So what's it gonna be?"

"It can't be helped. We can't leave them."

My sister and Tiffany were getting on that bird first; I'd already worked it out in my head. Next came Amanda and me. In a real *Sophie's Choice* kind of moment, my mind started culling girls. But I knew when it came down to the nut cutting, I couldn't do that. Neither did I want to be the one left behind.

"I'll handle it, toots. You owe me."

"My daddy will pay you."

He let out a roguish chuckle. "Not in it for money."

The desk clerk moseyed back to the counter, intent on cutting short my phone call.

I talked fast. "What time do you have, so we can synchronize our watches?"

"Two thirty-two."

Same as I. "Just be there at three o'clock, Mr. Richter. I can't call you again. I won't have access to my phone."

"No, *you* just be there at three."

The lady at the hotel desk didn't sever my connection. She didn't have to. Chopper Deke did it for her.

CHAPTER THIRTY-FIVE

My watch said 2:35. My heart pounded, and the pulse in my neck throbbed. I wanted to vomit. When I relinquished the phone to the desk clerk and turned around, Amanda was holding out a candy bar. We deserved a "Last Supper" if things turned out badly, but I didn't want junk food to be mine.

Besides, it wasn't like it'd go to waste. Amanda had already finished hers and was peeling back the wrapper to the one I'd rejected.

At 2:40, we corralled all the girls and placed the keys on the only table in the room. They didn't have anything but their clothes, Amanda only had her money and passport, and I only had my book and a few bucks left, so it wasn't as if we needed to check for items we'd left behind.

At 2:45, we walked through the hotel doors and headed across the street toward the park. Teensy rode slumped over in the wheelchair, dressed like a babushka, with dark pancake makeup covering her hands and face and a shawl draped over her head and shoulders in folds. She'd tucked her chin into her chest as if she'd nodded off, but I knew she didn't want anyone to see the deep purple bruises that had left her with raccoon eyes, or her split lip and swollen jaw. I felt confident about the disguise. So many people ignore the elderly. But I figured this made good cover for her—like a disabled person nobody wanted to be caught staring at, or a mentally challenged person made invisible by the attitudes of the people around them.

Children who should've been in school dashed across the grass, barefoot and in tatters, and up to no good with their sticky fingers and panhandling ways. Young lovers and older couples strolled hand-in-hand past the fountains, while others hung out beneath the huge palm trees. Many wore T-shirts with my picture silk-screened onto the front. Some of the girls we'd rescued bartered for more, shrugging into the tees right next to the vendor carts. Others carried theirs around in recycled plastic bags with various logos on the sacks.

At first, we milled about in pairs, as was the plan, sticking close enough to each other to be able to band together in an emergency, but not so close as to call unwanted attention to ourselves as tourists. Because of Amanda's dark skin, I let her push Teensy's wheelchair in the event someone recognized me, even with my dark hairpiece. If I had to flee, or took a bullet, I didn't want to endanger my sister any more than necessary.

Amanda bought the girls popsicles and frozen fruit bars from those little ice cream carts with *Helados* stenciled on the sides of the cooler; the kind with three wheels, jingling bells and a push bar that could be easily steered through the park. I declined, and warned Teensy not to eat one either. With no way to tell whether they used purified water to make the frozen treats, the last thing I needed was to invite another gastrointestinal explosion. I'd had my fill of that.

There were also drink peddlers on tricycle carts hawking flavored sugar water in bright colors, the kind that comes in glass bottles with a spout on them that you pour over shaved ice to make snow cones. Didn't need that, either. When I got home to the USA—if I made it home to the USA—I was going to buy a 12-pack of Diet Dr Pepper and ice it down in a cooler. Then I planned to suck down as many in a row as I could hold without making myself sick.

T-shirt vendors popped up every so often like dandelions at

the botanical gardens. *"¡Viva Danny Prescott!"* tees were selling like hotcakes. I admit it—I wanted to take a stack of them back to my recovering sorority sisters and the rest of my TCU mafia. When I told Amanda, she shot me a look hot enough to wither shrink-wrap. But so many people in the park had them on that I couldn't afford to stand out by not having extras.

I selected one from the small sizes in an eye-pleasing shade of robin's egg blue, and slipped it over my shirt. Then I put on one in lilac. Then I chose two from the medium stack, one in a shade of yellow and one in green, and layered them over the others. That took care of my three best friends. Plus, I looked like everybody else strolling through the park. Birds erupted from the ground in a flap of wings so intense that my ears shivered. I barely had time to pocket the change when I heard the *whuppa-whuppa-whuppa* of rotor blades overhead. Shielding my eyes against the afternoon sun, I looked skyward.

Chills swarmed over my body. I gave my sister a long, hard look. With her chin tucked into her chest, she'd drifted off to sleep like an old lady. The other girls stopped eating their frozen treats in mid-bite. I hurried to my sister's side and shook her by the shoulder. Confusion swam in her eyes. Then she smiled through swollen lips.

"It's almost over," I reassured her. But I had a bad feeling and it knotted my stomach. "Teensy, if I don't get to ride with you—"

"Don't say that."

"—you'll go on ahead. Chopper Deke will take care of you."

"I don't understand. Why wouldn't you be able to come . . ." The rest of her words were drowned out by the increasing noise of the helicopter.

The chopper didn't fly directly across the border like the people coming in at the border crossings. It angled in from the east, from the Mexico side.

My heart thundered. For a moment, my legs moved like my shoes had been weighted with lead. The girls were moving toward the aircraft while the rotor-wash swirling around us blew back our hair, clothes and facial skin. I looked around for signs of police or military, then pushed my sister toward the middle of the park.

Chopper Deke spotted us. He quickly stopped in mid-air before flying the chopper backward approximately fifty feet. Grass flattened around the helicopter. While hovering, the bird did a pirouette, mid-air, spinning on its axis in a way that allowed our pilot to see 360 degrees as he followed a straight path to the ground.

He had another person with him in the front passenger seat.

Gus Quintanilla.

An emblem of an upside-down, equilateral triangle with the flat surface on top and the tip pointing toward the ground had been duct-taped to the side of the chopper. Think: colors of the Mexican flag, with a green triangle superimposed over a larger white triangle, superimposed over an even larger red triangle. Suddenly, Chopper Deke's question about whether I knew what the Mexican President's helicopter looked like made perfect sense. I assumed this was the VIP emblem of the Fuerza Aérea Mexicana—the Mexican Air Force. I also imagined some general in Mexico City scratching his head as the calls poured in wanting to know why *El Presidente* just landed in the middle of Chamizal Park.

Clearly, this Vietnam veteran possessed a high level of skill to keep that machine from ending up on the ground like a wounded or dead bird. Despite the heavy crosswind, he held that chopper steady.

I broke into a dead run, pushing Teensy's wheelchair toward the aircraft.

The bird touched down; Quintanilla jumped out. He loaded my sister into the front passenger seat. Tiffany climbed in on top of her, while the rest of the girls hustled into the back.

"You have a mole in your operation," I shouted over the percussion thump of rotor blades. "The man who stayed to guard us tried to sell us into white slavery. And I think he hurt Mr. Cordova." He needed to know about events at the slaughterhouse, but it'd have to wait.

I saw an advancing blur out of the corner of my eye.

My breath caught in my throat.

Instantly, I felt a brick of ice where my heart should've been. A Humvee at the far end of the park jumped the curb and roared up the promenade with soldiers in camouflage holding AK-47s.

The last girl was halfway inside. There was no more room for Amanda and me, and there was no time left for Chopper Deke to hover.

"See you on the other side," I yelled to my sister. Then I shouted, "Go, go, go," and grabbed Amanda's hand and backed away.

Tension lined Chopper Deke's face. Then he saluted me. On some level I figured he was trying to tell me I'd done a selfless act.

I, myself, thought I'd lost my mind.

The rotors spun, producing lift as they cut the air. The aircraft rose vertically. As the spinning rotors tilted, the bird swung away. It moved laterally, made a sharp turn, and changed altitude. Its prop wash battered the palm fronds, and then it was gone.

Tears streamed down my cheeks. My stomach knotted with the notion that I'd rot in this effing place.

We'd passed the margin for error, and made a run for the crowd. We needed to assimilate into the group of people wearing Danny Prescott tees, and drop off the radar of the Mexican *federales*. I had no idea where Quintanilla went. Once we started running, I didn't look back. Neither did Amanda. Absorbed by the throng of stunned bystanders, we sprinted toward the grid-lock of rubberneckers who'd stopped their vehicles in the middle of the street, hoping for a glimpse of *El Presidente*. Blend-ing into the crowd, Amanda and I threaded our way through the cars, fanning away fumes from belching exhaust.

We flung ourselves through a side door to our hotel, which put us in the middle of a courtyard. After passing the ornamental iron gates, we entered the lobby, picked up a spare key and caught the elevator up to our third-floor room overlooking the park. As the door slammed shut behind us, Amanda toggled the bolt and shoved a chair under the knob.

My chest burned from oxygen deprivation. I collapsed onto the bed and listened to the thundering in my chest.

This time, I cried myself out.

Mexico sucks.

There is no remedy.

CHAPTER THIRTY-SIX

"You okay?" Amanda asked without turning my way. She had the curtain pulled back a smidge and was watching the goings-on out on the street.

I didn't bother to answer. The thought of the jack-booted Mexican military storming up the stairs, yanking me out of this room and depositing me in a Mexican prison where I'd spend the rest of my natural life behind thick iron bars, evacuating my bladder into an open sewer pipe, was enough to put me into a catatonic state.

"They're rousting people wearing Danny Prescott T-shirts," she deadpanned. "I take it back. You were smart to get several."

For no good reason, I wrangled out of the cheaply made tees, not to mention shameless capital venture of some enterprising manufacturer exploiting my picture without my consent. The colors were nice, but like everything else about this rotten place, they'd probably fade out with the first washing. I tossed aside what had become just another fashion reminder that I'd entered a third-world country with no way out.

I started to think in terms of taking Quintanilla's advice—run for the border.

And where was Quintanilla? It wasn't like the big man could slip into a "Danny Prescott" T-shirt and move undetected through the park.

"Do you think Gus is dead?" I asked dully.

"He's like a cat. He's got nine lives."

I took a deep breath and slowly let it out. "I want to make a run for it." My tongue felt thick against my mouth. My eyes traveled up to the ceiling and back down again. I settled my gaze on a really bad canvas of revolutionaries with bullet straps crisscrossing the front of simple white clothing. This large painting covered a quarter of the wall—swarthy Mexicans with beards, wearing ponchos and sombreros—and was done in muted turquoise and salmon that actually complemented the pale mustard-colored stucco troweled onto the walls. "I want to throw the last of my money into the air and let it rain down on the street, and hope people rush to pick it up. That's when I'll crash the crossing. I don't care if I'm arrested. At least there's a thing called due process. At least I'll have rights. Have I told you lately how much I hate this place?"

Amanda smiled. "I'm off to take a shower. Not that you've taken my advice since we got here, but don't leave while I'm in here tidying up. I'll think of something. And stay away from the window."

"Why?" I wasn't going to check out what was happening outside, but I had to ask.

"Remember that guy who came into the slaughterhouse to talk to our guard?"

"What about him?"

"I saw him out there. He's in uniform, and he has a gun."

I closed my eyes. Could anything else happen? My lids immediately snapped open. I fanned the air in front of my face, and even did a little voodoo finger wiggle on the off chance it'd zap that thought right out of the universe. I didn't need any more trouble. Nosirree Bob.

I flopped back onto a pillow, then abruptly reconsidered. God only knew what sort of *invisible-to-the-naked-eye-without-phosphorescing-liquid-and-a-UV-light* sort of nasty, germy residue covered this bedspread. I yanked it away, and then pulled back the top sheet scanning for signs of bedbugs or "curlies" left by the last inhabitant of this room. The linens looked surprisingly clean. I sat on the mattress and fell back against the pillow.

Momentarily, I closed my eyes and concentrated on listening to the street noises filtering up through the windows.

I wanted a shower, too, and I was hungry. I also didn't want to leave our room, and fleetingly wondered if they had room service, and whether they could send up a houseboy ferrying a tray full of tacos.

Amanda came out of the shower wrapped in a towel, naked from the waist up. Despite the fact that she had no breasts, she still looked androgynous enough to pass for either sex.

She said, "I have an idea. Remember when you asked me if I thought Quintanilla was dead, and I said he was like a cat, that he had nine lives?"

I had no idea where this was going, nor did I care. This gawd-awful place reminded me of those topiary mazes you couldn't find your way out of. I just wanted to go home. I wanted to see Bruckman, and to find out which hospital my daddy was in so I could crack a chair over Nerissa's head.

Amanda was talking. Whatever she'd said, I missed it. "What? I'm sorry. I have a tendency to drift in and out when you're talking." This time I smiled when I said it.

"Pay attention, diva. I said that my previous cat comment made me think of a way out of here."

"How so?"

"My cousin has a friend down here with a big-ass yellow cat. And even though I haven't worked out all the details, that's how we'll escape." And then, "By the way, are you hungry? I'm starving."

CHAPTER THIRTY-SEVEN

I was thinking Amanda had lost her mind.

How in God's name could her cousin's friend's big-ass yellow cat get us out of this mess?

"I'm ordering room service, diva." She mulled over the paper menu on the night table next to the bed. "Hey—listen to this: they have *empanadas, chilaquiles* and *chorizo.*"

What I heard was: blah, blah and blah. I arched an eyebrow.

"*Empanadas* are those little fried pies with fruit or pumpkin in them. They have other pastries, too. *Chilaquiles* are those green chili peppers they cut up on top of chicken and eggs and cheese. Good stuff. By the way, you're looking a little green around the gills. You sure you're okay?"

"I'm not going to be okay until I'm home in my own bed, with my Italian sheets and my very own cell phone."

"Speaking of, never mind about the room service. I'll go downstairs and order it myself. I need to use the phone to call my cousin. So, you want some *chorizo*—Mexican sausage?"

"Bring me chips and *queso.* Or something else that's hard to screw up. Or that won't give me food poisoning."

After Amanda walked out, a frightening thought flashed into mind—that an intruder might manage to breach our little homemade security system while I showered. Images of crazy hotelkeepers and sharp knives kept me fully clothed until Amanda returned a half hour later.

Okay, I admit it. She had me worried and my voice might've

come out a bit strident when I yelled, "Where have you been?"

"Running through the lobby naked, with your panties on my head, singing 'I Feel Pretty.' " She held out a grease-stained sack. "You owe me for the food, diva."

I owed her more than that and we both knew it. "Run a tab. Where's my snack?"

"You're eating chips and guacamole, and I brought beef and bean burritos. You're looking kind of puny, so I brought you two."

Peeling back the paper wrapper on the first burrito, I inspected it for foreign objects and other questionable substances that didn't come standard in a beef and bean burrito. This one had white cheese. I let it slide. I'm an equal opportunity cheese aficionado, all colors welcome. Well, maybe not green . . . or black. That's just disgusting.

And it had *salsa* on it—or *tomatillo* sauce—or Satan's drool. The chef who put this together used the hottest peppers in the world to season it. One bite and flames shot out of my eyes. No kidding. But hey—good news—it cauterized the stomach ulcer I'd been developing ever since I set foot in this country, so I figured I could quit sucking down Maalox.

Between bites, I quizzed her. "What'd your cousin say?"

"Man of few words."

"Is he calling his friend?"

"Already did."

"Is he going to help us get out of here?"

"Already working on it."

"You're being pretty cavalier about it."

She lifted one shoulder in a noncommittal shrug.

My eyes narrowed into slits. "How come you're so calm?"

She chuckled. "I have my passport."

I licked my fingers like a field hand—a no-no for ladies of The Rubanbleu—but Amanda didn't seem to notice. She was sitting on the bed, working her way through a stack of soft chorizo tacos like a log through a wood chipper.

Finally stuffed, I wanted every niggling detail.

"Your time would be better spent cleaning up, or you're not going to like your mug shot when they arrest you for border jumping."

Made sense.

I didn't want her to leave me in the room alone, but I didn't want to tell her not to go anywhere, either. I got an unwelcome sensation that came from anticipating the many ways she could scare me. It'd be better not to put ideas into her head.

I checked the time on the clock by the bed, and saw that it was already five o'clock. I wanted desperately to go back downstairs, pay the cow at the desk another ten dollars American money, and call Chopper Deke's cell phone. But Amanda said we were leaving in one hour, and that I'd better be ready to walk out the door.

Hot water with a slightly fishy smell ran over my head and body. For several minutes, I let it pour over me, washing away my troubles and whisking them down the drain. Then the water turned tepid, and I wrenched the faucet off before it went cold.

A small space heater warmed the bathroom, and I stood in front of it to towel-dry my hair. Chagrined about having to re-dress in the same ripe-smelling clothes, I stuffed my blonde hair beneath the brown wig. By the time I'd finished preening, we'd run out of time.

"Please tell me what to expect."

"The less said, the better."

"Where are we going?" It was a stupid question; we were going to a border crossing, but which one? And was her cousin's friend bringing his big-ass yellow cat? "Amanda, stop." I grabbed her wrist as she opened the door. "You have to tell me the plan. I need to be in on the plan."

"No," she said, "you don't. Would you please, for once, just trust me? You don't have to think about this. When the time comes, you just have to do it."

My stomach sank. "Please tell me we're not going on an overnight train trip complete with livestock and overflowing toilets . . ."

"Girlfriend, relax. We're not taking the train."

Outside the hotel, the winds whipped our faces, stirring up pollen and igniting my fear. I looked at the purple Texas sky, dotted with stars, and sensed infinite possibilities in the full, luminescent moon.

"Are we taking a cab? Because I really don't think it's a smart idea to get anywhere near the queue." I kept thinking about the customs officer who'd come into that nasty room at the slaughterhouse to have a word with our guard. Let me tell you, I didn't want to go near his post.

"There he is," Amanda said, pointing across the street to an old beat-up truck driven by a young boy who didn't look old enough to have a license. "Come on."

"Wait—who's that?"

"My cousin's friend's son."

From my place on the sidewalk, I memorized his face. "You know him?"

"No, we've never formally met."

"Listen up. There's no damned way I'm getting into a truck with somebody I don't know."

"Is that your final answer?" Amanda said, looking a bit puckish, her mouth pinched.

I debated . . . no, couldn't happen. "Yes."

"Then we'll walk," she said tightly. "At night. In the dark. By ourselves."

CHAPTER THIRTY-EIGHT

Apparently, Amanda's cousin's friend's son had been told not to leave without us, so he rolled along next to us as we walked past the park.

"How much farther?" I asked, knowing the distant firecrackers that just went off weren't fireworks at all.

Amanda had accusation written all over her face. I pretty much just stared.

We had no business out on the street now that the sun had set, and I was smart enough to understand my miscalculation. Wait—let me rephrase—we had no business out on the street whatsoever. Period.

"Do you have the . . . you know?" I formed my hand into a gun.

She nodded.

"Then I'll ride along. But you have to sit next to him."

Approximately two bumpy miles later, he cut the headlights. We rolled the length of a football field by the light of the silvery moon. Without applying the brake, he shifted into neutral gear and let the pickup coast along until it eventually slowed enough for him to yank up the emergency brake without putting us through the windshield.

He'd let us out near the Rio Bravo.

"Now what?" I didn't like the way the shadows moved in this desolate area.

"We wait for the big-ass yellow cat."

The boy who'd brought us here stood by the passenger door, propped against the pickup with his arms braced across his chest. I sensed that we made him uncomfortable, and gave him a half-smile. He didn't ask to be here and I hadn't acted very nice since I'd come to mistrust just about everyone in this town. If whatever was about to happen worked, I'd be eternally grateful to him and his father for helping to get us out of here.

So was this a spot where illegals crossed the "tortilla curtain"? I didn't see how. The fence had to be at least twenty feet high. You couldn't climb it or pole-vault over it. Couldn't cut a hole in it without a couple of hours and a blowtorch, and by that time, the surveillance cameras mounted on the distant, barely-visible towers would've made it a cakewalk to apprehend anyone from the U.S. side of the border. Even now, it concerned me that night cameras might be pointed at us, tracking our every move.

Good news, though—Border Patrol hadn't cruised by.

A chill rippled through my extremities. I wondered if we'd tripped those seismic sensors that were supposed to be sophisticated enough to tell whether an animal or human had triggered them. We'd been out here—what, thirty minutes?—skulking around, honing in on the creepy sounds of nightfall with the intensity of a police canine.

I remembered one of the few pieces of advice Amanda gave me on the ride out here—if I saw headlights or flashlights on the U.S. side of the fence, I was to hit the deck, face down in the dirt, lay perfectly still no matter what disgusting reptile or amphibian moved past me, and not utter a sound.

The lemonade to be made from the bucket of lemons I'd been handed in this latest ordeal was that the river in this particular location was narrow and shallow.

Gunfire erupted in the distance. The sound carried over the music leaking out of various nightclubs and filtered up into the night. I wondered again where my sister was, and whether she and Tiffany and the other girls were safe.

And I wondered about Daddy. About whether Nerissa'd managed to kill him off like she'd done my mother. I still had *The Ladies' Guide to Homicide* with me, and I wondered whether I'd come across a chapter about luring your enemy into a third-world country, or other areas where travel advisories warned against tourism.

Across the city, sirens bleated. Then they fell silent, and the swishing of traffic took over. A low, steady rumble eclipsed the traffic noises. I looked the length of the fence, expecting to see Border Patrol descending upon us, but saw no headlights.

What the hell was that sound?

The boy who'd driven us out here must've heard it, too. He reacted to the commotion by removing several long, wood planks from the bed of the pickup and carrying them to the water. He placed one end on dry land, and slowly lowered the opposite end across the stream. It didn't reach the other side, so he slid out the second board and walked halfway across the first one before lowering it in such a way that they met in the middle. A quick image of chivalry in medieval times popped into mind, when a man would remove his cape with a flourish and cover a puddle for a lady to walk across.

Now we could cross the water without getting muddy. But what of it? Once we got to the opposite bank, we still couldn't penetrate that fence.

The long, pulsing, clicking, sputtering sound of metal stress grew louder. The chugging, clinking, maneuvering noise had an odd cadence that was beyond my realm of experience. The closest comparison buried deep within my memory bank was the sound of a cement truck idling.

No, that wasn't it.

Beyond my field of vision, heavy metal blades scraped against concrete, creaking and grinding, and sometimes even purring as the loud noise closed in on us.

My mind hearkened back to similar noises made by heavy military tanks on old WWII reels, designed to stretch and crawl over hostile terrain by moving along metal tracks.

Or an excavator stirring up a racket.

My heart pounded.

Yes! The rattling, clattering din came from a heavy construction vehicle as it crawled along its metal tracks.

I stared into the dark abyss until my eyes almost dried out. In the distance, an apparition rose from the shadows and I could make out the form of construction equipment.

"There it is," Amanda whispered, "my cousin's friend's big-ass yellow cat."

Then she explained that the big yellow cat was a Caterpillar crawler, a self-propelled crane that moved on caterpillar treads. As it closed in on us, I could see it had a steel boom mounted on a platform. Because of the hydraulic mechanism, I assumed that this was a telescoping boom that could extend the crane to different working heights.

In this particular case, the crawler had a demolition ball attached.

Bewildered, I felt an unpleasant lurch in my stomach. "He's going to bash a hole in the fence?"

My lungs instantly tightened. I'd already encountered the trifecta of trouble back at the police department. That jailhouse sewer pipe sprang to mind again, and I couldn't catch my breath. If this turned out to be my fate, I'd have to taunt the Mexican officials until they put me in front of a firing squad.

"He can lift us over the fence," Amanda said, interrupting the gloom. "Why're you looking at me like that? It's a good idea."

"Have you lost your mind?"

"Think about it. How else do we cross without calling attention to ourselves?"

"I'm reconsidering our options," I said, trying to keep the thickening dismay out of my voice. "I think the inner tube in the river's definitely the way to go."

"No, no, no. Look—what we do is straddle the wrecking ball. The telescoping crane will lift us over the fence and lower us to the other side."

This is not happening.

But what *was* undeniably happening were two sets of emergency lights in the distance, bearing down on us from the Mexico side.

CHAPTER THIRTY-NINE

"I'm not going to jail. Not a Mexican jail." No need to ask who said that.

Amanda shouted in Spanish. A flurry of activity ensued as the father worked the hydraulics and the son steadied the wrecking ball.

"Ladies first." Amanda gestured for me to climb on.

"No, you first." I didn't like this idea at all, considering my paranoia instantly dredged up an ugly visual of a snapping cable, followed by me plummeting twenty feet to the ground, crushed by the ball.

Amanda straddled the big iron ball.

Red and blue lights flashed down the roadway. They—whoever they were—closed in on us.

I handed Amanda *The Ladies' Guide to Homicide* while I hiked up my grungy skirt and straddled the demolition ball. Then I retrieved the book and shoved it into my waistband. Amanda and I sat face-to-face as the crane shrieked and the pulley lifted us off the ground.

Headlights from the U.S. side closed the gap. We were seven feet . . . ten feet . . . fifteen feet in the air as Border Patrol vehicles bore down on us.

"The gun," I yelled. "Get rid of the gun."

We hovered in the air, maybe as high as twenty-five feet before the crane swung us toward the top of the fence. Amanda pulled out the gun and yelled something at the boy. Then she ejected the magazine. It dropped to the ground as we swung over the fence. Then she did an over-the-shoulder slow pitch, and the gun sailed back over onto the Mexican side.

The wrecking ball drifted to the ground with featherlike precision. We disentangled ourselves and jumped off. As soon as our feet touched the ground, it seemed to float back up into the air and over onto the Mexican side of the fence like a big black balloon.

"I'm an American," I screamed. "I'm American." Then I laughed so hard my face hurt, certain that these Border Patrol agents roaring up would think the Mexican government had found a way to rid themselves of their criminally insane, like the Mariel boat people from Cuba during the Carter administration.

Suddenly, the beacon from a television camcorder spotlighted me. Then I heard the *whuppa, whuppa, whuppa* of rotor blades overhead and the granddaddy of all spotlights engulfed Amanda and me. It lit up the satellite news-gathering truck behind the photographer that was beaming the event up to a satellite and back to the metroplex.

Son-of-a-gun.

J. Gordon Pfeiffer, my boss and the station manager at WBFD, really had sent a TV crew out to cover Teensy's and my story.

Border Patrol agents in green uniforms ran toward us, guns drawn. The ghost rings of their flashlights spotlighted our hands and faces. They shouted contradictory commands at us from all angles and directions, and in all intonations, none of them very nice: *"¡Acuestense!"* or *"¡A sus rodillas!"* or *"¡Boca abajo!"* and even *"¡Sientense!"* Which I think meant "lie down" and "on your knees" and "face down" and "sit down," because that's what Amanda did, and not necessarily in that order. And by "guns drawn," I meant M-4s, service weapons, Remington shotguns, tasers and FN 303s—projectile launchers—which may look like paintball guns on steroids, but I didn't want any part of it.

I did, however, recognize the *"¡Manos arriba!"* command from every low-budget western I'd ever seen. My hands shot straight up in surrender.

"I'm an American," I shouted over the din. "I'm Dainty Prescott from Fort Worth, Texas." While I had my hands raised, I yanked off the brown wig and let it drop to the ground, exposing my pale blonde hair, made incandescent as beacons of light hit it.

Then I gave Amanda a sidelong glance. "Amanda's from El Paso." My eyes thinned into slits. I asked the million-dollar question of my sexually ambiguous friend. "Really, who the hell *are* you?"

She gave me one of her gap-toothed grins along with a coy little chin duck.

Then, before she could answer, I remembered this would appear across the metroplex in HD. With my book in one hand, I re-fluffed my hair as best I could, but one of the Border Patrol agents had holstered his weapon and was ratcheting handcuffs onto my wrists

Not that I cared.

I'd made it home.

American born, American made, and proud of it.

I looked past the glare of the spotlight and saw Jim Bruckman.

My eyes welled. I felt a sharp prickle in my nose.

I slipped out of the agent's grasp—I'm mostly obedient, so he wasn't expecting it—and broke into a dead run. And that's how they captured it on camera for "Breaking News" back home in the metroplex. So if my blue-haired grandmother happened to be watching, she saw Bruckman hug me tight, pick me up and twirl me around like we were part of a figure-skating pair. Then he slid out of his jacket and whirled it across my shoulders. And as for Stacey and those other women who kept calling Bruckman's phone, well, if they were watching WBFD-TV that night, they got to witness the most mad, passionate kiss ever.

Very un-Rubanbleu.

Again, not that I cared.

CHAPTER FORTY

Instead of taking me to "port," the port-of-entry at the bridge where they processed illegal aliens before returning them to Mexico, Border Patrol agents drove me to one of their substations.

Fine by me. The farther away from that spiraling vortex of misery and stink, the better.

In a small interrogation room, seated across the table from the agent who'd handcuffed me and another Border Patrol officer, I laid out my story like a bad hand of Spades. I told them how I got to Mexico by way of El Paso, and broke down the chronology of events. When I mentioned Gus Quintanilla, the agents exchanged awkward looks and one left the room.

By the time I wrapped up the facts—I omitted the part about dragging Chopper Deke into the drama, and finding my sister—the officer who'd excused himself returned with several important looking documents. The one I'd been telling my story to pushed back from the table, and the man with the documents switched places with him.

I did a subtle lean to make out the paperwork. One of the documents looked amazingly like a copy of a birth certificate.

This agent wanted to know where I was born, my parents' names, my date of birth and the name of the hospital where I was born. Then he asked where I went to high school, and if I'd attended college—I swear he had a copy of my transcript, and a high school picture from my cheerleader days—and he wanted to know how I knew Jim Bruckman. With a heavy eye roll, I told them how I'd run a red light in Fort Worth and he pulled me over on a traffic stop. At no time did the agent show me the documents. Each time I leaned in for a closer look, he'd reposition them so I couldn't see where he was getting his information.

The door swung open. Bigger than life, Gus Quintanilla strode into the room. He tipped his hat before turning his back to me, and proceeded to carry on a long, drawn-out conversation with the agents that had nothing to do with me being here. For all they cared, I could've been elevator music.

Then Gus turned my way. "Dainty, Dainty, Dainty. You're a mess. Ready to go?"

I looked up expectantly. "What happened to Mr. Richter?"

He shot me a wicked look, and I froze.

The Border Patrol agent holding what I assumed to be documents that verified my history gently chastised me. "Next time, you need to take better care of your passport—"

Won't be a "next time."

"—and the rest of your identification. You can go, Miss Prescott."

Instead of taking me directly before a magistrate, the agents gave me shoulder shrugs of the *No-harm-no-foul* variety. I scraped my chair against the floor, pushing back from the table.

"There are tons of reporters outside," Quintanilla warned, "so you'll probably want to clean up before you talk to them. The ladies' room is around the corner." He pointed the way to the corridor bathroom, and I struck out in that direction.

Inside the restroom, I looked in the mirror. My reflection appeared as diaphanous and spectral as a ghost. I washed my face and blotted it dry with a paper towel. Then I wet my "wig" hair in an attempt to take out the creases, and tried to give my pathetic locks some lift by fluffing them under the hand dryer.

Just when I was ready to speak to the media, I changed my mind and set out to find Bruckman.

I never got a chance to say good-bye to Amanda before I left the CBP substation. Border Patrol agents were still grilling her when Bruckman and I sneaked out a side door with the help of the agent who arrested me. The CBP officer said Amanda would be there a while. It seemed the El Paso police were on their way over to interview her as a person of interest in a stolen dog case.

Taking the bichon frise from that ratty house in one of El Paso's colonias the first day we met suddenly made perfect sense. Amanda didn't steal that dog, she rescued it—much the same way she'd rescued the American girls and me. Her methods may have been unorthodox, but she did the right thing. I felt a twist of affection for her as I gave a backward glance at the closed door to the interrogation room.

The CBP agent who arrested me gave us a ride to a real five-star hotel, where, while Bruckman took a shower, I fell into bed without even bothering to inspect the bed linens.

CHAPTER FORTY-ONE

The following morning, I wandered next door to a boutique wearing my *¡Viva Danny Prescott!* T-shirt, my pitiful threadbare skirt and those ratty sneakers that helped save my life, and tried on a couple of skirts and cashmere sweaters. Bruckman had given me cash, but when I tried to check out, I came up short for the pieces I wanted. The lady at the cash register, who also happened to be the shop owner, must've been following the news and recognized me. She offered me the extra pieces, gratis, in exchange for a photo.

I agreed. I slipped back into the dressing room, shrugged into my new ensemble and allowed her assistant to take our picture together. I handed my old clothes over the counter and asked her to put them in her trash basket. I watched as she tossed them, but when I left the store, I glimpsed her fishing out the T-shirt. She'd probably make a tidy profit listing it on eBay.

I didn't have time to buy shoes, but the hotel had a little gift shop that had ballerina-type house slippers, so I bought them with Bruckman's cash. All in all, I pronounced myself present-able. Bruckman called me a living doll.

At first, Jim seemed pretty flamed out that I'd left his cell phone behind, but when Gus showed up at our hotel to give us a ride to the airport, he had my purse with Bruckman's cell phone in it. I traded his phone for mine, then scrolled down my list of numbers and called my grandmother while we waited to board our plane. Gran didn't answer, so I called Teensy's phone number. A swarthy-voiced Mexican answered and I immediately hung up. Then I called Daddy's house. Again, no answer. I no longer had Deke's phone number—it was buried in Bruckman's dead cell phone. When I called the TV station to get it, Rochelle practically sung out one of her fake greetings, then put me on hold without bothering to find out what I wanted, and left me orbiting in multiple-personality hell until I gave up and disconnected.

Seriously, I wondered if she had trouble filling out all of her nametags when Mr. Pfeiffer sent her to conferences.

But on some level, having to deal with Rochelle suggested that things were returning to normal for me. Which is by no means my way of saying Rochelle is normal. That woman's anything but.

The actual flight home took all of an hour and a half, but I slept through it with my head nestled against Bruckman's shoulder. As soon as we landed, I asked him to drive me over to WBFD since we weren't all that far away. I'd received no reports on Chopper Deke or my sister, and I was beside myself. If I went to the TV station, I'd get answers. If he hadn't returned, well, I'd be a mess until I learned my sister'd made it home safely.

Once we were back in the metroplex, rolling down the freeway, my mind cast back to Amanda. My eyes welled. I blinked back tears.

"What's wrong, Dainty?"

"I never realized the depths of Amanda's bravery until just now," I said, waxing nostalgic.

"Brave? Let me tell you how close you came to getting killed. Border Patrol agents told me that lunatic had a million-dollar life insurance with a double-indemnity clause. That screwball you call Amanda took your job planning to get killed so the kids would have money to live on for the rest of their lives."

My mouth gaped.

"Yeah," Bruckman chuckled without humor. "It came out in the interview." Between flashes of anger, he related what he'd gleaned from the CBP. "Amanda Vásquez, or whatever in the hell that pygmy's real name is, isn't even a cop, much less a police lieutenant. The only ties that asshole has to law enforcement comes from the number of arrests you can count on the criminal history sheet. 'Amanda Vásquez'—" he let go of the steering wheel long enough to put air quotes around the name "—just got released from jail that morning on a prostitution charge, and overheard you telling the watch commander you needed an interpreter to take you across the border. That scumbag heard just enough of the conversation to take advantage of you."

Humiliation crept over me. What a fool I'd been.

At WBFD, I asked Bruckman to wait in the car. I had no idea whether Deke was there, but I had visions of Bruckman coldcocking the guy who med-evac'd my sister if he got fresh with me.

When I walked into the foyer, one of the TV monitors mounted at various intervals near the ceiling flashed the weather. The station's weather girl, Misty Knight, stood in front of the chroma key wall—what people in the industry called the "green screen"—pointing out the rain showers showing up on Doppler radar.

Rochelle had her finger hooked into her cowl-neck, periwinkle-blue cashmere sweater and was airing out her cleavage with a tiny hand-held fan. When she saw me, she discarded the fan, abandoned the bleating telephone, and walked over with her long legs straining against the hem of her black leather pencil skirt. She gave me one of her trademark "seal hugs," the kind where you barely embrace and then use your hands like flippers to pat the other person's shoulders.

"Aw, what the hell? Glad you're back, kid," she said, and hugged me like there was no tomorrow.

Rochelle's a menopausal nut job.

Even though I hate mixing business with revulsion, I forced myself. "Is Chopper Deke here?"

"I'll get him for you."

So he is here. Thank God. Then that must mean my sister's safe.

Rochelle angled over to her desk, stabbed out an extension on the telephone key pad, picked up a coffee cup and tilted it to her lips. "There's someone here to see you," she said, and quickly put all of the unlit phone lines on hold.

As Rochelle sat back in her chair looking like she was about to enjoy the greatest show on earth, tension drained from my body.

My boss and the station manager of this media zoo, J. Gordon Pfeiffer, bolted from his office like a bull out of a chute. He wore a rumpled suit in an undesirable shade of brown. I wondered if this new and disturbing look meant he'd spent another night on the cowhide sofa in his office until the temporary restraining order for his divorce was in place; or if the ball-busting female attorney he'd recently hired managed to remove his cheating wife from their impressive home, and he just didn't care how he looked.

"Prescott." A grin gashed his face. "You nearly gave me a heart attack." Then he threw his bearish arms around me, temporarily suffocating me with a hug.

"That was nice of you to send a crew out." I wondered what I'd have to do to convince him to stop airing last night's footage. We'd be moving into sweeps month again soon and I didn't want viewers seeing me at my worst.

"Get back to work. You've got interviews scheduled. Aspen Wicklow's putting together a piece about your ordeal for sweeps, and you're the interviewee. Man, you looked like hell warmed over last night. But I guess I don't have to tell you that. You might want to look your best from here on out when the camera's on you. Getcha something in a bright blue, and stop by wardrobe-and-makeup. Have them put some color on your cheeks. You look like shit."

"Thanks for everything." *But especially for reminding me how I look.* "I'll be here tomorrow. I've got some rat-killing to do."

"And call your grandmother," he said, making a beeline for the front door. "The old bird's worried about you. And tell her to stop calling here. This is a business."

What a bastard.

I couldn't help it. I cracked a smile.

I adored my boss.

I still had no idea what I'd say to Chopper Deke, but as I rehearsed a little speech in my head, he sauntered out of the studio door and moved toward me in his pilot's swagger, reeking of cigarette smoke. We stood face-to-face, making quiet assessments, with Chopper Deke's eerie blue eyes taking an unauthorized tour of my body and me trying to figure out how to say thank you without the mushiness.

Nearby, Rochelle paused and considered an empty coffee cup. Clearly, she had no intention of giving us any privacy, and truly, I figured it'd be safer if she stuck around.

"I came to say thank you, and to pay you back for helping me and my sister." The real meaning of this conversation opener distilled down to: *What's it going to take to zero out my debt?* "So what do I owe you?"

I love my sister, I'll do anything for my sister, this man saved my sister . . .

For a long, uncomfortable moment, Deke looked up at the ceiling and pretended to meditate on that thought. Then his eyes fixed on mine in that spooky ringed gaze, and he punctuated his decision with a head nod.

"Show me your tits."

Ew.

That called for an emphatic *No.*

"Then let me touch 'em through your clothes. Ten seconds. You can time it: one-Mississippi, two-Mississippi, three-Mississippi . . ." He lifted his hands like he was about to measure cantaloupes.

"No."

"Give me your panties." His nostrils flared "I'll bet you wear a thong, don't you? You don't have a panty line. Give 'em to me."

A disgusting visual of him threading my underwear up the legs of a plastic blow-up doll popped into mind. Then, still locked in the most tepid part of my wild imagination, I saw him wearing them over his head while strutting around the station, bragging that I'd performed sexual favors for him.

I love my sister, but . . . Big headshake and a resounding *hell no.*

Out of the corner of my eye, I saw Rochelle yukking it up. Her muted laugh sounded like a submachine gun with a silencer.

The lobby acoustics echoed with Chopper Deke's rakish chortle. "Then let me cup my hands around those magnificent buns of steel." His eyelids fell to half-mast. He sucked air between his teeth as if he were already doing it. "Just a quick squeeze. One squeeze on each side. Promise."

Again, *No.*

"Fine. I'll take a thousand dollars to cover the gas."

I sucked air.

Go on, take it. It's a fair deal. I'm getting out cheap; after all, I owe him so much more.

"I don't have it, but I can get it. It may take some time, but I'll start working on it right away."

"Not interested in a payout. What else you got?"

Absolutely nothing.

"How 'bout this: I'll settle for a one-minute kiss. With tongue."

Ew.

I debated. *Uh, not gonna happen.*

I discerned a blur of movement in my peripheral vision. When I turned to look, Rochelle vehemently head-bobbed while tapping a manicured fingernail to her watch crystal.

"I'll time it," she mouthed without sound.

I looked Deke straight in the eye. "That'll even the score?"

"Even-Steven."

Ew, ew, ew.

I must love my sister.

She's safe now, and he's the one who saved her.

I really do owe him.

Ever the instigator, Rochelle put in her two cents' worth. "Bet he kisses like a stroke victim."

I waited for the trap door to hell to spring open and swallow me up. When it didn't, I said, "One minute. And not a second longer."

He held up a nicotine-stained finger and gave me the fish eye. "With tongue."

My gaze dipped to his blue jeans. I swear he'd taken a Viagra.

I sealed my eyes shut, and tried to visualize myself being kissed by my favorite actor after a "take five" for a smoking break.

Ew, ew, ew . . .

Hmmm, wait a minute.

He tastes sweet. Like cinnamon and vanilla.

This isn't nearly as bad as I thought it'd be.

He's actually a good kisser.

Ohmygod, what am I thinking?

Ew, ew, ew!

Finally, Rochelle called time.

Admittedly, it could've been worse—Bruckman could've walked into the lobby.

As soon as I un-suctioned my lips from his, I took a backward step, raising my pointer finger as a warning. "Don't think *that* will ever happen again, because it won't."

Deke chuckled. "I'll understand if you want to call me later."

"You'll understand when I don't." I quickly excused myself to the ladies' room. I was washing my mouth out—*ptui, ptui* and *ptui*—when Rochelle burst through the door.

"*J'accuse!*" I said. "You were supposed to call time at one minute. That's the longest minute I ever spent."

She made a sour face. "I took you up to thirty-four seconds before I called time. I just couldn't take it anymore. By the way, there's a free clinic on your way home. You should get a tetanus shot—he probably has trench mouth."

Which was like saying, *Oh goodie! Trench mouth—the best of the flesh-eating bacterium . . .*

"Thank goodness he didn't want you to screw him," Rochelle went on, with a twinge of disappointment in her tone. "I expect him to come down with Fournier gangrene any day now." Her attention and her voice drifted thoughtfully up to the top of the restroom mirror. "Little known fact: At the time of his death, King Herod the Great of Judea suffered from Fournier gangrene—necrotizing fasciitis of the groin and genitalia. But don't worry," she said, acting like she'd done me a huge favor, "I've been monitoring Chopper Deke's health insurance claims in case he comes down with it. You'll be the first to know about it . . . well, okay, not the first. The second. Oops, not the second, either. The doctor will be the second. I'll be the third. You'll be the fourth."

I blotted my lips with a paper towel, figuring I'd done the best I could do without actually ingesting germicide. I admit it:

I couldn't help what I said next, knowing she'd be chomping at the bit to test the theory.

"Don't tell anybody—" I darted a glance at the space underneath the stalls, pretending to take extra precautions to prevent anyone else from overhearing "—but Deke's an amazing kisser."

CHAPTER FORTY-TWO

I spent the remaining time on the drive into Fort Worth watching the scenery fly by, and calling area hospitals on my cell phone. After the fourth or fifth call, I learned Daddy had been admitted to Our Lady of Perpetual Suffering and was in ICU.

While Bruckman drove, I read excerpts from *The Ladies' Guide to Homicide.*

"I think she killed my mother, and this book proves it. I also believe she lured Teensy down to Mexico so she'd never be seen again, knowing I'd go looking for her. And I believe she means to kill my father to get her grubby hands on his money."

"Settle down. We'll get with a detective as soon as we find out how your father's doing."

"Easy for you to say." I had blood in my eye.

When we arrived at the hospital, I practically ran to the elevator. As soon as the doors opened, I sprinted past the nurse's station to room 520. Pushing the door ajar, I saw Gran slumped miserably at my father's bedside. Then I saw my daddy hooked up to monitors, with tubes from oxygen tanks shoved up his nose and needles sticking out of his arms. For a man who'd always been larger than life, he looked old and incredibly small.

I'm in the wrong room. This can't be my daddy.

"Dainty," my grandmother cried out. Then she explained in a loud, slow voice, as if we'd never met and she thought I might be retarded, how her son had come out of a coma that morning but still hadn't been able to talk.

303

I wasn't conscious of having left my place at the doorway, but the next time I blinked, I was stroking my daddy's hand and the corridor lay behind me.

The commode flushed, and the bathroom door swung open. *Teensy.*

United, we stood; Teensy with her horrible raccoon's eyes and split lip, and me wearing shoes that were about to fall apart. I'm pretty sure we shared a simultaneous thought: *I told you so.*

I looked at Teensy. "Where's Nerissa?" I said in a ventriloquist's voice.

"Gone," she whispered. "I think Gran had her killed."

A soft knuckle rap made me turn toward the door. *Bruckman.*

He cut a striking form, filling up the doorway with his GQ good looks, and his eye-candy body. I motioned him over.

"Hiya cutie," he said to Teensy, and gave her that little grin I love so much. To my grandmother, he gave a polite nod and said, "Good afternoon, ma'am. I'm Jim—Jim Bruckman."

She gave him an aristocratic sniff. "Eugenia Prescott."

Then he looked over at my father, and didn't have to say a thing. Because, about the time Jim started introducing himself, Daddy cracked open his eyes, and we were all treated to a glimpse of a self-made man who'd spent his early years as an oil field rat before making it big on his own without taking so much as a dime of Gran's money.

"Are you the son-of-a-bitch who let my daughter go to Mexico by herself? Girls, help me up. I'm gonna whip his ass."

EPILOGUE

One week later, after I finished the last series of interviews for sweeps month about my harrowing experience in Mexico, I walked out of the TV station in my cranberry pink sweater dress, and headed down the block to the coffee shop for a large hot chocolate. Several times, the hair on the back of my neck stood on end, and I frequently looked around to see whether I was being followed. I still had nightmares and restless sleep, and I wasn't at all convinced that I might not wake up in the middle of the night to find a human trafficker in my bedroom, ready to finish the job and take me back to Mexico.

By the time I got to the coffee shop, I'd broken a sweat. I knew, in part, it was because I hadn't had a leisurely walk. But when I got inside and the place was hopping with activity, I reined in my paranoia and bellied up to the counter to order my cocoa.

"Do you want whipped cream on it?" The name monogrammed on the coffee meister's green apron said *Amy,* so I assumed this was Amy.

"Yes, but not the kind that comes in the can. I want real whipped cream. Unless you have chocolate whipped cream. If you have chocolate whipped cream, I'll take that, even if it comes in a can. Otherwise, I'll just take the regular whipped cream. The kind that doesn't come in a can. Do you, by chance, have fresh whipped cream?"

She blinked. Then she called over her shoulder to someone

beyond my field of vision. "This one's yours," she said, tossing a cup towel down on the counter and walking off.

The line had backed up behind me, so I stepped aside and picked up a newspaper someone had left at an unoccupied table. For the most part, the Prescotts are private, but the newspaper had a bulldog reporter named Garlon Harrier who reported the police beat, and I figured it was just a matter of time before he got wind of the case the District Attorney was fixing to take before the grand jury on Nerissa. I flipped through the city-state section and held my breath a few seconds.

Nothing.

The line had thinned out, so I got up from the table and reordered my hot chocolate. This time when Amy asked if I wanted whipped cream, I heard a voice coming from behind and to my left. "Hell, yes, the diva wants whipped cream, and it'd better be fresh."

I stiffened. My mouth rounded into an O. I slowly turned to see only couples. Except for a newspaper held up in front of somebody's face.

Behind the society page, words sang with laughter. "And put those chocolate shavings on top. Not sprinkles—shavings. And make sure they're thin shavings because if they're too thick, they don't melt, and when you chew them, they taste like wax."

Silver platform thigh-high boots that were sparkly enough to damage my retinas confirmed my suspicion. I felt my face creasing into a smile.

"Amanda?" I said on a whoosh of air.

The paper came down to reveal long platinum hair that cascaded past her shoulders in a tangled mess of curls. She looked like a baboon wearing blue eye shadow. Instead of a sheer black blouse with a red lace bra underneath, or the short, red latex skirt that screamed *streetwalker* so loud it assaulted three of my five senses, she wore a tasteful cobalt blue tube skirt with a black Chanel-style jacket that had to be a knock-off.

"Amanda." My mouth split into a huge grin. "Ohmygod, Amanda, I tried to find you. Bruckman even got some cops at the El Paso PD to look for you. What are you doing here?"

"You owe me twenty dollars." Her broad nose flared when she talked.

"What are you doing here?" I asked again in disbelief.

"You told me I should visit the metroplex if I ever got the chance. Well . . . here I am. Besides—" she spoke in exclamation points, and gave me one of her flamboyant hand gestures "—I came to get my twenty dollars."

"But I don't have twenty dollars on me. How about a latte and a friendship that'll last a lifetime?"

"Hey, diva, the last time we were friends, you almost got me killed. I'm not sure it's safe to have a friend like you around."

"Well," I said, a little on the contrite side, "you know how I'm a debutante?"

"And you know how I'm a runway model?"

"And you know how you could use a bit of fashion advice from somebody who actually has impeccable taste?"

"Hey, diva, I've got a picture of you looking like a scarecrow."

I sucked air. "You *wouldn't.*"

"Yeah, well I just might if you get out of line. You shouldn't judge a book by its cover."

I couldn't help it. I'd really missed hearing that exaggerated, over-modulated drag queen cadence.

"Come on, you crazy lunatic." I welcomed her with open arms. She dropped the newspaper and got out of her chair. I hugged her so tight it's a wonder I didn't squeeze all the air out of her lungs. Then we linked arms and walked to the door, leaving everybody in that coffee shop slack-jawed and staring. "I'd like you to meet the rest of my family. Let's start with my blue-haired grandmother . . ."

ABOUT THE AUTHOR

Texas native **Laurie Moore** received her B.A. from the University of Texas at Austin and entered a career in law enforcement in 1979. In 1992, she moved to Fort Worth and received a degree from Texas Wesleyan University School of Law in 1995. She is currently in private practice in "Cowtown" and lives with a jealous Siamese cat and a rude Welsh corgi. A licensed, commissioned peace officer, this sixth-generation Texan recently celebrated her 32nd year in law enforcement.

Laurie is the author of *Constable's Run, Constable's Apprehension, Constable's Wedding, The Lady Godiva Murder, The Wild Orchid Society, Jury Rigged, Woman Strangled—News at Ten, Deb on Arrival—Live at Five,* and *Couple Gunned Down—News at Ten.* Contact Laurie through her Web site at www.LaurieMoore Mysteries.com.